a *storm* of *ice* and *stars*

Also by Lisa Lueddecke:

A Shiver of Snow and Sky

Lisa Lueddecke

a *storm* of *ice* and *stars*

SCHOLASTIC

Scholastic Children's Books
An imprint of Scholastic Ltd
Euston House, 24 Eversholt Street, London, NW1 1DB, UK
Registered office: Westfield Road, Southam, Warwickshire, CV47 0RA
SCHOLASTIC and associated logos are trademarks and/or
registered trademarks of Scholastic Inc.

First published in the UK by Scholastic Ltd, 2018

Text copyright © Lisa Lueddecke, 2018

The right of Lisa Lueddecke to be identified
as the author of this work has been asserted.

ISBN 978 1407 17404 4

A CIP catalogue record for this book
is available from the British Library.

Printed by CPI Group (UK) Ltd, Croydon, CR0 4YY
Papers used by Scholastic Children's Books are made
from wood grown in sustainable forests.

1 3 5 7 9 10 8 6 4 2

This is a work of fiction. Names, characters, places, incidents
and dialogues are products of the author's imagination or are used
fictitiously. Any resemblance to actual people, living or dead,
events or locales is entirely coincidental.

www.scholastic.co.uk

For Mom

No coward soul is mine.

— EMILY BRONTË

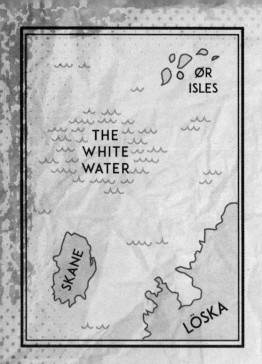

ØR
ISLES

THE
WHITE
WATER

SKANE

LÖSKA

N

NW

NE

W

E

SW

SE

S

Chapter 1

Skane was a silent land. The ancient trees stood tall and still, whispering to one another now and then. The ground lay heavy with snow, enshrouding its secrets of a time gone by. It had been walked by people not quite like us, but not so different either. It had seen things we would never know, been in the presence of immortals who had disappeared like a breath into winter air.

But Skane as we knew it was still young. The Skane of my people: the frightened, wide-eyed survivors who had seen it through fog and crashing waves out at sea, who had cried with relief at its form silhouetted against the stars. Who had thought its frozen shores and mighty forests held the one thing they had been longing for on their treacherous flight from home: safety.

Well, safety never lasts for ever. What my ancestors

did not know, when their boats ground on to the beach, was that Skane had a secret. Its sky held a power, and when it flushed a burning red, when it engulfed our island in a fist of blood that lasted only minutes, it meant that for many, death was certain. Imminent. Time would begin to count down, and while we could wait and watch and pray to the Goddess above for salvation, we had a greater chance of counting every star in the night sky than stopping it.

They had escaped Löska. They had escaped the Ør. But they hadn't escaped death.

Winter had settled into the very bones of Skane. Nights were bitter and sharp in that way that made every breath ache and every bit of exposed skin burn like a licking flame. Thick snow clung to the fir trees, cloaks of white to keep them warm. While all others were huddled beneath soft blankets and warming animal skins, waking now and then to stoke the fire and rub their hands together against the chill, I was deep in a cave outside the village, scratching away at rock. My fingers ached, both from the bitter cold and from gripping a writing stone for hours.

I sat back on my heels and flexed my hands, staring up at my work. Perhaps in the years to come, no one would find these stories of me and my love interesting or worth reading, but knowing they were there, written in stone, filled me with all the comfort of a warm blanket on a cold night.

The countryside around Skane was riddled with caves just like this one – dark, frigid places that offered both a place of quiet and a surface like the one before me. When I had first discovered it, it was no more than a wall of rock, uneven here and there, but unblemished and unadorned. Ready for my writing. For my stories and etchings.

Not any more.

I had been coming here for seven days now, each day adding more and more scrawls. Even on the days when I should have been collecting berries to eat or wood for fires, I would steal in here and continue my work with aching fingers and stinging lungs. No one would think to look for me here – or no one would bother. I had shirked enough duties and responsibilities to flee into the woods for solace so often that it was unlikely that anyone would bother reprimanding me. I wasn't the only one: there were several of us who spent much of our time in the caves, although for the most part, they were reading the writings of people long dead. Even though many of them had told their stories to their children, there had been a sense of urgency early on, to write down the things that had happened, what sent them fleeing from Löska, and the things that were waiting for them in Skane. How they had survived the winters, or built their homes, or started a new life. They were afraid, back then, that one by one they would all die off and there would be no record of them having ever existed.

Many did die, but many also lived.

I was still writing, still telling stories in a way that could transcend time. Paper could burn or rot to pieces, and spoken words only mattered so long as there were still people around to speak them. But these caves would remain long after I and everyone I knew no longer drew breath. I would one day be ash and lost to memory, but this stone would live on.

A gentle rush of cold air blew against my cheek, and I looked around, a weight suddenly pressing on me. I couldn't explain it, and I didn't tell the others, but sometimes I could still feel his presence around the village, under the trees, in the caves. A breeze would brush past, bringing with it a faint impression of him, the tiniest hint of his scent. It was in my head, no doubt; I dreamed it up to feel a slight ease in the pain, to find some small amount of comfort for a time. Heartbreak is a room with no light and no air, and I'd spent the past year just trying to breathe.

I ran my fingers over where I had carved his name into the wall beside mine, sharply, so it would never fade away.

Janna and Sølvi.

The hour had to be past midnight. There was more

4

to say, more to write, as there would always be, but my hands were cold, and the night was growing ever deeper. My veins ran with moonlight and my heart beat for the stars, but no matter how inviting these dark hours were, with their bitter cold and creeping frost, I couldn't survive being outside all night. If I stayed out much longer, my mother and father might send out a search party, and it was better to avoid that for everyone's sake.

I stuck the small stone I used to write into a crevice in the rock and stood, shaking out my sore limbs and expelling a long breath in a burst of white. The lantern on the floor flickered with my sudden movement, sending my shadow dancing and quivering around the cave.

Pulling my fur cloak tighter around my shoulders, I took my light and moved down the narrow cave tunnel towards the exit. As I neared it, I froze. My feet would not move – a shadow, I was certain, darted out of the exit and out of sight.

I stood still for a moment to calm my pounding heart, imagining how the thick walls of the cave and the snow beyond would mask my screams. An animal, surely. It had seen the glow from my light and entered out of curiosity but grew frightened at my approach. Nothing more. I pushed it from my mind, unwilling though it was to go.

Somehow, the air seemed less frigid the closer I got to the opening. It made sense: the inner tunnels and cavernous rooms never saw daylight, so the cold was given free reign. I opened my mouth to yawn as I passed through the opening of the cave, but I froze as my eyes were drawn to the sky.

No.

Something was wrong. Something I had never seen in my eighteen years. Something that sent dread bursting from my heart and into every vein in my freezing body. The night sky, filled with stars as always, was glowing red.

Red.

I stared until the colour was all I could see, until it stained every inch of my vision and I was drowning in blood.

Red.

From time to time, the sky shone green, sometimes blue. We had learned to associate the blue lights with snow, because without fail, when the lights glowed blue, a fierce storm would come rolling in from the sea within a day or two. But this … this was different. Red was different, and as the tales and songs came crashing back into my mind like a wave on to a shore, I knew what it meant.

Somewhere in Skane, death was creeping closer like winter frost.

Chapter 2

Faces shone pale in the harsh light of the torches, eyes full of fear. The alarm had been sounded sometime before I arrived, fists pounding on doors and shouts echoing off the walls of homes.

Red ... lós ... sky... The words reverberated through my bones as I seamlessly joined the shuffling crowd that was making its way towards the village centre in a jumble of tears and uncertain whispers, necks craned back to examine the now-harmless night sky. I glanced up at the tangle of stars far above. No sign of the blood it had shed not half an hour ago. It had done its part. Sent its message. Now it was up to us to act upon it.

I caught my father's eye as he emerged from our home, both hands on my mother's shoulders. *We will discuss your whereabouts later,* his face said, but he was soon distracted by the frantic voices of the villagers all around us.

More and more people stepped out of their homes, still wrapping cloaks and shawls around themselves, eyes wide. A faint wind picked up, whispering of approaching snow. I remembered, as I waited for someone to begin speaking, how my father had once said that if we didn't listen to the words of nature – the whispering winds, the rushing rivers, the cries of birds warning of nearby predators – then we were as good as dead. *The trees, the animals, even the air has its own language. We must learn to speak it, or our existence will fade away.* It reminded me of a child's tale I'd heard long ago: *Beware of the föss's fiddle,* they said. *He plays a song with the wind and snow, rustling the leaves just so as to pull you in, fill your mind, and drag you under. If the rushing of a river ever sings to you, beckoning you just a bit closer, the föss's spell has begun its work, and it may already be too late.*

I stared away through the ghostly houses to the forest beyond, cloaked in darkness and bewitchment. I would have given anything to be there in that moment. The breeze ruffled a few needle-ridden branches, and a shadowed bird darted from one tree to another.

Soon. I would be there soon. For now, I would stay for this grim show of togetherness, this stony-faced gathering to discuss how much time we had left, as Skane began another game of which only a few would see the outcome.

I shuddered.

My father – Sívar – was huddled together with Oben and an aging man named Alff, speaking in hushed tones. The rest of us clustered around, whispering and pointing to the three men, whose conversation was so animated we couldn't help but stare. I edged my way closer to those gathered and moved to stand beside my father. Everyone hesitated and glanced at me, but I remained. Why shouldn't I?

"It's been so long," Oben said, his voice breaking. "An entire generation has grown old with no sign of the lights."

"Yes, and the sea is deep and salty, yet stating such facts is hardly a resolution, now is it?" Alff snapped.

"We can argue among ourselves until said sea freezes over," my father said. "But people are seeking comfort, so comfort we will give them."

"Why give them comfort when there is no comfort to be had?" Oben pressed. "What use is false comfort?"

"If it keeps us from falling into disarray, then it will be worth it, just until we can calm our fears enough to form a plan. Speak to the other villages. Organize."

"And what will that comfort look like?" Oben asked. "What falsehoods will you feed them? Tell them that all will be well? Tell them to tuck away in their beds tonight, and pay no mind to the hundreds who have died in the past? To think nothing of how many of us will be dead in the coming weeks? Where is the comfort in that, Sívar? Answer me that."

My father held Oben's gaze for a long while, in a way that was somewhere between commanding and menacing. "Where is the hope in telling them there is nothing to be done? If people want to survive, why arm them with discouragement and death? Answer me *that*, Oben."

Oben crossed his arms and shook his head but fell silent. Alff offered no input.

My father turned to find me standing there, his eyebrows knitting briefly in confusion, and then he addressed the crowd, his voice bathed in a kind of fortitude no one else present seemed to feel. Children held fast to the hands of their mothers and fathers, and all eyes bore a heaviness like I had never seen before. It was as if a weight had descended from the sky and pressed down on every one of us gathered in the village, one that was too heavy to push away. That was how fear worked, breaking down your mettle and resilience until there was little left of you but a brittle frame that could be blown away by the wind. Somehow, that crushing fear that had paralysed me when I had first laid eyes on the lights had evaporated, the minutes bringing with them a replenishing sort of renewal, like waking up after a good night's sleep. I wasn't unafraid – far from it – but my thoughts had cleared, and my head felt lighter as determination mixed with a faint bit of acceptance grounded me. I would not let my fear worsen whatever grisly events were soon to crest the horizon.

I stood a little taller, squaring my shoulders and breathing deeply.

An elderly woman named Unna, who rarely came outdoors and walked with a wooden cane carved with the head of a bird, gently pushed her way through the throng of villagers. I stepped aside to allow her access to the group of men beside me, who grew silent as she approached.

Unna stopped to catch her breath, stray pieces from her long grey braid flickering in the breeze.

"If any of you were alive last time," she said with a voice that shook, "you were too young to remember. But I do. I remember it all, every day. I remember eyeing my own children as though they were strangers, waiting for their brows to start sweating, for their lungs to start coughing up blood." A few eyes darted to the children around us – even mine. I couldn't help it. "I remember my neighbour killing his own wife with a hunting knife when she began to show signs of the plague, dragging her body from the house to burn, only to die himself four days later. And I remember travellers from Isåvik, escaping their own village to find safety in ours – until one spewed blood on to the child of his host, and it spread like hungry flames from there. You don't know what it's like to remember. I relive it here every day" –

11

she tapped her right temple with a finger – "don't make me truly relive it again."

A man coughed in the otherwise-silent crowd, and those close by him crept away, leaving a large gap all the way around him.

"I'm so sorry, Unna," my father said, gently touching her shoulder. "I cannot imagine what that is like for you."

"You'll be able to imagine soon enough," Unna told him firmly. "In the time between the lights and the first signs of the plague, there is much fear and crying and planning – all to no end. But what there isn't much of, is time."

"We know," Alff said, with a less-than-subtle roll of his eyes.

"I am returning to my home," Unna said, gripping her cane again as though ready to depart. "And I shall do what I did last time: stay indoors. No wanderers from other villages will see me fall ill. I shan't let them in."

She slowly walked away.

After a long pause, heavy with uncertainty, the meeting went on. I let their words – about staying vigilant and how they would discuss measures they could take to ensure safety – fade away. My thoughts wandered as I gazed around at the crowd, wondering how many of us would be left in the weeks to come. . .

A set of eyes met mine and didn't look away.

Eri.

If I never saw him again it would be too soon. He was an accomplished hunter, and the son of a village widow, Svanhild, whose husband had died last winter along with ... the others. Little bad could be said of him: he cared for his mother and her broken heart when he was not in the woods, and his general knowledge of the weather and the forest had garnered him a good deal of respect throughout the village. He had even found a lost child a year or two ago, wandering alone through the trees sobbing, as snow threatened us. He brought her back to the arms of her mother and father to great acclaim from the villagers. But he and Sølvi had been like brothers, always close, and always together. When you thought of one, you thought of the other, and that's how it had been since they had met as children. After Sølvi had passed on, seeing just one was too much, sending me into fits of tears behind a house, or beneath the safety of my blankets. I couldn't bear the pain of it, so I had avoided him for months.

Then we just never spoke again. Even if it was small, he cost us happiness that we could never make up, and I didn't think I could forgive him.

At first it was strange to transition from seeing someone so often to never seeing them at all, but over the time since it had happened, I'd adjusted to it. And in the year since Sølvi had passed on, I'd grown accustomed to being entirely alone. Did I enjoy only the company

13

of my own mind? I had found that there was a sort of energy required when interacting with people, and so often I was too drained to even offer a simple greeting.

But now Eri stood staring at me, his arms crossed, hood down and light hair being tossed by the wind. He had matured in the year since we last spoke, into a man I hardly recognized. He bit on his top lip, a habit I had once come to associate with him being nervous. Somehow, I had managed to forget about him as my heart and mind were consumed by Sølvi's death; as I relived the whole of our relationship every single day.

But there was some small part of me that considered walking over to him. Asking how he'd been since his best friend had died. I'd forgotten that he, too, had lost someone last year. I was not the only one who'd felt that crushing pain, like someone had reached into my body and ripped my heart from its resting place, but death can blur things, make the obvious seem obscure.

A gust of wind whipped my hair into my eyes, and by the time I'd brushed it from my face, Eri had looked away.

Any warmth I had felt from my layers was sucked away as I watched a woman by the name of Ragna push her way through the crowd. Her severe features were only barely softened by the billowing hair that hung down to her chest. She stood tall, taller than me by at least an inch, and faced the three men with her chin held high.

14

She cut a forbidding figure, and always had, perhaps the reason she had long been avoided.

My reasons to avoid her were different.

Four years ago, her son Orri was six years old. A sweet but quiet boy, he kept to himself and stayed close to the village. I had assumed it was on the instruction of his mother – always the suspicious, fearful type. I was fourteen years old and meant to be collecting firewood with some other villagers, Ragna included. I had wandered far from the path so I could work by myself, and as I found pieces of bark and placed them in my basket, I heard a long, lonely howl from the north. It was too far away to cause alarm, and I was still close enough to the village for safety, but it caused a pang of longing in my stomach. I wanted to chase it, to sing with it, to run away to the distant mountains and never come back.

On a whim, I cupped my hands around my mouth and howled back. It meant nothing to the wolf, of that I was certain, but in that moment, I felt deliciously wild and free.

I collected my basket once more and turned to find Ragna watching me through the trees, mistrust burning fierce in her eyes. She would tell the others, I knew it, and the whispers about me would grow in number, though I had done no harm.

Until late that evening, when a trail of blood was found leading from the village and into the trees, and we learned that Orri had been dragged away by a wolf. We never found him, and through Ragna's shrieks and cries that lasted for days on end, she pointed a finger at me nearly as often as she drew breath. The others pitied her, sympathized with her, but even their suspicion of me wasn't strong enough to believe that I had called upon a wolf to kill her child. Eventually, the story died down, until it was only whispered about infrequently, and never in her presence.

"I do not believe that we can be so weak in the face of the red lós," she said, ensuring her voice carried over the crowd – and it did, strong and resounding, like a scolding none of us deserved. "When predators are on the hunt, the weak are the first to be feasted upon." She had a way of talking that secured everyone's attention.

Not far off, I saw my mother breathe deeply.

Alff cleared his throat. "Do you have suggestions to back up those words?"

Ragna looked around, her eyes seeming to smile as she realized everyone was waiting for her to continue. No, not smile. Smirk. A second later, her face hardened once more. "Sívar has already alluded to it, to safety measures to ensure our survival. We seal off the village," she said, her voice carrying the crushing weight of waves during a winter storm. "No one should be allowed in or out, with perhaps the exception of the hunters, and rarely. No trading with the other villages, no scampering off into the woods" – her eyes darted to me, and my skin prickled – "and no taking in wanderers. We all heard Unna's story about the visitor from Isavik; that *will not* happen again. We set up guards around our perimeter, taking turns on the watch. We can ensure that no infected persons go in or out of our village."

A breeze blew. Someone in the crowd coughed. But no one spoke for a long moment.

"Ragna, you..." my father started, and his words revealed that he was rocked to his core. It took him a moment to find his words, Ragna's biting words and ideas having no place in our village. "Why would we do this? And who would listen?"

Again, that smirk pulled at her eyes, and anger flared in my chest like a dragon's breath. "Fear," she said, and she was right. There was no question about it. "People will do anything when they are afraid, if they think it might save their lives." She motioned to the crowd and spoke of them as if they were too far away to hear her. "Suppose you put it to a vote. You know the result as well as I do."

A hush fell, disturbed only by the distant call of a raven.

Where there had been bow-string-taut tension before, Ragna had begun to pluck at it with a finger.

It was my mother who broke the silence. She stepped forward, her eyes never leaving Ragna's face. "I think perhaps not," she said, moving until only a foot or two

17

of space separated the two women. She had a way of sounding her most polite when she was the most upset. "The sickness will likely come whether we protect our village limits or not. You know nothing about where the plague comes from, or how it enters our bodies. It could be in the next sip of water you take, or your next breath of fresh winter air. That is not meant to stir terror – it is simply the truth. What sort of people would we be if we cut ourselves off from the rest of the world, refusing to even see or speak with those around us?"

"We would be survivors," Ragna replied. She drew herself up, standing even taller than before. Her eyes were ice. "We could be the only village in a few weeks' or months' time with no casualties. How can you deny these poor people safety?" She gestured to a nearby child, a weak play at garnering sympathy for her cause. "How can you insist upon inviting death into our numbers?"

"How can you insist upon leaving others to die without help?" my mother asked, her voice rising sharply. "There are children just like this in other villages. Children who might soon be motherless. Fatherless."

"They are not our children," Ragna said simply. "We must care for our own first, just as the others must care for theirs. We shoulder our own burdens in this harsh world. You know that as well as I do."

"I know no such thing," my mother breathed. "All I know, in this moment, is that you know nothing of love."

Something swept across Ragna's face, a kind of emotion I couldn't place, but it took me back to her boy, dragged away by wolves. Surely she had loved him, once upon a time, or she would never have blamed me so cruelly for his death – yet this woman standing here, stony-faced, I could see nothing in her that spoke of love, or compassion, or anything that resembled empathy. The people of Skane had long been divided on our purpose. *We live for freedom*, said some. *For courage*, said others. But if we didn't live for love, we lived for nothing.

"I am with my mother," I said, steeping my voice in the same ironclad strength as Ragna's. "Cutting ourselves off is selfish and cowardly." I put an extra stress on the last word and spoke it directly towards her. Her stone face didn't flinch, but her eyes bore into mine in a way that almost made me look away.

Almost.

My father nodded, and so did Alff, but Oben remained quiet, looking from one person to the next. His obvious silence sparked a question from my father.

"Oben, what say you?"

He eyed Ragna for a long moment, a wordless conversation seeming to pass between them. "I have heard far worse ideas," he finally said. A sound of disgust escaped my father's throat, and he rubbed his eyes with both hands.

"Do not be a fool, Oben," he said, frustrated. I could

see it starting to happen, the fear and uncertainty igniting a sense of frenzy and self-preservation. Some said self-preservation had helped us to survive, but others argued that it was a sense of community, of bonding together with the aim of not just surviving, but of thriving. I always thought it was a bit of both. There was no harm in protecting your own, but not at the expense of others. *Never* at the expense of others.

"Just entertain the idea for a moment, Sívar. All of you here must see the sense in it. Chances are great that the plague will not come from somewhere within our village. It will be brought here by something or someone, and we can prevent it from happening. Cut it off before it has a chance to reach us. If closing it off could indeed keep us safe, keep us from spewing blood until our bodies run cold, could you deny us all that?" He shook his head. "My father told me what it was like, only a year or two before I was born. How he saw his sister drown from the *inside*, blood draining from her face. She couldn't talk or cry, and he watched her die slowly, her eyes still wide and round with fear long after she had passed. He never forgot it. Ragna speaks the truth, however hard to hear it may be."

Ragna's eyes glistened at the support as she sent a challenging look to my father. The tension was a fog in the air, thick and unwelcome.

"And you think no one before us has had a similar

thought?" my father asked. "You think you have, at long last, solved the problem of the plague that has haunted us for generations? Or do you think, perhaps, that you are shit-scared and behaving like children who have just been told a ghostly bedtime story? Locking yourselves away is not a solution; it's putting a fingertip on a laceration and hoping to stop the bleeding. Pull yourselves together."

Another grim silence slipped by, until Alff said, "Let us take this discussion indoors. We will bring our solid arguments back to the village later."

There were a few objections from the crowd, but the children had grown distracted and faces were tinged with fear from their proximity to others, as if the plague had already crawled up from the ground to claim them. When I moved to follow my father and the others into Oben's house, Ragna held my shoulder. I jerked out of her grasp and turned to face her.

"No children," she said, and swept past me through the door.

"She's eighteen—" my mother started, but Ragna interrupted her.

"No children," she repeated.

Fire burst through my veins, but I fought to quench it. Children cried when they didn't get their way, and I was no child. So instead, I faced Ragna for a short moment and challenged her with the one thing I knew she would despise: the same smirking smile she had bestowed on everyone earlier, like I knew something she didn't.

The sour look that shadowed her face nearly brought a true smile to my lips as I turned away.

The shadows darkened as I put more and more distance between myself and the village. In the wake of the meeting and seeing Eri again – really seeing him – a pressing need to be far away had propelled me into the woods. I had been dismissed as nothing more than a petulant youngster, forbidden from speaking with the adults. My temper flared hotter and hotter, and though I worked to keep it in check, the sight of Ragna's face shutting me out would not leave.

Now my path was steep as I worked to climb higher and higher, up to a towering point on a familiar cliff too far from the village to be safe. If my mother and father knew, they would likely lock me in the house indefinitely.

Enjoy your freedom while it lasts, I thought bitterly. If Ragna and Oben had their way, I might be confined to the village in the weeks to come. And if there was one thing I knew about Ragna, it was that she generally got her way.

I was not the only one out and about in the woods. Between the trees I saw another girl picking her way through rock and limb, the sound of a tune she hummed just barely reaching my ears. Enja. I swallowed when I saw her face, its lines of familiarity that pulled at my heart. She was Sølvi's sister, not quite two years younger. We'd been so close, of course, what with spending so much time with her brother... But as with most of my friendships, it had crumbled away last year. I hadn't thought much about how she might have needed a friend after her brother died, only about my own pain, which made me feel selfish and ashamed to the point that I kept away from her even more. How can you take on someone else's pain when you can hardly bear your own? I had needed to be away from everyone, alone with my wounds to allow them to start healing before I could help anyone else. And no doubt, she had done the same.

A ball of white fur walked close at her heels, and I remembered a time not all that long ago.

Sølvi and Eri had been tracking a large hare – Sølvi wasn't much for hunting, and Eri had offered to guide him – unaware that Enja and I were trailing them. It hadn't been on purpose. Not at first, anyway. We were meant to be gathering kindling for our homes and had strolled off into the woods together but had quickly been distracted by their voices through the trees. I knew Eri well; knew how adept his senses were and how wholly aware of the woods he became the moment he stepped into them, so I made sure to keep us downwind and out of sight. But with every glimpse of them, we knew they were both far too preoccupied with their work to notice two girls spying on them.

23

They spoke in low tones and walked carefully, slowly, trying not to scare off their prey.

"Poor Sølvi," Enja whispered, smiling. "I am sure he'd rather be walking miles alone naked at night than this. He's no hunter." It was true. When he wasn't writing on cave walls with me or herding and shearing sheep, his carving skills could have filled entire days from start to finish. He whittled elegant arrows and knife handles, spoons and other cooking utensils for the villagers. A few months ago, he had etched the rune for love – or perhaps it was family, though; it was difficult to be sure – into a smooth bit of wood and hung it on a string. I'd worn it every day since then.

He had a bigger top lip than bottom, which sometimes – like right then – made him look almost as if he was about to cry, until his face lit up with a smile that could reignite life in the dead.

"Should we be following them?" I whispered, keenly aware of the annoyance I would feel at such a discovery. "We can slip away now, and they'll never know we were here."

Enja held up a hand. "No, no. I want to see if my brother succeeds. It's about time someone around here dethroned Eri."

It sounded as if it was meant to be a joke, but as with many jokes, it was riddled with truth. Eri's name was frequently found on the lips of the villagers, who praised his skills and strong heart. "A warrior's heart," my father had

24

said, although I hadn't figured out why that was something to be desired.

So we carried on following them, and perhaps ten minutes later, the two boys froze and stared at something through the trees. Then Sølvi raised his bow and let an arrow loose.

"No," Eri said, but it was too late. Something nearby let out a yelp, and on instinct, Enja and I hurried out of hiding.

The heads of the two boys snapped in our direction, confusion and annoyance rampant on Eri's face, and horror alight on Sølvi's. He hadn't killed a hare; he had killed a fox.

"I saw the white fur and..." Sølvi began, but he stopped, shaking his head.

"It was a good kill, and one we can use," Eri said with a sigh. "Just not the one we were after." He looked to me. "Why are you even here?"

"We were meant to be collecting kindling and started following you." My desire to keep that a secret had evaporated the moment his annoyance with us had become so clear on his face.

"And no part of you considered the dangers of following two hunters, carrying bows?"

I shrugged. "We kept behind the trees."

Enja, seeming to have noticed something a few yards away, knelt to the ground. I made my way over to stand beside her, and saw a little white face peering out of a burrow in the ground, mostly hidden by shrubs.

"She was a mother," Enja said.

"Oh, damn me," Sølvi cursed to himself when he saw the little creature. He shoved his bow at Eri, who took it with a look of surprise.

"You know you make the arrows I hunt with," Eri said, slinging the extra bow across his back. "Not being the one to fire them doesn't absolve you of responsibility."

"I can change that," Sølvi shot back. "I came out here to learn how to track a rabbit, not to kill a mother."

"Welcome to Skane," Eri said. "People like you are the first ones to go." Then he turned and strode away through the trees.

When I turned back to Enja, she had the baby fox in her arms. It was trying to climb back down, yipping in fear and confusion, but she held it firmly. "He's coming home with us," she announced, looking her brother square in the face.

"Wonderful," he replied.

Eri's words to him would haunt me later in life, after this wretched island had indeed claimed Sølvi's life, but I thought little of it in the moment.

Enja was carrying a basket on one arm, probably out collecting berries or kindling to dry. Her faithful fox followed at her heels. I should talk to her, see how she had been. But I turned away. A hundred thousand excuses floated around in my mind, all bumping into one another.

I didn't need to pick just one in order to avoid speaking with her. I had been doing it for a year now. One more day would do no harm.

If I was being honest, I would have acknowledged that I wasn't ready to be the broken leading the broken. I hadn't found enough pieces of myself yet to make a whole person, someone she could lean on, and I wasn't sure if I would ever be that way again.

My foot slipped on an icy rock, and I flailed my arms to find balance. I had been climbing higher and higher up a ridge, and it was a long way down to the stony ground below. That would be a fall I would never survive.

I had tucked all my hair into a fur band that wrapped around my ears, just barely keeping them from going numb. My breath still hit the air like smoke from a chimney, but there was just enough warmth from the sun beyond the clouds to keep frostbite from my limbs. I had so many layers wrapped around my frame that the cold would have to fight to reach my body.

At the top of the cliff, I took in a deep, refreshing breath and planted myself on a rock close enough to the edge for a good view, but just far enough that I would not tempt fate. Around me, boulders and rough precipices and fir trees stretched for miles, until the forested horizon met the grey sky far to my left. To my right, tiny curls of smoke rose from the houses of my village. I knew that sight should have been comforting – home, familiarity,

27

warmth – yet those were feelings I got out here in the wild, not surrounded by four walls.

Not far to my left, the sea churned and seethed. I didn't travel to the shore much, finding enough distraction in the caves and forests of the land. Furthermore, Mother and Father had forbidden me from going there at a young age, and though I was generally happy to prowl about in places I shouldn't, that was one instruction I had always heeded. Things outside our village did not often frighten me, but that turbulent sea did.

I turned slowly as I sat there, and let my eyes wander to the north. There were only snow-clad trees as far as I could see, rising and falling and hiding the horizon from view, a green and white sea of its own. Sometimes, on a clear day if I stood tall, I could just barely make out the tiny, shadowed forms of the mountains, impossibly far away – or perhaps I imagined them. Perhaps all the stories I had heard and the longing I felt about them morphed into those tiny black smudges that sometimes disappeared when I blinked. Sometime after arriving here, my people had named them the Kalls, an old word for cold. Simplistic, perhaps, but the mountains were in the north, and the north was undoubtedly even colder than here, where our little village sat.

We had stories about the mountains, of course, but because we knew so little about them, they came largely from the wandering minds of storytellers, with little to no basis in fact. *They are the tombs of a people much larger than us, and far more ancient. They are the wall between our world and the other one. They are where all the evil things in Skane were gathered long ago, and they are better off left alone.*

In the early days, a scouting party had headed that way, but they were run back by a pack of wolves, larger than the ones they had seen in Löska. Then when I was a child, an old man named Geir had left to travel to the mountains, but he'd never come back. After that, we stopped talking about them. Stopped thinking about them.

Sølvi always said that one day he would go, that one day he would set our village behind him and strike off to the north, and that he wouldn't return until he had reached the mountains and collected stories to tell. And I ... I wanted to go with him. I wanted to explore uncharted territories, to lay eyes on sights our people had never seen. I wanted to breathe in the cold mountain air and see what beautiful, wicked things they held. See silvery peaks that challenged the sky, soaring above the land like a fortress that either kept us out, or kept dark things within. I had dreamed of it, once or twice. Dreamed of the two of us traversing the distant mountains together, living out adventures we would grow old telling our children.

And then, one day, Sølvi was gone, and those dreams broke apart like a fallen icicle, shattered into myriad shards that could never be put back together. I stopped thinking about them, pushed away all thoughts of what we had wanted, what we said we would do, and let the idea of the north, of the mountains, fade away into the dim and be lost to thought. How could I, one person, want the same things we had wished for together? How could I hope any longer for a life that had been dreamed up when everything was different? But now... Now the call of the north sang to me again, and those thoughts and memories took in giant breaths of air, sending them spiralling back to the surface.

Trying not to move on from a loss is like staring at the stars at sunrise and willing them not to grow faint until you are merely staring at a lightened grey sky. Sooner or later, the parts of yourself you thought you lost begin to find their way home again.

"What's in the north?"

A voice splintered the freedom of my thoughts. Eri stood a handful of yards away, a bow in his hands and a full quiver strung across his back.

"Am I your prey?" I asked, without answering his question. I pulled my knees up to my chest and hugged them.

"No. I found your footprints and followed them here."

"You shouldn't have."

He stood straight, arms at his sides, but absentmindedly patted down the snow around him with one foot. "I saw you at the gathering. I know you saw me. You didn't say hello."

"We haven't spoken in a year."

He picked up a small stone from the ground and tossed it over the edge of the cliff, a sort of frustration behind every move of his muscles. "I know." Silence. "I saw the lights for myself. They . . . they nearly made me sick."

"I would have thought you were in bed at such an hour."

He ran a finger along the string of his bow. "And I'd have thought you would be." A long, heavy pause, and somehow I knew I would not like what was coming. I held my chin up, ready to face it. Whatever he had to say couldn't be worse than the wretched year that was already behind us. "I was in the woods at the time because. . ." He cleared his throat and breathed deeply. "I knew you were in that cave. I knew because. . . Because I had followed you there. Into the woods. And back home." The look on his face said he regretted saying it immediately – as he well should have. "I was worried about you, as your parents are, and I had seen you leave the village." He spoke faster and faster, as if any of his words made it any better. "I would have felt terrible if something had happened to you and I was the only one who had known."

I stood slowly. "You followed me?" The memory of that shadow darting out of the tunnel resurfaced.

"It was the right thing to do."

Something broke inside me. I took three steps forward and poked a finger against his chest. "The right thing to do," I whispered, shaking, "would have been to leave Sølvi and me alone. The right thing to do would have been to forget about me the moment you met me. The right thing to do would have been to apologize to him for what you said when you killed that fox's mother, about people like him being the first ones to go. Because he's gone now, Eri, and I can't get him back. You were right: this Goddess-forsaken island did take him, and your words haunt me every day of my miserable life. The right thing to do would be to never speak to me again."

He turned away towards the village, his eyes glistening with tears that would fall at any moment. My gentler side whispered I had been too harsh, but my anger snapped back that I had not been harsh enough. He gripped his bow with both hands and hugged it to his chest. "I regret those words every waking moment of my life, Janna," he whispered. "But no matter what I do, or how I feel, I can never take them back." One of the tears ran down his cheek, but he didn't seem to notice it. "All I have left is you, and making it up to you, and keeping you safe. He asked me to, once, long ago. He said that if anything ever happened to him, to make sure that you were looked after. I can't let him down. I can't."

Words got caught in my chest, and I had to turn away

32

for a long moment, breathe in and out and collect myself. "You aren't my guardian, Eri," I said at last. "You are an anchor around my neck." The thought of it, of a weight pulling me down beneath the dark and violent waves of the sea wasn't unlike how I felt on most days, like I was struggling for air that was just out of reach.

The words cut at him, I could see it in his eyes, but he pressed on. "I hunt with your father, you know. He talks. He's worried. He says you haven't been the same since ... since last winter."

"None of us have been the same since last winter." He'd lost a friend in Sølvi. Enja had lost a brother. And I had lost my love, my future. How could any of us be the same after that?

He held my gaze, fir-needle-green eyes piercing through mine, waiting for me to respond. I kicked a large rock with my boot so hard that pain shot up my leg.

"I don't follow you for any reason other than to keep you safe, Janna. To keep your parents from worrying. You are lucky to still have both of them, and lucky that they care so much for you." His voice broke, and he cleared his throat, but didn't bother wiping away the tears that sparkled in his eyes. "I'm past hoping anything – I don't think of you in any way except as a friend worried for another friend. That is all."

My sharp edges softened. It wasn't truly Eri himself that angered me so much – even though he had tried to divide us. But that was ages ago. What I hated deep down was how seeing him reminded me of Sølvi. They were always together, one right behind the other, and when I saw Eri walking through the village or the forest, I almost felt like Sølvi could be right behind him.

Although he never was.

"Will you come home soon?" His voice was quietly hopeful, but the word *home* stung my ears.

I turned slowly away for another deep breath, then back to look at him, to take in his whole demeanour. He didn't want to be out here any more than I wanted him here. I was being harsh, but with a cause. He was not just someone from the village looking after a neighbour. There was a history that burdened every word we spoke; memories that invaded every second I spent in his presence.

"Yes," I replied. Part of me meant it, part of me didn't, but I made sure it sounded honest. "I'll be home soon."

He nodded twice. "Thank you." After another moment or two of hesitation, the silence bursting with unspoken words that I could feel he wanted to say, he left me.

The air seemed to grow colder in his absence, and I hugged myself tighter. The night grew darker and darker somehow, though the sun had long since set. Overhead, innumerable stars sparkled and glistened, and when I looked at them, it was impossible not to feel hope. I stared for so long they consumed the world, and I was floating far away from this island, from the ground, bathing in starlight and shadow. Far in the distance, the howl of a wolf echoed through the woods, the siren song of a lonely forest. I tilted my head to determine where it came from. North. That was the second time I had heard it from that direction, yet they never seemed to move further to the south. They just cried on: the call of a wild animal which I longed to answer.

The call sounded again, and I stood, slowly. I knew these woods. I was light on my feet and I could climb a tree if need be. I stared to the north, pushing fallen bits of hair from my eyes. A wind from the south pushed against my back, propelling me forward. I shouldn't go. My mother and father would be angry, and they would likely send Eri back out after me, but in that moment, it didn't matter. I took another step.

Bright is the moon on a cold winter's night, my grandfather once said. *And bright are the bones it illuminates.* It was a warning I had never forgotten.

And yet.

I could face their anger later, but tonight, I wanted to dance with a north wind and run with a wild river that rushed off to distant shores. Tonight, the north was calling.

It was the midsummer bonfire when I was thirteen, and all the children were playing a game where they split into two teams and tried to capture each other until one team came out the winner. The adults sat around the fire in the centre of the village, eating roasted meats and swapping stories of hunts or winters past, while we played on the outskirts nearer to the woods. They worried less during the summer, when the bears and wolves were fat on the plentiful smaller beasts found roaming the woods, and the air was far warmer than in the harsh winter months. Having been overlooked while teams were being chosen – I wasn't sure if it was the fact that I stood a good few centimetres taller than most of the girls and some of the boys, or if it was the whispers I'd heard that my excursions alone to the forest made them uneasy – I was standing on the lowest branch of a tree inspecting an abandoned nest. That was how my mother always referred to my hair. As a bird's nest.

Broken shards of speckled blue eggs lay among the grass and twigs. A raven's nest, then. One that had served its purpose. Perhaps they were somewhere else in the same tree, watching me inspect their old home as they learned to live and fly. Judging by the pieces of shell, they had all hatched—

"Do you not want to play with us?"

I nearly fell off the branch at the sudden voice below me. A boy I only knew through Enja, Sølvi, stood under the tree, his hands folded behind his back. I didn't know how long he'd been standing there, but staring at birds' nests would do little to quell their concerns about me.

"I don't have a group," I told him, backing away from

36

the nest to sit on the branch. "I'm fine."

"You can be in my group," he offered, beckoning for me to join. I saw a girl stop running to listen and stare. "I must not have seen you during the choosing. I'm sorry." He looked genuinely apologetic, but his green-brown eyes had a way of always smiling even when he was serious.

I shrugged. "I'm happy to watch."

"It's midsummer. We should all be enjoying ourselves."

"I was enjoying myself."

"What were you looking at up there?"

I glanced back up to the bundle of twigs. "A raven's nest. It's empty, though. They all hatched and left."

"Ah. It's that time of year, I suppose. Anyway, will you join us or not?"

The girl who had stopped running came to stand at his shoulder. She cupped her hands around her mouth and leaned in to whisper something in his ear. Somehow the cupping, meant to muffle, only amplified her words. "My mother said she's a witch. You must have heard the stories of when she called the wolves to kill poor Ragna's baby. Leave her be. It's best for everyone."

A frown knitted Sølvi's brows together, and I swallowed back a lump in my throat. It was not the first time I had heard those words, and it certainly wouldn't be the last. They had heard me speak to the animals from time to time, even though the animals never spoke back, and I spent more time out of doors than within them. Children were meant

37

to behave, meant to come when called and meant to play with one another daily in the village, scampering about after their chores. Chase rabbits. Learn to hunt together. I behaved well enough, but I didn't enjoy their playtimes, with wooden toys and games of hiding behind houses, waiting to be found.

"I wonder, then, how your mother is so familiar with witches," Sølvi said as though he was deep in thought. The girl blanched. "Perhaps I should go and ask her." He turned towards the village and craned his neck, as if searching for her.

"You shouldn't," the girl said quietly. "Mama says we should listen to adults. If she thinks the girl is a witch, she must be a witch." There was defiance in her voice, but also uncertainty.

"And what if I told you my own mother thinks you are a witch?" Sølvi continued, cracking the knuckles on his hands one by one. The lines around his eyes and the way his mouth kept twitching like he was trying not to smile said that he was enjoying this more than the girl realized.

She swallowed and stared at the ground. "Then she would be wrong."

"But my mother said it, and so she must be right. Perhaps I should warn your group. . ."

Without another word, the girl ran off, back into the village.

I stared at my feet as they dangled in the air, feeling

the burn in my ears and cheeks. I still didn't know exactly what a witch was capable of, though they came up from time to time in our stories and poems. Perhaps I was one and didn't even know it. If a witch meant someone who preferred the woods to a house and the wind in her hair instead of the smoke of a fire, then I would wear the title with pride.

"Well, witch? Do you want to play with us, or not?" Sølvi's smile melted the uncertainty growing within me, and I hopped down from the tree to join the game.

Chapter 3

Through the tangle of needles overhead, I caught glimpses of the stars as the darkness danced between the treetops. I kept glancing up, vaguely afraid that the sky might once again be bathed in red. I didn't have much by way of a plan, but I needed to be away from the village with the same kind of urgency as when awaking from a nightmare, convinced that it was real. Away from Ragna and the others. Away from Eri. Away from where everyone would be talking about the red lights. If I had days left to live, I couldn't spend them in captivity, and I couldn't spend them reliving the feeling of dread that had flooded my body at the sight of the red sky. I would rather the forest be my walls and the wind be my music than ceaseless chatter about approaching death.

A howl split the air again, and a rabbit darted across

my path and away – away from the sound. It wasn't as distant as last time. Either I was nearing them, or they were drawing ever closer to me. Whichever it was, I allowed myself to be on my guard, though I wondered why my fear had been kept largely at bay. Perhaps over the course of the night, between the red lós and the village meeting, and my conversation with Eri, danger no longer frightened me. Perhaps I didn't care what may come.

Weapons were cumbersome to carry, but I always kept a small knife tucked down my boot, just in case. My father had taught me to wield it many years ago, as all of us children had learned. I felt its pressure as I moved along; a faint comfort, though I hoped I would never have to use it.

Stillness crept through the trees. The call of the owls and the rustling of night creatures all seemed to quiet at once, even the chilling caw of the crows. The wind softened to a faint rush high overhead, and even I stopped walking as an unseen force bid me be still. As if the forest were thirsty, silence seeped in, filling every nook and crevice, every cave, every recess in the ground. Something was changing, and my very skin tingled in response.

I turned in a slow circle, taking in the woods around me. There was a tree nearby that I could easily climb if the need arose, but not yet. I tried to understand why this sudden silence and close proximity to wolves had not left me shaking, but I couldn't find an answer. There was no logic to it, so instead I forced my mind to focus on the present. Clarity and determination were the pathway to survival.

Far away through the trees, seven or eight large shadows moved towards me with the slow grace of creatures that feared nothing.

I didn't move. I didn't breathe. A lock of hair fell across my face, but I didn't dare brush it away.

The forest was dark and dim, details scarce at a distance, but their size could not be mistaken. Though they drew closer, their footsteps made no sound in the snow. Every lithe, deliberate step seemed almost human in its grace and purpose. When the shapes had nearly reached the spot where I stood, they fanned out, moving to stand in a circle with me at the centre. Was this how wolves hunted? I had imagined running and chasing, howling and snarling, but perhaps that was only when faced by quarry that dared to fight back. They must have known how many of them there were, and only one of me.

Their watchful eyes tore into my soul with the force of a winter storm that should have rendered me powerless. I turned to meet each of their gazes one by one. Some of the wolves were dark grey, the colour of the sea at night or before a storm. Others were white, little more than a disturbance in the snow. And some were in between, patches of grey and white ebbing and flowing from head to tail. I was cut off from the tree I had chosen as an escape, and I would likely not have the time to reach for my knife before at least one of them was upon me.

If these wolves were out for a hunt, this would be my end.

One – fur almost wholly white with grey strands flecked throughout – threw back its head and howled to the stars. At such a close distance, the sound was sharp, deafening, resonating somewhere deep within my core. I kept my eyes on its face, vaguely remembering not to show fear. They may have outnumbered me and been raised in these woods, but I had intellect and agility. I could use those to my advantage.

And yet, a sensation swirling in the air around me made me think I would have no need for it. These were wolves, and I had seen wolves before; seen them ripping into the fur and flesh of some crying, helpless animal. But these weren't like those wolves. Somehow, they were different.

With another howl that ended in a yelp, the white wolf took a few graceful steps towards me, eyes still boring into mine. I drew in a breath, my hand flexing as I thought of reaching for my knife. The distance between us closed slowly – now I could see all the details of those icy eyes, the individual whiskers growing out from its snout. My window of time to react was shrinking, and yet I stayed as still as the trees around us.

An arrow flew through the trees from my left and lodged into the wolf's right shoulder. It took a stumbling step sideways before it fell over on its side. I turned, shrieking.

"Stop! Don't shoot!" I waved my arms wildly, searching for the source of the arrow, and a few metres away, Eri stepped out from behind a tree.

Anger burned through me.

"Monster!" I screamed, but before I could speak again, the other wolves were already off and running through the trees, disappearing with silent steps into the clouding north. Eri darted off after them, but I knew they could outrun him.

I dropped to my knees beside the wolf with the arrow – it was panting, trying to catch its breath, eyes searching mine. "I'm so sorry," I said, unsure if I should remove the arrow or leave it in. Either way, it would almost certainly die. "I'm sorry."

My head swam. Too much energy and worry and fear all at once. The world lit up in a flash, and then darkness clouded my vision and the ground gave way to nothingness.

Chapter 4

Do not let her die.

Fire crackled. Light pressed against my eyelids. I blinked once. Twice, climbing out of a deep dream where there was something I had to do. Someone I needed to save.

Home.

I sat up quickly, my head spinning, and imagined I saw a wolf and an arrow and Eri holding a bow. And those words weighed heavy in my mind, though I didn't know why.

Do not let her die.

"What happened?"

It was my mother's voice that answered. "Eri brought you back last night. You'd fainted."

I collapsed back on to the bed, pure frustration making

my skin flush. "I have to go back," I said, and then moved to get up.

"You can't, Janna," Mother said softly, and something in the way she said it gave me pause.

"Why not?"

Before she had even answered, I remembered the village meeting. The cold resolution in Ragna's face. The things that had been said. The last time I had seen my mother, she was entering Oben's house to discuss Ragna's proposition. I should have forced my way in, insisted on being a part of the discussion, but I had given in to Ragna's words and turned away for a walk in the woods, like the child she thought I was. I kicked away all blankets and furs, too warm.

"We put it to a vote among all of the villagers," she said. Her voice was rife with sadness, weighed down by whatever she was about to say next. "They voted overwhelmingly to seal off the village. It's happening today."

"I wasn't here," I said quickly, jumping to my feet. "And neither was Eri, or Enja, for that matter. We didn't get to vote."

"Your votes would not have changed anything, Janna. Only a few voted against it."

I could see all their faces standing there the night before, see the fear and the worry and the frustration that haunted their features, and I could picture the vote in my

46

mind. Picture them choosing the option that might – just might – give them a chance. Fearful minds are quick to search out hope, even if it's false, and Ragna gave them what they craved. She painted a picture of safety and life, and they ate it up like starving creatures would, giving no thought to anyone else. A scream boiled up in my chest, but I quelled it before it had the chance to escape. The plague could take days or weeks to arrive, and weeks or months to leave. The thought of being trapped here for so long – and trapped with the dead and dying, blood melting into the snow, spluttering coughs the only sounds to be heard within miles – made me sick deep in the pit of my stomach, and worse, the thought of what sort of message it would send to the other villages. Granted, we rarely saw them, did almost no trade with them, and especially now in the dead of winter found very little reason to make the long trek through the snow to the nearest one. But if someone came calling, if a fisherman came to trade for deer meat or some of our stockpiled wool, if they *needed* something, word would spread around like fire through straw that we had closed off. That we had left everyone else to die while we stayed safe and secluded within our own walls.

"How soon?" I asked.

"Now. Today. They are already working to divide up the watches and light fires around the outside of the village."

I thought my heart would stop altogether as the walls seemed to reach out towards me, sealing me in. "Now?"

"Now."

The forest. The hills. Open stretches of undisturbed snow. That was what I needed; what had given me hope and strength over the last year. They had got me through the darkest part of my life to date, and the thought of not seeing them again for weeks – or never, if the plague found me – was suffocating. "What happens if someone leaves the village?"

Mother spoke each word carefully, ensuring I received their full meaning. "Then they will not be allowed to return."

I collapsed back on to the bed, as the wood of the roof fractured and spun overhead.

The sun was harsh, glinting off the snow and threatening to blind me as I all but stomped through the village towards Enja's house. It was the first place I had thought to go after waking up; the first place I had *wanted* to go. But was it Enja I truly wanted to see, or was it an old habit that had yet to die, from the days when I made this walk to visit Sølvi? I avoided answering myself, because I didn't know.

There was a comfort in making this walk, and in these hours between the red lights and the plague, when our village was collapsing in on itself and fear had climbed atop our trembling bodies to reign over us, I was desperate for comfort.

All the houses were alike, although they varied in size. Wooden walls lined with mud and rocks kept out the harsh winds. The streets that wove between them were little more than packed earth from frequent walking, now smothered with trampled snow. Most homes housed several generations, the elderly living with their children until their death. My grandfather and grandmother on my mother's side had passed away nearly ten years ago, from a great sickness that had swept through the village and claimed many of the older folk. Of our family, only my father's father remained, though he lived across the village with my uncle.

One by one, the homes slipped by, all the same. The door to Eri's family home was closed, but I couldn't help glancing at it as I passed, tempted to kick it open and wring his neck for what he'd done to the wolf. But all in good time. I would have nothing *but* time to deal with him when we were all locked in the village for the foreseeable future.

My hands shook as I stood outside Enja's – Sølvi's – house. I had been here so many times before, for dinner, for games, to spend time with his family, to ride out snow storms, or to bring him over to our house. Memories hung thick in the air around me, threatening to choke me and rob me of air. Was that a faint scent of him? His hair always smelled of leaves in the forest, and his clothes carried the soft scent of dried kitchen herbs. But – no. The sight of his home, the echoes of a bygone time that my mind wished to once more make real, made me almost believe he was here. And the understanding that he wasn't here was an anchor weighing my soul to the ground.

After four knocks, the door opened. It was her mother. His mother. They were his eyes, staring back at me in surprise. A sad sort of recognition settled into her features. "Janna?"

I drew in a steadying breath and brushed my fingertips along the door frame. "I just came ... to see Enja. Is she in?"

Hildur shook her head, but I didn't miss the surprise in her movements. I had not come here seeking out Enja's company in what felt like a lifetime. "She went to walk along the perimeter, to see if there was someone who would let her out. I tried to stop her, of course, but you know how she is. I might as well try to tame the wind." A sad sort of *what can you do?* passed across her face, and for a moment, I could see just how tired she was.

"No one will let her out," I assured her, taking a step back. The overwhelming familiarity was seeping into my skin, finding its way into my bloodstream and making me nauseous. I wanted nothing more than to turn and run, but I wouldn't. Not in front of Hildur. I swallowed heavily and gripped the door frame for support.

"If you find her," she said, "please bring her home."

I nodded, then spun around and walked away as quickly as I dared, until I had rounded a handful of other homes and his was out of sight. The world tilted and spun, left and right and up and down blending together until my knees met the ground and I fell.

I tried to breathe. *There's no air.*

I tried to stand. *Your muscles are too tired. They've been tired for a year.*

I lay down and rolled over to stare at the sky. *There's no beauty in a sky that gives host to the red lós.*

It was the voice I had been fighting since last winter. I couldn't stand the sound of it, whispering in my ear every dark and wicked thought I spent so long trying to push away.

Slowly, I struggled to climb to my feet. When I was certain no one was around, I leaned back against a tree trunk set between two houses on the outskirts of the village and closed my eyes, focusing on the rustle of leaves and call of birds to calm my racing heart.

The house looked the same. It smelled the same. He could so easily be there, sitting just inside the door, working on a pile of arrows or stringing a bow. He could have been only a few feet away and turned to look up at me when I knocked, his eyes shining with firelight and the scent of dry leaves wrapping me in an embrace. He could have.

51

But he didn't. And he wasn't. That was the worst part: how nothing had changed except that he was no longer here, which meant that somehow, everything had changed. Life in Skane was a game which everyone ultimately lost, but some lasted longer than others. I was not ready for his part to be over. I was never going to be ready.

What would he say if he were here, knowing, as we all did, that somewhere on this island, the plague was alive and well again? That the next person to cough could be the first person to die, and that in one of these quiet homes around me, someone could be staring at bruises forming beneath their skin. Could see the redness in their eyes reflected in a pool of water. Those stories that had once made my skin crawl with horror, of blood and death and pyres full of bodies, were real, and they were here.

"Janna."

Slowly, I opened my eyes and looked to my left. I knew that voice.

"Enja."

A bird called overhead. In the distance, a man's voice echoed off the trees.

"You look unwell," she said. Both hands hung at her sides, her white-blonde hair tied up behind her head. Shorter than me by a few inches, she still somehow managed to cut an imposing figure when she stood still, icy eyes unmoving in their search of your soul. Her long grey cloak, lined with fur, danced in the gentle breeze. I'd had such a fondness for her, such a respect for her once upon a time, and those familiar feelings, like being in the presence of family, came trickling back.

But so did a sense of discomposure as I was gently reminded by a voice in my head that I had forgotten how to be around her. That I had abandoned her when she needed me. *She abandoned me first*, I shot back.

I pushed off from the tree and crossed my arms behind my back. My ears burned, though whether from the embarrassment or the frustration that warred within me, I didn't know. "I just came from your house."

A breeze toyed with her stray hairs, and her eyes wandered briefly before finding mine again. She didn't nod or move, she just said, "I see it every day, you know. Her face. His face." She flexed her fingers one by one, perhaps working methodically to stave off tears. "Some days I hardly notice it, and then she'll say something that he would have said, or make a face like he would have made, and then it's all I see. It's like my lungs slowly start to fill with water until, all of a sudden, I can't breathe. She doesn't know, because she doesn't see herself, but we all see it. I see it."

It was a rebuke, in her own way, reminding me that I wasn't the only one to hurt when he passed on. But pain had made me inconsiderate. I had retreated into myself after he died, searching for comfort in the safety of my own mind, though I had found none. Could I have been happier if I had run to her, instead?

A year of unspoken words formed a fog between us, and I was half tempted to use it as cover to turn and run away.

"She asked me to send you home," I told her. Somehow, steering the conversation to the present kept me from fleeing.

"I'm sure she did." She bent down to pick up the white fox at her feet, who nestled into her arms and closed his eyes. "They are sealing us in as we speak, stringing rope and twine between trees to outline our perimeter, since so few of them know their way around these woods. They are setting up patrols to walk along it, to watch for anyone trying to pass in or out. We're no better than sheep."

That pressure in my chest returned, a crushing sense of suffocation and helplessness. "Even sheep find ways to escape." I brushed a piece of frizzy hair from my eyes and breathed deeply. "I wasn't here for the vote, or I would have fought it."

"Neither was I."

"Wouldn't have made a difference."

"I know."

Footsteps grew louder close at hand, and two women with armfuls of rope moved by at a careful distance, casting furtive glances our way. I knew that look so well, the one that reminded me the village would always keep me at arm's length, never trust me enough to let me in. But I didn't want to be let in. The villagers didn't trust people they didn't know, and none of them had tried to get to know me or Enja. They had seen wild girls with wild ideas, who hated the village and loved the forest, and had slapped us with a stamp of witchery which we would never be able to remove.

Once a few paces past us, the two women began to whisper to one another.

No one trusted anyone after the red lights, least of all us.

"They won't look at us the same until it's over," Enja said. She tried to sound matter-of-fact, but there was a shake to her voice as though tears were not far off. I wanted her to find her strength, to drip with it, even if it was only skin-deep. To let the words of the villagers run down my body like rain and fall away. "We aren't to be trusted." There was a devilish twinkle in her eye.

I nodded, and shrugged, watching as the women disappeared into the trees. "I'll never look at any of them the same way again, either."

I walked Enja back through the village but said goodbye before her door came into view. I couldn't bear to look at it again so soon. When she had disappeared into her own house, I should have gone home straight away, gone to speak with Mother and Father about what I could do to help the village prepare. I'd heard voices as I walked back towards home, echoing in the woods and emanating from doorways, speaking of funeral pyres that would need building and sunset prayers to plead with the Goddess for mercy, but all it had done was make me vomit behind a house. I'd felt ashamed after that, like I was too weak to do anything of value, but when I'd stood up again and taken in the cold night, that sickening fear had been overshadowed by something stronger.

I held my chin high for a long moment, collecting my thoughts as this new fire, this sense of purpose, kindled to life in the darkest corners of my heart. Voices and whispers hissed around me as I walked, and now and then, words reached my straining ears. I was curious about this village now, curious about those who had come to a decision I so despised. Now, more than ever, I wanted to understand the people I lived with. It had only taken eighteen years.

"... should have done this last time. Goddess knows what they were thinking..." The words were spoken by a man to a woman as they carried armfuls of wood from a shed towards the open door of their house.

"... always been underestimated. I've long said she should be a leader. She knows what's best for us. Always has..." spoken by one of two men who sat inspecting an array of weapons laid out before them. Bows and arrows and knives. I prayed silently that they were not speaking of Ragna. And when would they have need for so many weapons? If other villages came calling? To end the misery of those with the plague? I wanted to ask, but I kept walking. It was better if I didn't draw attention to myself.

I pulled air into my still-healthy lungs and stopped near the centre of the village. Was there anyone on this island, at this exact moment, who had yet succumbed to the plague? Anyone who felt blood seeping into their lungs and eyes and nose and mouth, who knew that the end was near. I didn't know exactly how it felt to have the plague, but I had imagined it more times than I should, out of either fear or wicked curiosity. But it had always been a distant thought, still under the safety of a blue or green or clear sky. It was never sure. Never imminent.

I gently touched my chest with a hand, that feeling of suffocation beginning to return.

The soft but distinct voices of children made their way to me on a light breeze. I followed the sound to a small grove of trees on the edge of the village and stayed out of sight behind a woodshed while I listened. One seemed to be telling a story to the others, who listened in silent rapture.

"... says the witchfolk still live among us, conjuring storms in the sky, or causing hunters to lose their way in the woods. They bring predators upon us and frighten away any game we could hunt. Because"– He sucked in a breath, drawing out their interest for as long as possible – "witches don't need food to survive. They live on human blood, stealing it from you while you sleep, over and over again every night, until one day, you just won't wake up."

I peeked around the shed to see the three children sitting on the ground gingerly touch their throats.

"And the worst part of it is, you won't even know when you meet one, because they look just like you and me. The only difference is that, on nights with no moon, you can't see them at all. They just..." The boy snapped his fingers. "Disappear."

The children gasped.

"But my father says that they live among us, that they walk the same streets as us; that they are the ones who bring the plague to our veins and watch us bleed to death one by one."

One of the children cried, and another asked, "But who are they?"

The boy who was speaking shrugged. "I don't know. My father never told me. I don't think anyone knows."

I should have gone in to break up this vile little meeting of theirs, but something told me that I did not want to insert myself into something like this. That it would be better if I stayed silent and out of sight for the moment.

"You there," a man called to me gruffly. He tossed

me a heavy coil of rope, which I just barely caught. "Take this to the southwest perimeter edge. They need more. Hurry up."

I smiled drily when he turned his back to me. When no one was looking, I tossed it into the first fire I could find.

When the veil of night settled over the village, Mother had asked me to return to the house – and I would, eventually. My breath was sharp and biting in my lungs, and the areas of my face that were exposed to the cold night air stung like a skinned knee. I wandered the edge of the village hugging myself, glancing up at any snapping twig or rustle of the underbrush. I was still within the perimeter, of course, but far enough that I felt the satisfaction of pushing the boundaries. I hated myself for thinking it, but with every breath I took in, I couldn't help but imagine the plague slipping into my lungs and spreading like floodwaters through every bit of my body.

Terror rose, but I stamped it down.

In the distance, through the silhouetted trees, I could make out the echoing voices of those on the watch, and here and there I could see the faint glowing of their campfires. In the space of a single day, my world had shrunk to the size of the village, and I had to breathe through the alarm that tried to swell within me. Now, more than ever, I wanted to hear Sølvi's comforting voice.

The village is what you make it, he would say. *Find a way to be yourself when you cannot be where you wish.*

His time with me had, for a while, sent him spiralling to the outside alongside me and Enja, but his friendship with Eri and his ability to hunt – a skill so highly valued in our village – soon saw him welcomed back into the arms of our people. He could walk that line in a way I never could; be the wild boy I loved, and the upright one they cherished, somehow without losing himself along the way. It was everything or nothing with me, outsider or insider, but no part of me wanted to surrender any of my freedoms to spend more time with people who whispered that I was a witch whenever I turned my back.

I wasn't unlike them, though. We were all working towards the same thing, all fighting for something that was never, for any of us, guaranteed: a future. It was why they sealed off the village, why they didn't trust the others dotted around Skane, why we hunted and gathered for the winters. We were all just trying to survive, but I did not want to survive in a world where the only heartbeat that mattered was the one in my own chest. Sølvi gave everything he had for me, including his own heartbeat, and I would not watch us devolve into a divided, fearful society that rose up only by standing on the bodies of the weak.

Something small – a rabbit, perhaps – scurried through the nearby shrubs and disappeared into the shadowed forest. The woodland was just coming alive for the night, and I wished with an aching heart that I could be a part of it.

Night-time had always been my refuge, my retreat from the glaring vulnerability of day. But tonight, the dark held wicked things with gleaming teeth, and the wind carried the whispers of the plague on its back, breathing death into my ear.

A door opened maybe ten yards away, and a man stepped out to collect an armful of firewood. He stopped when he saw me, staring for long enough that my skin prickled. His eyes, what I could see of them in the faint light from his doorway, glittered with distrust. A moment later, he returned to his house, and I was again alone. Superstition ruled the village, and I, considered an odd outsider from childhood, was the easiest one on whom to lay their suspicions.

As if I could conjure the plague from the frozen air around me.

Early the next morning, they found a body.

Chapter 5

I could sense death nearby before I had even opened my eyes. It hung in the air around me, in the tone of my mother's voice, in the faint cries outside the house. Death is a force of nature for which the world around it must make room.

"What happened?" I asked, sitting up and kicking off the blanket.

"There's been a death," my mother replied with a face as white as snow. "One of the men from the watch."

A sinking fear weighed down my heart as I asked, "The plague?" I hated it, but dread rose up within me as I pictured blood and bruises and burning bodies.

"I don't know. I don't know." She shook her head and rubbed her face. "Your father's gone to find out more. I do not even know his name."

A parade of familiar faces swept through my mind,

grandfathers and fathers and sons. Could the plague have cropped up so quickly? Could it have found some secret, silent way into our veins, and be hiding there, even now? I looked down at my hands as though they would tell me something, looked up to my mother's white face. Even if the plague never came, the creeping disquiet and suspicion were enough to set us all against one another. I couldn't trust my own blood, and that realization set my body to shaking.

Mother stood and grabbed a heavy wrap. "Come. If someone is in mourning, we must comfort them."

Even in the midst of death and uncertainty, duty called, and I forced myself to oblige. I pulled on my warm clothing and boots, staring into the flames of the fire. All had been well and still last night before I had come home. *What had happened?*

A grey day accented the grey mood of the village when we stepped outside. The streets were largely empty, but a few people stood in small groups, whispering to one another or dabbing at their eyes with bits of cloth. I rubbed my hands together against the morning cold as we made our way towards the centre of the village, where we found my father with a cluster of people. He glanced at us quickly, and there was something in the look he gave me that made me stop walking. A warning that only lasted for a fraction of a second. Loud whispers reached my ears.

". . . no sign of the plague," my father was saying. "No

proof whatsoever. You've let your imaginations run wild."

"A man is dead," someone shot back. "A man is dead, and soon the rest of us will follow."

"His neck was broken," my father said, gentler this time. "That is not the work of the plague."

A few pairs of eyes snapped towards me – including those of the man I recognized from last night. The one who had stepped outside to gather firewood and had seen me. Something was happening, a layer to this conversation that I hadn't yet comprehended, but it made the hairs on my arms stand up.

"I saw her outside last night, prowling around the village after dark." Hate burned strong in his eyes. "And now Fiak is dead."

There was a roaring in my ears – anger or terror, I wasn't sure which – and for a terrifying moment, my vision clouded. "How ... dare you?" I hissed. I hadn't seen Fiak last night, or any of the people on the watch. I had stayed close to the village, as my mother and father wished. For once, I had mostly listened to them, and yet...

A woman moved a step away from me, drawing her shawl tighter around her shoulders. When she turned to look at me, my heart sank. Ragna. Those bitter eyes told me that, in a way I didn't quite understand yet, she had won. "Perhaps it is time to acknowledge what many of us have long known, Sívar," she said gravely to my father. "Your daughter is a witch."

64

My breath caught in my throat as the gathering fell silent. They were surely jesting, in a frightfully unfunny way. Surely. "Don't be a child, Ragna," I nearly spat at her, fury ruling my tongue.

"Bedtime stories have no place here," my father said with deadly calm.

"I've seen her and that other girl, Enja, wandering the tree line around the village, whispering together," said another woman. "They planned this together; I would bet my home on it."

I hated the way they spoke about me as if I wasn't there, as if I was an invisible target at which they had all come prepared to shoot. This was all circumstance, accident. I hadn't intended to see Enja yesterday, it just happened, and we spoke of nothing of substance other than her mother. Clearly they hadn't heard *that* part.

"This is nonsense," my father said quietly, his hands shaking. "There is nothing but happenstance to suggest my daughter has done anything wrong. She is still grieving from a loss of her own; she is hardly one to take a life."

"And therefore the perfect one to do so," Ragna said, as though she were stating a fact. Others nodded in agreement. I could see it happening, see an idea taking root in their minds and flourishing, like they had been waiting for it. That was how suspicion worked. How blame worked. Find someone with a weakness and then exploit it until it makes sense. But I knew something they didn't:

I *hadn't* killed Fiak, which meant that someone in this village had.

My father folded his hands together and looked at the ground for a long moment. "We will discuss this more formally this afternoon," he said. "We will gather the whole village, and we will talk and discuss in truth and fairness." He looked at Ragna and repeated, "In truth."

"And in the meantime," Ragna replied, never one to relent without a stipulation, "the two of them should remain indoors. The village isn't safe while they are allowed to roam free."

"I cannot speak for Enja, but as for my daughter, she will not be a prisoner until she is guilty of a crime," my father said, very slowly and deliberately. "And if you would like to challenge me on that, you know where I live."

He turned back towards home, taking my mother's trembling arm. I should have kept quiet and simply followed them back to the house, but I paused first, drawing close enough to Ragna to ensure that no one else heard my words.

"And if I were a witch," I said softly, "I could do just as much damage indoors as out."

Her face paled as I turned away, vaguely satisfied, but knowing I should have stayed silent.

Our friendship grew faster than a dry twig snaps in midwinter. I knew somewhere in the back of my mind that he only played with me out of pity, but then there was a sort of genuineness to his joy when we ran into the woods for a game of hide and seek, or when we raced each other to the top of a nearby hill and crashed to the ground out of breath. Once we lay there through the evening until the stars came out, and then spun stories to each other about the constellations, growing wilder by the second.

"What if the horse," I said, pointing to the great horned beast, "is sad because she can't find her foal, and she's cursed to roam the skies for eternity, never giving up."

"Too sad," Sølvi replied, shaking his head against the ground.

"Then maybe the giant was the king of the jōt, and when he died, they sent him up to live in the stars so that they could always see him. Maybe the other giants truly loved him."

"I suppose it's possible," Sølvi said. "But what if all of the constellations"– he swept his arm up to the night sky – "are gods and goddesses of their own small islands? Islands we can't see. Maybe he's the god of an entire island of giants just over the horizon from Skane, or maybe the horse rules an island roamed by nothing but more horned horses. Maybe right now, on another island, another boy and girl are lying down looking at the sky wondering if the woman is a goddess somewhere. Maybe the whole world is just a series of islands with stars for gods."

I blinked and stared at the stars, finding no reason why

that might not be the case. In fact, I loved the idea that we weren't alone on our own little island, and that there were many more hiding just over the horizon, waiting to be found.

"I wish we could send them a message," Sølvi mused, waving as though his vision of another boy and girl could see him right in that moment. "You know, 'hello, we're here, come find us.'"

"I'm sure they are happy on their island," I replied. But as if the sky had heard Sølvi's wish, faint bits of green light began to dance overhead.

Mother and Father stared at me from where they stood a few feet away. I sat on a stool, arms folded in my lap, wishing myself hundreds of miles away from the looks of uncertainty and scepticism on their faces. Were they frustrated that I had got myself into this mess, or did they at all suspect me of being guilty? It was difficult to tell, but I refused to wither under their glares.

"I had nothing to do with it," I protested, although I had said it several times before.

"Then why were you out?" Mother asked, and the way she spoke, the way the words of doubt from the villagers had wormed their way into her mind, made me cold.

"Because I always go out at night," I replied, keeping my voice calm. I didn't want the growing desperation I felt to be revealed. Didn't want it to seem like I had something to hide. "I never laid eyes on Fiak. Never even got close enough to hear his voice."

"You can see how it looks," Father said. The tone of his voice made evident his attempt to walk the line between giving into his suspicions and maintaining my innocence.

"Just tell me," I said, hugging myself tighter, "why I would kill that man. I barely know him, I never speak to him, and I couldn't even pinpoint his house in the village if my life depended on it." I stopped to draw in a calming breath. "Yes, I can see how it looks," I agreed. "But I know I didn't do it, and someone else did. Enja and I ... we're the easiest ones to blame. I wouldn't expect anything less."

"If we can't find a way to prove you had nothing to do with it..." My father's voice trailed off, but I stared into his eyes, imagining all the ways that sentence could end. *I can do little to help you. The village will punish you. I fear what will happen to you.* "I won't force you," he said presently, "but I would advise you to stay indoors and out of sight. People will be looking for an opportunity to press their point. Do not give them another reason to show others your guilt."

"There is no guilt to show," I said. "Any proof they come up with is of their own devising."

Father tilted his head to the side and let out a long, tired breath.

"Do as he says," Mother told me. She spoke in that

69

tone that she used to use when I was a child, the one that dared me to disobey her. But back then I was often wrong, avoiding my chores or disappearing for hours without telling her where I was going. Looking back, I could understand her frustration, but now ... now, I knew I didn't deserve it. I didn't know how Fiak had ended up dead, but I'd had no part in it.

"Fine," I said after a long moment. *Caged animals are known to grow vicious*, I wanted to add, but thought better of it.

Chapter 6

Father led me to the village gathering in the afternoon. The way I followed him, trapped in the village as we were and made to stay indoors all morning, no part of me felt free. A prisoner, that's what I was. A prisoner in the home I had known all my life. Fear was my captor and the villagers were the bars to my cage. People stared at me as we walked past – but they glanced at one another furtively; quick, sharp looks as if to ensure just by looking that the plague hadn't yet taken root. A child coughed as we walked by, and even her mother took a step away, eyeing the girl with unease. The death was an easy enough distraction for the moment, and one that had captured the attention of everyone in the village, but it was already wearing off, as all were reminded that, somewhere on this island, sickness was creeping closer.

Ragna hardly waited for us to finish walking before she spoke up, her voice strong and steady, as though lies were as easy for her as the truth. "Last night, this girl was seen wandering around the outskirts of the village alone, and hours later, a man was found dead."

A few people in the crowd shook their heads, slowly, as if they simply couldn't believe it. *Such evil*, their faces said. *She deserves to suffer.*

"I need not remind you, surely, of the grisly circumstances that have followed this girl around like a shadow. She witnessed the drowning of Finni, the death of the good-hearted Sølvi, and"– she ensured her voice trembled some – "saw to the violent death of my own dear son. There are other matters to which we must soon attend. The plague will be upon us any moment now, and we must be on our guard. And yet, we cannot let such dark times as these distract from evils like murder. Therefore, I propose that this matter be closed with haste and ease. A simple vote should do." She rested a hand on her hip and looked to the crowd. Confidence dripped from her, chest out and chin high, as though challenging anyone to stand up to her.

"Ragna, perhaps—" my father began, but she silenced him quickly. Her might and wrath were wasted on a village as small as ours. She could command armies if she tried – vile, wicked armies.

"There is nothing to be said for your unfortunate

daughter, Sívar. Save your breath before we begin to suspect you, too." Her eyes sliced into him, sharper than icicles at the mouth of a cave. Then she turned back to the crowd.

"How many among you find this girl guilty of murder?" she asked. Such a simple question it was, but the words cut through the air like a knife through flesh, and they hurt every bit as badly.

Air all but left my lungs.

"A moment, before you vote," I heard myself saying, although the world danced around me, and the edges of my vision were growing dark. I worked to breathe through it, to maintain my clarity, but the struggle grew more intense by the second.

Ragna began to protest, but Alff waved a hand through the air. "A minute or two won't hurt anything, Ragna." She whispered something vicious, but my eyes were still too blurry to see her face.

Everyone stood facing me, ready to hear me speak. I cleared my throat but ended up coughing and spluttering.

"I don't know most of you except by name," I began, too quiet at first, but gaining strength. "Most of you know who I am, because most of you knew Sølvi." My voice broke at his name, but I pushed on. "Sølvi died last year, a loss I, along with his sister and mother, are still recovering from." Sølvi's father had died many years ago, slipping on ice and taking a fall from a cliff. Enja had

73

only been two. I tried to find them in the crowd, but the faces all blended together into one mass of anger and distrust. "I was there when Sølvi died, and he died protecting me. He died so that I could keep living, and breathing, and going to sleep and waking up. I sat with him while he took his last breath, and I sat there, alive, my lungs still filled with air, and my heart still beating, while the boy I loved slipped away."

Something tingled on my face. Tears, perhaps, but I had gone numb.

"I witnessed death in the most intimate way possible, and I would never, ever, wish it upon anyone else. I would never take someone's life away from them. And if you don't believe that, then I have nothing left."

There was only silence from the crowd, but I didn't know if it was a good, tearful silence, or one of continued unease. Ragna broke it.

"This girl," she said, sweeping an arm out to me, "was there for the death of the beloved Sølvi. She was there for the death of my own dear son, Orri. And now she was there for the death of Fiak, a well-respected man who met a too-sudden end. How dare you believe each of those to be happenstance? This is her witchery at play, entrancing you with stories of pain and heart to play at your softer sides, while she gets away with murder. Do not play the parts of fools. Now, I ask you again, how many of you here find this girl guilty of murder?"

It happened slowly at first; a single hand here, a few fingertips peeking over someone's head there, and then, in the time it took for me to draw in a long breath and release it, the village centre was a sea of raised hands, all condemning me for something I hadn't done. I forgot how to breathe, briefly. Forgot how to balance myself enough to remain standing. A hand grabbed my shoulder and kept me upright – my father, probably, but my vision had grown dark and the shadowed world swayed around me.

This was fear, alive and writhing and black as soot, villagers fighting for control at a moment in time when they had none, when death was imminent for many and the most they could do was point their fingers at me and damn a life that at least wasn't theirs. So twisted. So wrong. And yet I was powerless, a dead leaf caught in a windstorm.

Satisfied, Ragna turned back to my father. "You know what must happen now, Sívar," she said, her voice colder than the air biting my cheeks. "You know what happens to murderers."

"You will do nothing to her," said my father, and he stood up taller than ever before. He cut a respectable figure, tall and lean but with a frame that had seen hard work. His grown-out hair was tied behind his head, that dear but hardened face painted with anger and heartbreak. Even through my wrenching fear and the sickness rising within me, I was proud to call him my father. "She is still my daughter."

A murderer. The word was shards of frozen spray from the winter sea. That's what they were calling me. A murderer. Only a day ago I had tried to save a wolf from Eri's arrow. I had helped Enja save the fox that now shadowed her every step. I had spent the past year in agony after the death of the one I loved. And yet they could call me a murderer.

Fear is a wicked beast.

I had never known a murderer in my lifetime. Respect for the island and our desire to push onwards and make the most of our lives after Löska kept violence and retaliation largely at bay.

"You would protect a killer, Sívar? Perhaps you should say as much to Fiak's wife, if she were present and not mourning the death of her husband. Because – need I remind you? – her husband is dead. All our prayers to the Goddess will not repair his broken neck."

"She is not a killer. You know as much, Ragna. Janna could not kill a spider if you held a knife to her throat."

The icy calm of Ragna's angled face was unmoved by anything my father said. My vision began to grow clear again, and I could see the faces staring back at me, see the faces damning me. They didn't know me, and I didn't know them. As hard as I tried, I could barely recall any of their names – that woman there, was it Elspa? Her son Anarr? In many ways, I had brought this on myself. I hadn't given them a reason to trust me, but then again, I had never imagined they'd be trying me for a murder I did not commit.

So eager, they all were. So ready to see me ruined, as though it would save their necks in the coming days. Even if they burned me now, I wouldn't live to feel my body catch fire from within, to cough blood from my lungs until it drowned me. I wouldn't watch those few souls I loved suffer in unimaginable ways until it took them and moved on to the next. Fiak's death was wretched and unforgivable, but far more deaths were creeping towards the horizon with every frigid breath they pulled into their lungs.

"She must be burned," Ragna announced, raising both hands up to the sky. "Punishments cannot be withheld for family. All must pay the price. And that other wretched girl, if she was complicit in this, she will burn as well. This is the price of evil."

I heard a cry from the crowd, but it took me a moment to single out Enja's mother. They would do it, and without thinking. They would take away the daughter of a woman who had only just lost her son. In her face filled with sorrow, I could see him, and I could see how desperately he would try to comfort her if he could. My heart nearly cracked in two at the sight, and I wanted nothing more than to embrace her, to tell her that I would not let it happen. I reached out towards her as tears stung my eyes.

But I was powerless. My words would fall on apathetic ears, and her tears would be brushed away and ignored.

Already people were closing in, and the protection of my father would not last long. I shook at the helplessness, the frenzied pain in her eyes that I couldn't extinguish.

"Tonight," Ragna said with a sense of finality that settled into my bones. "Prepare a stake."

It was too much. Too much. My knees gave out and I fell to the ground, but even before I was done falling, hands were pulling me up, roughly, yanking me through the village at a pace my weakened legs could not keep up with. Then it was dark, and I was in a room I didn't recognize. A lock clicked. Voices sounded outside, and then footsteps faded away.

And I was alone.

Chapter 7

I wouldn't – couldn't – let myself think of my approaching death. It lurked in the shadows around me, tried to snap at my ears with pointed teeth. I pushed it away by telling myself stories I had heard as a child, fables parents told us to help us fall asleep. They reminded me that the world was bigger than our small village, than this island, where we were both unfettered and prisoners of the sky.

The Löskans had told of Maåd, an ancient deity who cherished the night so much that she surrendered her skull to the sky, becoming the moon we see today. I thought of it nearly every time I looked up; every time I saw a full, bright moon illuminating the dark sky and, as a child, I used to wonder at how someone could love something so much. I never knew, when I heard such stories, how much truth they held, superstitions steeping everything in mystery and myth. When we left Löska, though, all other deities fell away, as the Goddess commanded our attention. Maåd, had she ever truly been anything at all, had faded away into words that warmed only the rarest of bedtime stories, living in the minds of those who heard them.

As we grew older, the tales became more frightening, to ones of the trees transforming on midwinter nights into great, terrible men with horns and swords of ice, who danced and hunted beneath a starlit sky, and who you could only see if you fixed yourself a crown of dead animal horns and waited quietly in the woods. I had wanted to try it, when I was younger. Wanted to sneak out in the bitterly cold midwinter and see if the tales were true, but I could never work up the courage. Or perhaps it wasn't a lack of courage, but a desire to let such stories be. To believe them, even without reason to do so. To believe that anything was possible. So I had lain indoors on many a winter's evening, staring into darkness and imagining the ghostly men with animal horns hunting beneath the glistening, distant stars.

I went through story after story, some light, some frightening, and some I had forgotten either the beginning or the end of. I worked, huddled in the gloom and hugging my knees, to remember each time I had heard them, recalling every word that cast a cloud of white into the air as we clustered around a fire and listened. There weren't enough of those nights, I realized. Not if I was about to die. Those stories took me places I could never reach on foot. An escape from the confines of the village. I didn't tell them, because when I tried, the words all ran into one another and got jumbled on the way out, but they stayed, for the most part, safe and whole in my head.

Sølvi used to tell me some ghostly ones under the stars, away from the village where the sinister things of which he spoke could so easily have come wandering out of the trees. But that was what made them so real. I would shiver and pull my cloak tighter around myself, clutching his arm as if to remind myself that I wasn't alone. I loved those times with Sølvi.

Sølvi.

My mind wrenched to another shadowed and frozen place, lying there waiting, *waiting*, listening with all my might to hear if he was still breathing. He always was – until he wasn't.

I choked on a sudden sob and fell back, an arm covering my streaming eyes.

"No," I whispered to the solitude. *Don't make me think about it.*

Time crept by. I had never given much thought to just how long a minute was, let alone an hour. My mind had gone blank as they'd dragged me in here; I didn't know where I was. How long did it take to gather kindling? Perhaps my father was still fighting for my life. It wouldn't matter. When a village like Sjørskall made up its mind about something, it never changed.

But Enja. Her disorderly whitish hair filled my vision, twinkling eyes still every bit the child on most days. Would she burn as well? Could they do that to her still-grieving mother? I liked to think that in any other village, the answer would be no, but here, it was simple.

Yes.

The walls closed in. I could feel them pressing against me, squeezing the air from my lungs. Thoughts of forest clearings and snowy fields seemed more like distant memories from fractured dreams than anything real. What parts of my life had truly happened, and which parts had I imagined to fill the gap after losing half my heart? The past had always been the one sure thing, the one thing I could count on, but now, locked away in blackness, I wasn't sure I could trust my memories. I dug through the memories, waded through the murky uncertainties until I found his face, and I gripped it with everything I had. He was there, and he was real, and he was smiling at me. I reached up to touch him, to run my fingertips along his cheek, and I could almost feel it. Almost convince myself of his presence in the room with me. Grey furs piled atop his shoulders framed a smooth face, earnest eyes delving into mine as though he wished he could take away my pain and suffer it himself.

"Wait for me," I whispered, and let my hand drop

back to the ground. "I'll be there soon." I reached into my pocket to find it, the thing I always carried with me but never looked at, but it wasn't there. I thought back, muscles frozen, to having tucked it under my pillow to sleep so I wouldn't crush it. When I had learned the news about Fiak, I hadn't thought to pick it up again, which was jarring, because I took it with me everywhere.

There was no knock, but at some point during the long stretch of time, the door cracked open, and Ragna stepped in. Bitter cold, delicious air flowed in behind her as she closed the door, along with the distant scent of evergreen. I sat straight, stiff and terrified.

"I have never liked you, Janna," she whispered in that harsh, loud whisper that sliced through the room. "As I think you know. And you have never liked me. If it wasn't for you, I would still be a mother. I would not have been robbed of love and joy these past few years. And yet, I have some pittance of respect for you. That is why your role in this will be an honourable one."

There seemed to be some greater point to which she was building, so I stayed silent, waiting.

"Sjørskall, and indeed all of Skane, has long been in need of leadership, but in a place like this, it cannot be earned through good deeds and kindness. Only through respect."

"And I suppose that leadership ought to come from you," I said through my teeth. "But many in this village despise you, and rightly so. Your journey to veneration has not even begun."

She prickled. "By condemning a murderer and executing a long-suspected witch at the same time, they will have no choice," she said. "Death has followed you like an incoming tide, and yet I had nothing to do with most of them. You laid the groundwork yourself; all I had to do was build upon it."

Ragna had killed Fiak.

"I have not yet decided if I truly think you a witch, and yet your hand in my son's death can be explained in no other way. But the village, as you know, made up its mind years ago. They have no room for sympathy with the growing pile of bodies behind you, and that is your own doing, my dear, not mine. Those who survive on Skane are those who understand how it works, and I understand this village in ways you cannot. You are the first step in my journey to leadership, and I thank you for that."

If I hadn't paused for a breath, I might have launched across the room to strangle her.

"I heard stories growing up of what happens to people like you when they die," I whispered, as though my words might conjure evil things from the shadows. "They were full of fire and teeth and suffering. Your path will be littered with bodies and bones, and you will pay for it when you leave this world."

"Yes, I've heard all the stories and even made up a few of my own," she said, turning as if to leave. "But they are just stories. I believe in the true world, in snow and stone and fire."

"Why?" I asked quickly, and she hesitated. "Why did you come here tonight?"

In the dim light from her candle, her eyes glistened. "I couldn't watch you burn without you knowing it was all my doing. The village will for ever believe you were the murderer, and my careful design would go for ever unnoticed. At least now it can die with you."

Though her words said otherwise, I couldn't help but wonder if perhaps guilt had begun to gnaw at the back of her mind, and she desperately needed to tell someone what she had done. Sjørskall was harsh and unkind, but people here were not prone to violence against each other.

"Rest easy on the other side, Janna," she said. "The Goddess will know of your innocence, even if Skane never does." She opened the door. "Again, if you believe such things." And she left.

Minutes or hours crept by, each second slower than the one before it, until again the door open, and Enja was pushed in. She stood still for a while, perhaps allowing her eyes time to adjust to the dimness or working to accept her imprisonment. As the light from the brief opening of the door faded away, I slid sideways to give her space to sit.

"What happened?" I asked presently.

She took a slow step forward and slumped to the ground. "Mother had locked me in our house to keep them from taking me, guarding the door with a knife clutched close to her heart. Little good it did her when they finally came, though she fought them off with her soul. I couldn't even cry as they pulled me away."

Though they may not have fallen, tears lurked just behind her voice.

"I'm so sorry," I whispered.

There was a rustling as she shifted, and a gentle thud as her head rested back against a wooden wall. "She's lost so much," she said softly. "Now she's lost everything. They'll make her watch, too. Watch as her last child burns. Ragna will make certain of that."

Half of me wanted to vomit on the floor, and the other half wanted to scream and raze this whole village to the ground. My hands shook; I sat on them.

"They speak of witchcraft and dark gods that are worshipped deep in the woods. They say it's why you and I venture out so often. Threads have been woven from one thing to another; from you to the red lights and the plague, and Fiak's death. They've seen all they want to see. They've made up their minds." Her voice shook at the last words.

My breathing was ragged, the way it was after hours of crying. The turmoil in my mind grew worse by the second, a never-ending sequence of thoughts and feelings that collided and fractured into a fog so thick I couldn't think through it.

"We could break down these walls," I said wildly. "Kick them to pieces and run like there's a fire behind us. We could do it."

She let out a rush of air that said, *It's a nice idea, but foolish.*

"We're the wild ones. Unpredictable. That's why we scare them, Enja. They built cages that we broke out of, and we can do it again. We can shatter this cage." I ran a hand along the wood, hardly wincing at the sharp pinch from a splinter. Beyond these walls was freedom, the forest, my beloved caves.

And the stake that sat ready for me on Døv Hill.

I buried my face in the fur of my cloak and screamed.

None of it was right, or fair, or just, but our village had started a whirlwind in which Enja and I had been caught up. We couldn't pull free or reach the ground to run away. And if only I could make them see that this would all be for nothing. Tomorrow, when our ashes were hardly cold, and with nothing left to distract their minds, thoughts of the red lights and the plague would return with a crash. Perhaps it was here already, making a home in someone's veins. Or perhaps it was still days away, our village merely in sight.

They came for us sometime later, hooded and hidden by darkness. Those who would light the fires beneath us preferred to keep their faces concealed, perhaps to avoid our judgment in the moments before we passed. My stomach bubbled and churned as I tried not to think of it, tried not to think of how long it would take; if I would pass out from fear first, or live until the flames had consumed me. On an island of snow and ice, death by fire was almost unimaginable.

The sun had long ago set as they led us outside, and the last few villagers were wending their way through the streets and up to Døv Hill. The name had settled in sometime over the course of its history of burnings – which were rare, but lingering. They were saved mostly for those who denounced the Goddess, and murderers. I had never seen one myself, but I had heard that a burning had happened when I was very young, during an especially hard winter when food was scarce, and a man had killed a hunter returning from the woods with a rabbit.

Two men had died because of a rabbit.

Here and there, I heard voices singing out of touch with one another, an old song about death saved for executions. I didn't know all the words, but I knew two lines, and they slithered into my ears like something cold and macabre.

May the river of death be shallow and calm

And may the god in the shadows forgive you your wrongs.

We didn't speak much of what came after life, not for people who didn't join the Goddess in the sky. Ascending to the stars was a reward, something joyous to look forward to and lighten the prospect of death. But for murderers and evildoers ... for people like Ragna, well, a far more lurid crossing awaited her.

The sky was starless and angry, a storm well on its way. In the darkness, faint, small snowflakes darted about on the breeze. By morning, all talk would be of the snow that had fallen and what sheep they had lost in the storm. We would be long forgotten, because no matter what distractions tainted our everyday lives, Skane would always fight to reclaim our attention.

I glanced around as we were ushered along, my eyes meeting briefly with Enja's. Even in the dim light, I could see the resignation in her face, where there had always been a fire. She knew nothing more could be done, and though I was older than her, seeing that acceptance stirred terror in my gut.

There were perhaps five or six men escorting us, more than was necessary. Did they think we would use our *witchcraft* to burn them where they stood, or call upon all the ravens in the forest to tear at their skin until nothing remained? It almost brought a twisted smile to my lips, the things they thought we were capable of. I half wished I could conjure some sort of devilry upon them for the things they were about to do, or at the very least, for some sort of escape.

The last of the houses slipped by as we walked, and my feet faltered. It had never felt like home before, but now, in what may well be the last moments I would ever spend here, a longing tore away at me. I wanted my bed. Our warm fire. My mother and father. I wanted one more night where things were the same, where I was safe and warm inside while a storm raged outdoors, the screaming wind lulling me to sleep. I wanted to wake to the smell of warm bread, to the sounds of my father wrapping up to help the village dig through the snow.

Why had I given my parents so much cause to worry?

The hand holding tightly to my left arm yanked hard, and I was forced to keep moving. I turned as much as I could while still walking forward, until the last of the familiar houses had been eaten up by the trees.

The ground rose up and away, on a path I rarely took. Up to Døv Hill. We were so close now. I could hear the hushed whispers and the voices of the gathered crowd, all eagerly awaiting such an enticing distraction. At last, the burning of two suspected witches. Girls they long worked to steer away from their children, who would work to enchant them or curse them or – as with Ragna's son – kill them. For those villagers, this day had been too long in coming.

Sickness had been building within me, but when we

rounded a turn and the crowd and the stakes and the men with torches came into view, sheer rage blazed to life, consuming my confusion and terror as fuel for its inferno. They were still singing the song of the death god, so happily damning me – so they thought – to the shadows of the underworld. Anywhere, so long as we weren't here. So long as they were safe and sound, for these final hours or days before the plague.

They were ready to watch us burn.

Excited.

My feet slowed again as they tried to push us up the hill towards the waiting stakes, and Enja all but stopped. I had been imagining it while locked away, unable to shove it from my mind, but seeing it now, all those horrors made real, nearly stopped my heart from beating. It couldn't end like this.

I could kick and scream and try to run away.

I could claw and tear at their faces and escape into the woods.

I had spent the past year learning how to escape. Why should now be any different?

But if it wasn't the fire, then it would be an arrow as I tried to run, or a knife thrown through the air. In those fleeting seconds, I couldn't decide which death I preferred.

They pushed us forward, roughly, and if I did not use my own feet, they would simply carry me. There was nothing I could do against so many.

The faces of the crowd were a blur as we stumbled past. I couldn't make out anyone I knew, but I could hardly recognize my own hand if it were before my face. In the hustle, I reached for Enja and just barely managed to brush her fingers before we were pulled away. Were my mother and father in this crowd? Would they be forced to watch? I did not want to believe that this village could be that cruel, but they were.

The stakes rose up before us. They weren't always here, but however much time had passed since our imprisonment in the shed had been more than enough to erect them. Tall posts stuck into the snow and tied by two ropes tugging in opposing directions to nearby trees, just far enough that they wouldn't be set alight. Atop the snow around the posts lay piled kindling and dried brush, the kind that would burst into flame from a single spark.

"No," someone said, almost in a whimper. "No. No. No."

It was me, I realized, though my voice sounded hollow and distant, like a voice from a dream that you can't remember clearly.

"This isn't right," I whispered. "This isn't right."

"Having my son torn apart by wolves wasn't right," said a voice behind me. I twisted as far as I could, despite the men who held my arms so tightly. Ragna stood with her head high, hair pulled back away from her face, and glistening eyes drenched with satisfaction. "Breaking the neck of an innocent man was not right. What had he done, Janna? Had he witnessed some sorcery for which you for ever silenced him? We will never know, because Fiak will never speak again. You've seen to that." She took a step closer, her eyes ripping into mine as though ensuring her next words would find their home. "Sitting idly by while Sølvi passed away *was not right.*"

The blade of her words sank into my heart. I thought I would die, then and there, standing atop Døv Hill only steps from the pyre that would burn me alive. I slumped forward, my body giving out, my head too heavy to hold up any longer. Everything about me was so *heavy*, like a stone had been added to my shoulders every day since Sølvi had passed, and just in this moment, it became too much.

But a tiny voice echoed off the bare walls within me, almost inaudible at first. I caught only fragments, a jumbled collection of words that drifted upward. *Stronger than this. Resilience. Find the might within you.*

I thought, at first, as the seconds stretched away, that it was Sølvi's voice urging me on, helping to pick me up and face the world for these last minutes I had left. But it wasn't Sølvi's voice at all, I realized, as the echoing fragments of words became a roar that thundered towards my mouth. It was my own. It was the pieces of me that had wandered off last year, that had been buried under snow or carried off by a freezing river. Pieces of me that

93

were too wounded and weak after I had lost Sølvi to carry on any longer. Pieces I thought I would never see again, but had somehow, against all odds, fought their way back home.

I could feel them slipping into place, working with the fuel of my new-found strength to once again make me whole. It wasn't everything – perhaps some of the pieces would remain lost for ever – but it was enough.

It was enough.

Slowly, deliberately, I raised my head to meet Ragna's gaze. There was such a glittering pleasure in her eyes, as though she knew how deeply she had wounded me. But like midwinter cold turning water to ice, I was healing with reckless speed.

"Ragna," I said, and my voice was strong and deep. On the edge of my senses, I heard the murmuring crowd grow silent. "My life has been a short one," I said. "Eighteen years on an island I love and hate, that loves and hates me. A blanket of snow and ice, of blood and broken hearts, and funeral pyres seeing off those gone far too soon. I love every moment, and hate every second, but when I take my last breath, I'll at least know that I *lived*. I breathed in the forests and sang to the stars, and I *loved* with a passion that ripped me limb from limb when I lost it. I am a thousand broken pieces that make up a whole girl, and when I die, I die with a full heart, and a mind as clear as ice. There will be no river of death for me, Ragna, but in a few days' time, when your heart only beats to drown you in blood, and your vision goes red as the lós, there will be a river for you. And as you lay choking and sobbing for help that will never arrive, I hope the last thing you see are the stars overhead, where I'll be looking down with an eternity of joy and light stretching away before me like the vast and unbroken horizon."

One of the men holding my arms loosened his grip momentarily, then tightened it again. The hush that had fallen over everyone remained, the only sounds the distant rustle of growing wind in the trees. Enja stood beside me, and though I couldn't see her directly, I could feel her eyes moving slowly between my face and Ragna's.

Ragna's eyes had gone hard and cold as stone. I imagined that every vile thing she had done and said was flashing before her, sparks from a flint stone that seared her vision. No doubt, some part of her, and many others gathered here, did truly blame me for Orri's death. It was as if she had spent so long pointing a finger at me, condemning me for this or that and spreading whispers around the village of my witchery, that she had grown to believe it herself. That she had been working to forget it was her who had killed Fiak, merely to use his dead body to stand higher than the rest of us.

"Burn her," she said, devoid of feeling. "Burn them both."

The time had come. My confidence wavered, but I couldn't let it show. Ragna would feed off that, bring that wretched smile back to her lips, and I would not let that be the last thing I saw before I died. They shoved me backwards against the stake, and as they did so, I tilted my head back to look up at the sky. The stars were hidden from view by the advancing storm, but they were there, hanging just behind the clouds, and knowing that brought me at least some comfort.

I wasn't ready to die yet, because I wasn't done living. I had made a promise to myself after Sølvi passed, after what he had done for me, that I would do something to thank him. Help someone. Pay off the debt I owed, in some way. I couldn't imagine myself truly dying, because my life wasn't over yet. But Skane seemed to have other plans for me.

Enja was silent beside me as they tied her hands. I looked over to see if she was crying, and our eyes met. Hers were dry, but there was the fear there of a small animal who had lost all hope. I wanted, instantly, to rip my hands free and cut her loose, to beg anyone who would listen to spare her life, but it was no use, especially not now that I had so enraged Ragna. Those gathered here would do her bidding in a heartbeat – partly because everyone feared her.

I wished, for a fleeting moment, that I could call upon wolves to come tearing up the hill, to rip apart these ropes and free us. But I couldn't.

Flames from a torch drew nearer. I couldn't tell who held it, because spots had begun to fill my vision as my hands and legs shook. Any second now. It would start any second now. The kindling. The flames.

An arrow whispered from the darkness and landed in the foot of the man who held the torch. He stumbled backwards and crashed to the ground, a rumbling groan rising from his throat. In the dim light, I saw blood dripping into the white snow.

"Stay where you are, the rest of you," said a voice I recognized instantly.

Eri.

Five of them came up the hill, cloaks cascading behind them in the wind, and bows drawn back and ready.

"Turn around," Ragna growled, facing them with her head high and her hands hanging straight by her sides. She was tall, but not as tall as Eri, who loomed over her as he advanced so close that the tip of his arrow brushed her nose. "We can set this whole village on you if need be."

"So help me, Ragna, I will sink this arrow between your eyes if you open your mouth again," he cautioned, his words on fire. She took a step back, but he followed, keeping the tip of the arrow against her head. "That's a promise."

"I will order them to tear you apart," Ragna whispered, her voice rasping and low. "They've come for a burning, and they'll do anything to see it done."

"They want what you've told them to want," Eri said coolly. "If I rid them of you, that won't be a problem. They will follow whoever looks the part of leader. Right now, that isn't you."

"Let them go," someone said beside Eri, motioning to the men beside me and Enja. It was the voice of one of the hunters, but I didn't know him well. Was his name Jonár? Why had I never bothered to learn it?

The village hunters were much like brothers, hours on end spent helping to ensure our village's survival. Eri was not a leader, but they respected him enough to follow him, to aid him, to come to our rescue. I was thankful for that.

"They've brought death and evil to our village," said the man to my left, but I felt his grip loosen some. "The plague may well be their doing, the witches. How can you bring that upon these innocent families?"

Eri had reached the end of whatever patience he'd come with. "If they could conjure the plague, they would have done so a long time ago, Dagur. Pull yourselves together. You're the one touching their hands and holding them prisoner. Who do you reckon will be the first to go if they are capable of such things?"

All the men standing around us backed away. My hands had not yet been fully tied, so the rope dropped into the snow, and I was free. I moved to Enja and worked to loosen the rope that bound her.

"You can't let them go," Ragna hissed.

Eri's only response was the sound of a bowstring stretching and pulling as an arrow was aimed.

"Don't shoot, for hell's sake," someone shouted from the crowd. I knew that voice.

My father stepped forward, his heavy cloak tied around his shoulders, and a travelling pack on one arm. Mother stood behind him.

"We'll soon have enough of death as it is," he said placatingly. "No one's life needs to end tonight."

"Agreed," Eri replied, moving around Ragna while keeping his arrow aimed firmly at her face. "Jonár, handle this for me. I'll be back." He looked to me and Enja and jerked his head for us to follow.

We moved to the far side of the hill, where the raven shadows of trees made it nearly impossible to see any detail. But with a burst of relief and comfort that set my eyes burning with tears, Mother, Father and Hildur all gathered around us.

"You have to leave," Father whispered, so quietly I barely heard him. "Both of you. You have to go far away where they won't find you, and quickly. Don't return until after the plague has come and gone. Their accusations will be long forgotten by then."

He said it so matter-of-factly, so directly. It was an order – albeit one from a place of love. The wave of relief began to dissipate, and confusion took hold. I had just been so sure of death, of fire and pain and an end just within sight...

Enja whispered with her own mother, and the sniffling of tears and muffled sobs cut at my heart.

"You're dressed for travel," I said, remembering his heavy cloak and pack.

"We're leaving, too. We'll find another village or somewhere we can survive until this has passed. They'll never forgive us here. The hunters may have an easier time of it, but not us."

"Come with us," I started, but Father stopped me.

"We can't, Janna. You were sentenced to death for murder and witchcraft. You have to run, and swiftly. We'll only slow you down. Run as far and as fast as you can, and do not look back."

"But—"

"Janna, you must go," my mother whispered. Her voice cracked with tears, and part of me realized the finality of this brief moment. These might be the last few seconds I would ever spend in their presence.

Voices reached us from the distance. Shouts, as though the crowd had grown angry and wild.

"There's no time," Eri whispered from a few paces away.

"I love you," I said, and tears fell fast. I threw myself towards them in an embrace that I wished would never

100

end. "I love you. I'm sorry."

"And we love you," they both said.

"Hurry, Janna. You have only moments." Mother shoved something into my hands, a piece of paper, I thought, but I couldn't see it in the darkness. I shoved it into my pocket, hoping with everything I had left that it was Sølvi's letter to me.

I turned to Eri, who stood with an arrow still strung in his bow. "Th . . . thank you," I said, words escaping me. "I don't know what else to say." I touched his shoulder hesitantly.

"Sølvi was my brother in almost every way," he said softly. "Of course I would help you."

Shouts rang out again.

"Go," he hissed, and turned, raising his bow.

I drew in a steadying breath and grabbed Enja's hand in my own, then we turned and dashed from shadow to shadow until the forest had claimed us.

Chapter 8

The dark fingers of the trees reached out for me, sometimes brushing against my skin like something far too human. In the distance I could see fires, where patrols sat guarding the perimeter of our village. We could hopefully slip between them easily enough, silent as a shadow, giving them no cause for alarm – but then again, if it were so easy, why were they there at all? Word would soon spread that we had escaped, and I expected they would soon be after us with all the might they could muster. We needed to be far away, and before the snow fell deep enough to hinder our journey. Where we would go after all of this, I didn't know, but I could decide later. For now, we had to get past the fires.

"Stay close," I whispered into Enja's ear, afraid to make even the smallest of noises. I didn't know how jumpy those on the watch were, or what sort of orders they had been given. I wouldn't put it past them to shoot us.

The fox, who'd been lurking nearby when we had fled into the trees, slinked and slithered before us, his feet silent in the snow.

The fires loomed larger as we crept along. Echoing voices sounded off the trees: those on the watch chatting to pass the time. They wouldn't know yet, wouldn't know what had happened within the village. To them, it was just a long, dark night on the watch.

Certainly, in some confused way, the plague might offer us a kind of protection. Those within the village, and those guarding it, may be less inclined to follow us with its threat looming large on the horizon. I prayed it was so as we slipped through the forest. I could make out huddled forms sat before the fires, long shadows of swords and bows leaning against trees, near enough to grab and make use of if need be.

Our steps slowed to an agonizing crawl. Any moment now, shouts could erupt behind us, villagers hurrying to raise the alarm after our disappearance. Hurrying to keep their prey from escaping.

The witches are on the run.

I didn't know what would become of Sjørskall in the coming days, but I knew with a relieving certainty that I would not be around to find out, and neither would my mother and father. Eri would see that they reached somewhere safe. He would look after them, and in these moments of terror and confusion, that was a grounding comfort.

Gradually, the last of the fires was behind us. We could quicken our pace now—

Shouts.

The voices rang off the trunks around us, coming from the village. Those seated around the fires rose quickly, grabbing their swords in the moments of uncertainty, ready for anything. I doubled my speed, using the cover of the shouts and the rustling of those rising to mask my steps. Enja followed barely a step behind me, and we ran as one through the trees. These woods were my home. Every hour I had spent out here, silent as one of the animals and learning every inch of its needle-ridden, snowy floor, was unknowingly preparing me for this night.

The snow was falling heavier now, and they could soon track us with little trouble – if they dared.

Footsteps close at hand snapped in my ears. Someone was giving pursuit, and although I was tall and long-legged and accustomed to running, a grown man with strength and vengeance fuelling his steps could easily overtake me. I focused on the midnight-dark woods before me, plotting my path through the trees and rocks in advance for a speedier course, knowing Enja could keep up. That was all I had: I knew these woods better than he did, whoever he was. I had to use that, or I would wind up back at Døv Hill with a fire growing around me.

"They're over here!" the man thundered, much closer than I had imagined. Surely if he just reached out an arm, he could grab one of us by the shoulder and end this chase any second.

A hidden store of energy rose up to the challenge, and I pushed my breathless body further, harder, pounding across the forest floor with a speed I had never managed before. Enja was a flash of blonde hair beside me, running with a fury that could so easily leave me behind. Faster and faster, between great, wide trunks and over rises in the snow where rocks were only barely concealed.

Until the thin, knife-like point of a tree branch sliced through my cheek and sent me spiralling for enough seconds that I toppled over, and the man caught up to me in an instant. Strong hands pinned my shoulder to the ground, and I heard him fumbling with a rope tied at his waist. My vision was dark and hazy after my fall.

The snow fell on to my face, tiny kisses from the sky that once upon a time made me feel better. The wind of the growing storm stirred the trees, and I listened, these last few seconds of freedom slipping by far too fast. I saw the stake, and the hill, and the crowd of faces, and my thin string of hope snapped faster than a brittle winter twig. Eri would have left by now to help my mother and father, and whatever hunters had remained would have their hands full in the village.

A sudden rush. A subtle thud. And the man before me let out a shriek so loud it nearly frightened me. He reeled back, dropping the rope he had at last mastered and gripping his right foot, where an arrow protruded from his boot. I didn't know whose it was – one of the hunters, perhaps, or a villager who had grown warm to my cause – but I didn't have time to consider it. I rolled over, jumped to my feet, and ran and ran and ran.

I didn't look back.

The shadows around us strengthened, and we had to pick our way through the woods even slower than before. My mind worked to trick me with every step – was that a shrub, or the hulking form of a wolf? Was that rustling from the wind that toyed with the forest around me, or were villagers slowly creeping towards me, and any moment now I would be tied in a heap on the ground? Shadows breed terrors and wicked things, I told myself. And what will be will be. One foot. Then the other. Every mile must be crossed step by step.

Still, a sort of quiet uneasiness settled over me, and I picked up my pace. Racing against the villagers was one thing, but a winter snowstorm was something else entirely. I knew the way the storms would arrive in what seemed like minutes, bringing furious wind and snow, and a cold so bitter your body wanted nothing more than to give in and give up.

I glanced sideways at Enja. How odd, that we should go a year with hardly a word spoken between us, to now be thrown together and flung from the village to survive on our own. We had hardly spoken since escaping the perimeter, just a brief *are you all right?* when I had caught up to her once more, but that was all. Silence had eased back in and made itself at home, and I wasn't sure I was ready to break it.

Through the uneasiness, a slow-burning sense of adventure began to flare up, as we ran headlong towards freedom. The village had always been a prison – a safe one, perhaps, but often vicious and closed. I had long dreamed of these moments, of being far away, and now, with the plague looming ever nearer, perhaps I could use this freedom to do something. If I couldn't stop it, I could survive it, perhaps, and help others to survive it. I would find a way. I would do something, whatever I could.

The possibilities were bright and beautiful. I just had to find them.

We carried on, stopping momentarily at a narrow stream, crossing by way of a few flat rocks, and picking up our direction again on the other side. I did not come this way often; it was a long trek to the sea and I had found plenty of caves in the hilly areas around my village, but once or twice the need or desire had arisen, and

I had made my way out to lay eyes on the sometimes glistening, sometimes bleak and murky Grey Sea. Those from other villages still sailed it, sticking close to the shore in their fishing boats, but sailing it, nonetheless. I had never been on a boat in my life. Never even seen one afloat, but each time I had seen the sea, rolling and angry and dark, I had less of a desire to do so.

It had been Enja's idea. There was a place we could hide, she had said, and after all the turmoil of the night, I had not bothered to argue. One hiding place was as good as the next, as long as it was far from the village.

I kept stealing glances behind us, around us, over each shoulder in turn. All the fear that had built up when I had thought I was about to die had yet to dissipate, and it made me jumpy. Uneasy. And then I remembered the terror they had all shown over the approach of the plague, and I realized again with a sinking sensation that Enja and I were likely the only two souls about on this island. Sjørskall had lost us, and they would soon give up. It was better that way.

With every step we took, the world seemed to grow darker. We moved faster and faster, until we were all but running as we fought to keep track of which direction we travelled. Far from village lights, and with no moon and no torch, I had to trust my eyes and ears more than ever before. Only the faintest flush of light illuminated my pathway, an ambience of the moon behind the clouds, perhaps, or something in the snow itself that caused it to glow. Something in my gut began to clench with worry as the wind blew harder and the village fell further and further behind. The wilds were around me, and they were my home. No more protective walls I had long grown to hate. No more warm fires and mother's meals. No more familiar faces for me.

No going back.

Raven shadows melted and oozed around me, caressing my shivering form as we picked our way over rock and root. Night-time had always held a charm for me, but tonight was different. Tonight, though I was happy to be free, the darkness held a dread, like something alive and waiting and watching, and I was its prey. As though the night had become a living, breathing creature. I could feel eyes on me in every direction, feel the sensation of being exposed despite the dark.

Tree trunks creaked around us. Boughs rustled and murmured.

Sometime later, the land fell away up ahead, and I could just barely see the billowing, wild darkness of the sea. Enja reached it first and stopped to take it in, gathering up Siiva in her arms. Out of breath, I closed the distance between us and stopped atop a cliff so high my head spun. The cliff face must have been at such a sharp angle that it hid the beach – if there was one – below.

All I could see was water and faint white crests where waves and swells crashed against one another.

The ground around where we stood was rocky, the snow thin and uneven. I couldn't see the loose rocks that tripped me up as I moved closer to look for a way down. Enja grabbed my hand.

"I know the way," she shouted, though I could barely hear her over the roar, wind and water consuming all other sound.

She returned Siiva to the ground and motioned for me to follow, though my head still spun from our height and the wind that threatened to push me over the edge. She took a few long steps to our right, where the edge of the land split off in a steep decline that hugged close to the face of the cliff.

I swallowed back a wave of sickness. It was just wide enough for a person to stand on – barely. I stared at it, at the sudden, unforgiving drop on one side and the thin strip of rock that meant the difference between life and death. One unsteady step. A sudden uptake in the wind. A single loose rock. That was all it would take to end our lives, to unceremoniously send us tumbling over the edge and to the sea waiting below.

"I can't," I said. Fear took hold and my limbs shook. "I can't."

Enja turned back to me and crossed the distance between us, gathering up my hands in hers and boring those icicle-blue eyes into mine.

"You *have* to," she said, and the resonant certainty of her voice, even over the wind, calmed me. I didn't even need her to carry on; my mind filled in the rest.

You have nowhere else to go.

The storm is too strong.

We will both soon freeze to death.

The last one was the worst, the thought of being so cold and afraid ... again. I couldn't let it happen. I wouldn't. No matter what.

Enja had come this way before. The descent could be made, and if she had done it, I could do it.

Drawing in a long, steadying breath, I placed one foot on the ledge behind her.

Chapter 9

My whole body shook as I painstakingly made my way down, which made it more difficult. I tried to breathe evenly, to keep my eyes anywhere but at the drop below, but I couldn't help the occasional glance, which would start a new round of shaking. Heights had never terrified me so much, but then again, I had never found myself clinging to a ledge far above the sea. I kept both hands flat on the rock face beside me, pressing my body up against it as much as I could without pushing myself backwards. In places, the ledge grew even narrower, barely wide enough for my feet, and in other places it spread out again, but only by a centimetre or two.

I tried not to count my steps so the time wouldn't feel so achingly long, but even that was difficult. Each step felt like an age, and the end of the descent did not seem to grow any closer. What I thought was rock could so easily be ice, so I had to test each step before I trusted it to my weight, tapping gently, pressing firmly, then moving forward. Slowly, surely, one foot after the other, the top of the cliff disappeared overhead, and the sea grew closer and closer. The waves roared below, louder now as it ricocheted off the cliff. If there was no beach waiting below, nothing but churning water and sharp rocks, I would have to turn around and climb back up the cliff face – and even now I didn't think I could do it. My energy was all but sapped, and I hadn't yet reached the bottom.

I could hardly see Enja further along the ledge between the wind flinging my hair about, and my intense focus on my own steps.

A little more than what I hoped was halfway down, my left foot skidded on a loose pebble and I lurched forward. Sea and rock spun around me as I swayed unsteadily. I tried to force all my weight down into my feet to anchor myself, my hands grabbing at the face of the cliff for any purchase they could find. After a moment, my fingers caught on an edge of stone and I stopped sliding, heart thundering in my ears. I stood perfectly still, shaking and breathing and telling myself over and over again, *you are alive*.

Even slower than before, cautiously eyeing each step, I began to make my way down again, the wind from the sea beating against me. It whipped my hair around so fiercely it felt as though a child was trying to tug it from my scalp. I should have thought to tie it back before beginning my descent, but I was pressed for time, and it was too late to attempt it now.

With time difficult to tell, clinging to the edge of a cliff, I reached the bottom after what felt like an hour. Jagged rocks and pebbles greeted me, a few solid metres of rough beach before the water began. The wild waves beat the shore, the thunder rising from my boots.

And Enja lay unmoving on the rocks.

I charged forward and crashed to a stop at her side. "Enja," I whispered. She was slumped almost wholly on to her stomach, so I gently rolled her over, fresh blood gathering at the side of her head and her cheek. "Enja, can you hear me?"

She made no response, and I looked around as if to find help from the wind and waves, but we were alone on this secluded beach, snowflakes teasing us as they made their way down from the sky.

Well, almost alone. A pair of eyes inside a splash of white fur watched us from behind a large rock. The fox.

A soft noise came from Enja's mouth. I patted her cheek lightly a few times. "Enja? Wake up. It's Janna. Wake up." I kept repeating myself, unprepared with words for a moment such as this one. She continued to stir some, her head lolling around and her eyes blinking in the darkness.

"Janna?" she said eventually, trying to focus on my face.

"Yes, that's right," I said, relief washing over me. Her

eyes were less glassy, her voice stable. "I didn't see it happen, but you've taken a fall from the ledge."

She pushed away from me and looked around at the waves and snow. "Where is Siiva?" she asked, pulling herself upward until she sat on her own. At his name, the fox darted out from behind the rock and crawled on to her lap, wary eyes watching me. "Good boy," she told him, scratching the top of his head gently.

"Do you know where you were trying to take us?" I asked, turning to examine the rest of the beach.

"Yes," she said, without looking up from the fox. She pointed at the cliff face further down the beach, where a shadow split the rock. "We can hide in there."

A cave. It had to be. As a shrieking gust nearly knocked me over, I stood and held out a hand to her. "Can you walk?"

Without answering, she urged the fox from her lap and climbed to her feet, swaying slightly. She was up and awake, but I didn't know the extent of her injuries. The worst wounds aren't always visible.

I held her shoulder for support, and at a slow but steady pace, we made our way towards the mouth of the cave. With each step she seemed stronger, and a small bit of hope burned to life.

Closer to the water, what looked like a pile of wood lay on the pebbles, though it was faded and old and oddly shaped, unlike firewood or the trunks of trees. I couldn't stare for long, as I turned my back to it and continued towards the cave.

I swept my hand wildly around through the darkness, ensuring that the path before us was clear. As I was trying to remember if I had brought any flint or candles with me, Enja pulled away and seemed to kneel, feeling around on the cave floor for something. A moment later, sparks lit up the darkness, followed quickly by a flame on the end of a torch.

I quickly examined her head in the light, using what feeble knowledge I had to assess the extent of her injury. It was cut and had bled, but it was shallow and would heal quickly – at least I hoped so.

"There's water in that jug," she said, pointing to the one she meant. "I always leave some here, just in case."

I used it to clean out the wound as best as I could, removing at least some of the sticky matting from her hair and flushing away most of the blood that had run down her neck. When she was as clean as I could make her, I collapsed on to the cave floor.

Since leaving the shed in the village, there had not been a full moment for true reflection, but now the weight of the day came thundering towards me with the power of a thousand horses. I saw the stakes and the torches, Ragna's shining eyes, my mother and father silhouetted in the dark, saying their goodbyes, and then endless snow and forest while we ran.

The fire that had run through my veins on that hill had all but vanished. Now I felt weak, my body shaking, as though if I had to, I would fail to even pull myself to rise off the ground.

"The worst is over," Enja said softly. I looked over to her, then back up at the roof.

"Is it?" Now we had to survive, to eat and sleep somewhere safe on an island where nowhere was safe, and that was if the plague didn't take us during the night.

"I hope so."

"Do you ever feel fear?" I asked, looking at her again. She turned her gaze to the fox in her lap and stroked his head. "All the time," she answered, then her eyes sparkled. "But I don't like people to know what I'm thinking." The way she said it, with a subtle smile, reminded me so much of Sølvi that I had to look away and breathe through a sob that swelled up within me. Perhaps this was why I had avoided her for so long. The constant reminders. The way I sometimes saw his face in hers when she smiled or spoke.

But that was unfair of me. Enja couldn't help it, and my pain at being reminded of him felt selfish and dirty, no matter how real it was.

Things littered the cave around us: scrolls, bits of wood, old shoes and buckets and broken pieces I couldn't even recognize. It was as if someone had been living in here, but someone with belongings just different enough from our own to look strange. I took in each peculiar item in turn, and then looked at Enja, who was still on the floor, stroking the fox.

"You come here a lot?" I said, phrasing it as a question despite the answer being obvious.

She shrugged. "It's my home away from home."

"What are all of these things?" I held up a broken piece of wood that had at one time been carved into a strange shape. An oar, I realized after a moment.

She was quiet for a moment before she said, "Do you honestly want to know?"

I nodded. Discussing the items around us meant delaying the inevitable conversation over the fact that any moment now, the village would be sealed off and no one would be allowed in or out. With the storm raging outside, there was little to be done about that.

"It was a shipwreck," she said, watching me to see my reaction.

A shipwreck. I spun the words around in my mind. "Of a fisherman?" I asked. "From another village?"

She shook her head. "Older."

"From. . .?" But I couldn't think of another possibility. No one in Skane would try to leave, not with the monsters that had chased them here lurking out there, waiting.

"A Löskan shipwreck," she said, and somehow, I'd known the answer already.

The words split through the room. I drew in a breath and

looked around again, each item holding a new fascination for me. "How do you know?" I asked, barely above a whisper.

"I assume most of what was on the boat was lost to the sea, but some things survived. Sealed barrels and boxes, a few leather satchels. Odds and ends that washed ashore on their own. There was a map of the Löskan shore, partly ruined but readable in places. Most of them spoke Agric but there's a label scratched into this barrel here in what can only be Old Löskan. *Pysk*. It has dried remnants of fish carcasses inside. And this ... well, this doesn't prove anything, but I saved them anyway." She held up a tiny pair of leather shoes that had lain nearby.

I stared, haunted by thoughts of the small form that had once worn them.

"How do you know none of them survived?" I asked, breathing away the pangs of sorrow.

"I don't entirely," she said. "But..." Her eyes moved towards a pile of rocks in the corner I had missed before. I took a step closer, something inside me urging me to stay away, and stopped when I saw a few bones peeking out here and there.

I turned away quickly and met Enja's eyes. She stood stroking the fox's head as he rested in her arms. "Did you bury them?"

"The ones I could find," she replied, staring at the pile of rocks and bones. "Which was only two or three. I think they all died before reaching shore, perhaps in a storm. Some of the bodies remained on the boat, and some did not. It eventually washed on to the beach here and lay hidden for generations."

I could understand why. It was hardly easy to reach. I knelt and picked up a partly rotted leather bag, turning it over. All these items lying about, they were all pieces of hope. The seeds of a new life that could blossom far from the death and carnage in Löska. And blossom it did, to which Enja and I were living proof, just not for these poor souls. What an end to meet after such a journey.

"Sov fridd dølaeth," I whispered to the bones. It was an old blessing for the dead brought over with our ancestors like these ones. I doubted if anyone truly knew what it meant any more, but it seemed fitting for those buried here. "Why haven't you told anyone about this?" I asked.

She shrugged. "I thought about it, but knew they wouldn't care. Not like you and I would. What would any of this matter to them?"

Her words were true, and they sparked a heavy sadness within me. All thoughts in Skane were on growing and thriving and looking ahead, which meant that lives like these, deaths like theirs, would go unnoticed, would disappear into time and be lost for ever.

I pitied them with everything in me, but I couldn't stare at the remains a moment longer, so I turned away. The rest of the cave was dark, although something seemed to flicker further inside – something that wasn't light.

My *senses* seemed to flicker, to notice something out of sight and deep in the tunnel. Something I could only feel. Enja must have felt it as well, for her eyes stared off into the darkness, the ears of the fox standing tall. Listening.

"Does anyone else come here?" I whispered, because keeping quiet felt suddenly important.

Enja shook her head. "I've never seen another person here before."

And yet it had not felt like a presence, strictly. I couldn't place it, but the sense made my skin prickle.

"I've never gone back there," Enja said quietly. "I've never left this room. But I've ... I've sensed this once or twice before, and I've always left when it happened."

We, sadly, did not have that option. "Are you armed?" I asked, and her eyes moved to a hunting bow in the corner, beside a quiver with a handful of arrows.

I pulled the knife from my boot, the handle comforting in my grip. "I would rather find it ourselves than allow it to surprise us during the night," I said quietly, as distantly the wind howled as the storm grew ever worse. "We're stuck here until the morning." Or longer.

Enja nodded, returning Siiva to the ground and moving to collect her bow. When it was firmly in her hand, an arrow at the ready, I took the first step towards the darkness of the tunnel ahead.

Chapter 10

The wide room we were in shrank into a narrow passageway. I wondered, as I did with most caves, how it had been formed. Naturally, during the birth of the world? By hand, by someone long ago? There was a sort of gentle thrill in knowing I'd never know the answer, that some secrets Skane would never give up. What things this island had seen before our arrival would for ever remain mysteries to us.

The torch rested steadily in my hand. With Enja injured, even slightly, I had to be the stronger of us two, refusing to show fear even in the face of the uncertainty I felt. That sensation had been ... unnerving. Even the fox had felt it, and though it had begun to diminish, some phantom of its presence still clung to my mind and body.

I took each footstep slowly, glancing all around us

and down to where my foot would land. This wasn't one of my usual caves that I could walk with certainty in darkness, and in the shadowed places of the world like this, it was impossible to be too careful. Every now and then I'd glance behind to find Enja a few steps away, bow strung but pointed at the ground, and Siiva haunting her footsteps. It was a good setup: whatever I missed in the front Enja could follow up on with her bow. Confident, I pressed forward.

The tunnel pinched ahead, becoming just wide enough for a body to fit through before opening up wider again. Turning sideways, we edged through, the walls seeming to close in even tighter as we passed by.

The tiny hairs on my arms, the back of my neck, all stood on end. I shivered despite the warmth of my wraps. Behind me, Siiva let out a low whine. Everything about this cave felt off but inviting, frightening but intriguing. I had never been so confused but so sure in my life as I came to a standstill and turned in a slow circle.

The light from my torch wasn't the only light in the room.

All around us, swirls and shapes and unfamiliar lettering lit up in a dull blue, pulsing and waving as though alive. It filled up every inch of the walls; every bit of space the cave had to offer was alight with writing I couldn't hope to understand. It was an art form just as much as it was writing – if indeed it was some form of writing – and for several long moments, it moved us to silence.

"Have you ever seen this before?" I whispered.

"Never." Disbelief and fright were heavy in her voice. "What is it?"

"I wish I could say. I've never—" I stopped short as the lights flickered heavily like the flame of a candle someone was trying to blow out. On and off, fading in and out and rippling around the walls as if they were nothing but water. They were reacting to something, and as daft as that sounded, I'd never been more certain of anything. "Hide," I said quickly.

I extinguished the torch and ducked behind a tall, jagged rock. Enja and Siiva did the same a few feet away, thankfully still in my line of sight. She held the fox in her lap, likely to keep him quiet, and then we waited, the room illuminated only by the blue glow from the walls.

It took a few long moments as the writing flickered more and more, dancing in a way that reminded me of the lós on a particularly cold and clear winter's night. The icy blue grew vibrant then faint, up and down, but it never went out. Then, from further down the cave, something slowly worked its way towards us. It was large and odd, but decidedly elegant, certainly not a person. As it drew closer and closer to the centre of the wide room, the realization dawned on me.

A wolf, just like the ones I had seen in the woods. Like the one Eri had shot. A large, peculiar wolf that now stood tall, its head up. I couldn't see details in the dim bluish light, but I was certain its eyes were closed. Could it sense us? Smell us? Animals could almost always sense humans and other animals, but perhaps in here, with no breeze to carry our scent, we would be safe.

A moment later, it threw its head back and howled. The noise cracked through the room, deafening in the silence and piercing my ears in a way that made me turn my head away. On it howled, the sound hungry and desperate to fill every inch of the world.

Then it stopped. Silence settled back in, and the lights dimmed. The wolf stood still for an achingly long moment, our eyes locked on its face as we waited for it to move, to howl again, to do anything at all. And when it finally did move, it slowly spun its giant, regal head – and met my gaze. I couldn't fool myself into thinking it couldn't see me. Its eyes bored into mine as if it could see beyond my face and flesh to the soul and mind beneath. My skin prickled from the cold but flushed from the heat. I was speechless and desperate to shout. Every emotion I'd ever encountered warred with one another as its gaze lingered, endlessly.

After a long, drawn-out pause, the wolf turned back the way it had come and left the cave with that hauntingly graceful walk.

I fell backwards against the floor, out of breath and dazed.

"It saw you," Enja whispered, shuffling closer. "It gazed right at you and did nothing." She turned to look back at where it had disappeared. "I don't understand."

I shook my head, still at a loss for words, and shuffled back on to my feet.

In the faint blue light, I struck the flint and relit the torch, motioning for Enja to follow me back the way we had come. Neither of us spoke as we followed the tight passageway back to the room with the Löskan items. When we were both there, Siiva darting around the room smelling everything to ensure it was all exactly how he had left it, I spoke.

"What was ... that?" But I knew she didn't know. Her eyes were wide, her face pale.

"I've never seen that before. I've never even seen a wolf that big. Once or twice while I was on my way here I'd hear their cries in the distance, but they were never very close. I didn't think they could find a way in..."

That piercing howl echoed around in my head.

"It isn't safe to stay here," I said, making my way back towards the mouth of the cave. "Not if we don't know what it is." I didn't like the not-knowing. Everything – the caves I frequented, the writing on their walls, the storms, even the red lights – were all explainable in some way, backed by history or stories or something we could

126

understand. But that... That, I knew nothing about. "It could come for us in the night." I stopped talking as I reached the cave mouth, to a wall of swirling white snow. The wind roared beyond the stone entrance.

Safe or not, we would be sleeping here for the rest of tonight.

"Janna, I ... I don't think it will come for us," Enja said carefully. She rubbed both hands together nervously, which was odd for her, ever the cool and collected one. "It looked at you. It *saw* you, and it simply walked away."

I sighed and dropped to the ground, crossing my legs. Enja took the torch and fixed it nearby, so I rubbed my hands across my face and thought hard. We could either brave the storm and almost certainly die, or brave the wolf and those lights and spend the night in here. Even if Enja hadn't been injured, going out in the storm was far riskier. The choice was already made.

Neither of us spoke much for the remainder of the night. I wasn't sure what to say – what could be said after what we'd seen – so I lay wrapped in my cloak staring at the roof, lost in thought. Outside, the storm raged on, howling and shrieking.

We always held that storms were the workings of giants: somewhere far away they fought with one another, their breath turning to wind and their voices rattling the ground. I imagined it now – a fight between two giants that could nearly bring Skane to its knees – if for no other reason than to avoid thinking about the wolf and the writing.

Life in our village was simple: hunt, gather food, knit, carve wood, prepare for winter, do not go too far alone. I knew what to expect from this life; from sun-up to sunset, everything was easy. Planned. And whether I liked that or not, it was the way things were. But this – the lights, the wolves – didn't make sense. It didn't fit in line with everything I knew about Skane, about life, about anything. I didn't understand it, and that ate away at the back of my mind like rotting wood.

"Why did you bring us out here?" I asked presently, looking at Enja who sat staring back through the tunnel at the back of the cave. "Why not hide in the forest, or a nearby cave?"

She tore her eyes away and looked at me. "This place has felt like a home to me since I first found it. I hide here sometimes, since no one else would climb down that ledge." A small smile. "They can shut their doors to the world, but I didn't want these things to be lost for good, for those who survived." She held up a scrap of cloth as if to illustrate her point, and then set it gingerly back down again. "Their story deserves to be heard, even if it's only by us."

"There are many stories that will never be heard," I said, and then regretted how harsh it sounded. "Some of them aren't meant to be known."

But I understood, I truly did, and if I had been in her place, I knew I would have done the same thing. "We can try another village, after the storm," I said, changing the subject. "Perhaps another one might be more friendly."

She nodded, but she didn't look convinced that we would be welcomed.

"Perhaps," she said distantly.

I fell silent and looked around the room, the realization beginning to dawn on me that this was now as much my home as anywhere else. That pile of blankets I had always called my bed no longer belonged to me. Those walls in which I had grown up were no longer my refuge. The people who lived there had cast me out into the snowbound world beyond. All my life I had wanted to escape, to find a life in Skane that wasn't tied to my village, and now here I was, with no other choice but to survive.

And survive I would, if I was forced to cling to life by my broken and bloodied fingernails. I would not be ruined by the people who had spent eighteen years casting false smiles my way, standing ready to accuse me of a crime I'd had nothing to do with. No, I would live, and I would endure long enough to outlast the plague and return to the village to see what havoc had been wreaked upon it. And evil though it was, a small smile pulled at my lips in the dying light of the torch.

Over time, even the hardest of hearts can learn to

forgive. Animals can forgive, or at the very least forget. But Skane did not forgive; its stone, its merciless winds that ripped and shredded and threatened to tear you limb from limb ... that was how I felt, like the ruthless wind of Skane, unflinching in its icy resolve. In being raised on this island, I had become a part of it, and the resolve and resilience it had engraved into my soul may be the one thing that would help me to weather the coming days.

Embrace the storm, Sølvi had once told me, while the wind shrieked outside. But I would do better than embrace it; I would become it.

Chapter 11

It was one of those springs that worked to deceive us, teasing us with a handful of warmer days before once again plunging us into snow and darkness. One afternoon we would be out of doors playing in the sunshine, casting off our thickest layers as the exertion warmed our bodies, and the next, we would be huddled beneath blankets and cloaks, rubbing our hands to keep them warm. On one such night, many of the village children, myself included, gathered in the home of my good friend Enja, Sølvi's sister, preparing to hear her father tell us stories while her mother offered us food and warm drinks. A great fire roared in the centre of the room, but I stayed on the edges, aware that most of the children knew little of me, and therefore mistrusted me. Enja dropped to the ground beside me and tossed me a hunk of bread, slightly dried out from the fire, but still delicious. Her father chatted with her older brother, Sølvi, whom I had hardly spoken to, but knew from the village.

"It's colder than a troll's bum," Enja said, then glanced to her mother to be sure she hadn't heard. "Perhaps winter is here to stay."

I shivered at the thought of winter refusing to release us from its frigid grasp, of never feeling warm again, and never seeing the ground hidden beneath the snow. "Then we should leave," I said, smiling a little to show it was in jest.

"Back to Löska?" Enja asked, flashing a smile. "I would rather stay here and be cold."

All sense of fun disappeared as thoughts of that continent and the carnage that had happened there emerged from the depths of our minds. Those stories were ingrained in us, a part of who we were after hearing them so often, but so disturbing that we pushed them away as often as we could, only remembering on the rarest of occasions as we grew older. The monsters, the Ør, cruel people from distant northern islands who had overtaken the homeland of my people, murdering, skinning, and driving them out. The jewellery made from human teeth. It sounded more like a ghost story told by a fire than the actual history of our people. We were, all of us, Löskan, new to this island for only a few generations.

"Welcome," Enja's father – Ulrik – said, rubbing his hands together. The room hushed, voices fading into whispers that faded into silence as we all stared at him, ready to laugh or cry or jump in terror at whatever story awaited us. There were some stories that were often repeated, ones we knew by heart, but some were new, saved for special or deeply cold nights where we longed for a distraction. Tonight, I hoped to be scared.

"Once, many a year ago in a small village called Setta, there was a woman who claimed she saw a man made of nothing but bones."

A few of the children shivered, and we all leaned in closer.

"'He was tall and bore no flesh or hair, only a black hat that never fell off in the wind,' she said, but no one believed her. It is impossible, muttered some. The cold has gone to your head, said others. But for days, the woman insisted that, in the middle of the night, her door had somehow been cracked open and the wind was whistling in, so she had risen to close it. As she was about to push it shut, she saw a man standing outside, nothing but waxen bone with no eyes or nose or lips. The wind rushed through him, howling all about the house, but the hat sitting atop his head didn't budge an inch. He said nothing, nor did he move. At last, thinking herself to still be asleep, she slammed the door shut and locked it, climbing deep beneath the blankets on her bed until well into the morning. When she rose to go outside, there were footprints outside her doorway, angled and sharp, like the bare feet of a man with no flesh. Her blood ran cold at the sight: chilling proof that it had not

133

been a nightmare as she had worked to convince herself. She tried to show the villagers, but they waved her off, supposing it to have been some animal lost out in the cold that had wandered off. Three days later, they found her dead in the forest, fallen from a cliff with a broken neck."

I drew in a sharp breath, jumping at his sudden rise in tone, then flushed, embarrassed at having been afraid. I glanced at Sølvi, worried he had noticed, and felt my face flush even further to find him watching me with a self-important smirk that said he had heard this story before. I sat up a little straighter.

"Not a week later," Ulrik went on, "a fisherman went running through the village during the night, shouting about a man made of bones who had visited his door, but disappeared into the swirling snow. Again the villagers wrote him off, assuming too much time on the sea had confused him, but this time, they locked their doors. Three days later, the man's body washed ashore, drowned somewhere far out to sea.

"Now the villagers grew afraid, worried that they, too, would find the bone man waiting outside their doors one dark night, heralding a death that would follow in three days' time. Weeks went by with no sign of him and eventually the village of Setta began to grow calm again, wondering if perhaps it had all been a misunderstanding, or perhaps a gruesome hoax. But then, on a particularly bitter night when snow swirled about in great white twisters and the *shadows were rich and deep, an old man heard a knock at his door shortly after he had gone to bed. As he opened it with shaking hands, he, too, came face to face with the bone man, who said nothing and made no movements. He stared at the man until he grew so afraid that he quickly shut the door and backed away. One by one, the bone man knocked at each and every door in the village, and one by one, three days later, each and every villager met a quick and sudden end."*

My hands shook, but I didn't want the story to finish. I fought the shaking by smoothing down my clothes and avoiding anyone's face but Ulrik's.

"Never again, in any of the surrounding villages or indeed anywhere in Löska, was the bone man ever seen." Ulrik's eyes gleamed at the looks of shock and enjoyment from his story, and he leaned back in his chair, satisfied. The children began to whisper again, and I turned back to Enja.

"Perhaps it is best to leave Löska be, after all," she said, smiling with a wicked twinkle in her eye.

My dreams that night were filled with lights that burned behind my eyes, the howl of a wolf never far away. My mind replayed climbing off that ledge to find Enja injured below, only this time it wasn't Enja, it was me, and I wasn't injured, I was dead. All the scares and frights of the day came crashing into my dreams in one dark, fractured gust of terror, and I awoke at long last covered in sweat.

The comforting form of my mother sitting by the fire was nowhere to be found, and the walls of my familiar home had been replaced by darkened stone. I shivered and hugged myself, haunted by night terrors.

Siiva sat alert nearby and watching my every move. Time was impossible to tell, so presently, I hauled my aching body to my feet, and made my way to the mouth of the cave. The snow was at least a foot deep, and the wind had carried it partway inside the cave in messy piles, but it was no longer as windy and wild as it had been the night before. Here and there the sky had cleared up, and faint bits of a grey dawn were visible.

Back in the room where we had slept, I gently shook Enja. She awoke slowly, exhausted after yesterday's events. Her face was still pale and there were a few new spots of dried blood where the wound had been irritated and opened during the night, but there was no sign of infection.

"We should get on our way as soon as possible," I told her, grabbing my cloak from where it lay on the floor, having served as my bed for the night. "We can find food and fresh water in the forest, and with any luck, a village that might take us in." In the dim light of morning, it suddenly didn't seem so bad. Surely we would be welcomed in somewhere. Only our village was so evil as to cast us out for ever.

Siiva darted around in circles, pausing every few seconds to stick his head up and look at us, clearly keen to leave the cave. When Enja stood up, she rocked a bit and gently touched her head. "It aches," she said, closing her eyes tightly.

I watched her for a moment. "Things always get worse before they get better," I assured her, because it was true. I had seen a good deal of injuries in my life, and nothing about hers told me that it wouldn't heal quickly. "But..." I looked back towards the mouth of the cave. "Enja, I don't think you'll make that climb. You didn't make it down yesterday when you were well. I wouldn't risk it while you're injured."

"It's the only way up," she told me.

"Well..." I started. "It isn't." I swallowed, looking towards the tunnel we had gone through yesterday. Her eyes grew wide, and I rushed to explain. "That wolf got in and out somehow, without using the entrance or the ledge. It didn't even bother coming our way because it didn't have to. If it was so sure, then perhaps its way is much easier."

"But what if we run into it?" she asked, her voice rising. "What if it's their den, or some sort of gathering place? One would be bad enough, but two? Three?"

"Then we're armed," I told her. "Climbing that ledge will be far more dangerous than taking the tunnel, especially after a snowstorm." I hated that I was right, because I didn't know what we would find, but right I was, and there was no mistaking that. I smoothed down my cloak and tried to think logically, pushing fear aside. "It's either the near certainty of falling from a cliff, or the possibility of running into wolves. We have to take the chance, Enja. We have to."

She drew in a breath and looked at Siiva, who still stood alert, ready to leave. Having an animal with us could only be helpful; he could hear or sense things approaching before we could, giving us – with any luck – enough of a chance to hide. The odds were stacked in favour of us taking the tunnel, and as the eldest, though not by much, I felt that it was my responsibility to make the decision.

"We're going through the tunnel," I said, as firmly as I could. "And we are going to be fine, and we'll find a village where we'll be safe, and someone can tend to your head better than I can. All will be well. We just have to get out of this cave."

Enja didn't bother arguing. She simply picked up her bow and quiver, adjusted her cloak, and nodded. I held my knife firmly in my hand, glancing around the room at the precious items that would have to stay behind. They were safe in here, for the most part. Safe from the storms outside and the waves from the sea. In a sinister, sad sort of way, they were the safest they had ever been. We would come back for them one day, but for now, the outside awaited.

We crept back through the tunnel, keeping closer together this time, walking side by side when space allowed. Siiva moved around slowly, ever on the alert, sometimes behind us and sometimes in front. I wondered what sort of things he could sense, what he knew about this tunnel and the darkness ahead that I didn't. I wondered if animal senses were anything like what we had felt yesterday, when something within us had flickered, acknowledging a presence that we could neither see nor hear.

Slowly, slowly, we inched back towards the cavern with the lights. The markings were still there, blanketing the walls in shapes I had no hope of understanding, but their bluish light and pulse had disappeared, and the wolf was nowhere in sight. Siiva sniffed around, interested, but gave off no warning signs.

We moved past the walls, past the place where the wolf had stopped and given off that piercing howl while the blue lights danced around it, and into the narrower tunnel beyond. All around us there was just cold stone, uneven walls, and the pressing darkness outside the comforting glow of the torch.

The passageway wound on, the roof sometimes so low that we had to duck to fit our heads, and then sometimes so high that we couldn't see it at all, even when I held the torch over my head. I was always surprised by the discovery of a new cave or a new tunnel, winding through the land like unseen veins that pumped with secrets and history.

On and on and on the passage went, until distantly, so faint I almost thought it was a trick of my eyes, there was a light. A blue-white light that could only mean one thing: day. The end of the passageway. Enja gently tapped my shoulder to point it out, and I nodded, smiling with relief. The bizarre nightmare of the cliff and Enja's fall and the inexplicable wolf in the cave was over.

Siiva darted forward, almost out of reach of the torch light which was fast losing its vibrancy. A moment later, I dashed it out on the rock. Pale daylight lit our way as we moved quietly towards the small opening, the fox guiding us onwards. Outside, I could see snow-laden trees and white drifts piled heavily against their trunks, like winter had breathed over the land during the night and left its mark on everything. Difficult as our walk would be, the sight of daylight and snow and anything outside this strange cave was welcome. Siiva stuck his nose into the snow and rolled around, overjoyed to be back outside and out of the darkness. As my boots sank into the piled flakes, I smiled slightly. This daylight felt like freedom.

Like whether we would spend tonight sleeping under the stars, or an unfamiliar roof.

It was always more difficult to navigate a forest after a snowstorm such as the one we'd had the night before. The ground was mostly hidden, the trunks looked just a bit different, and some of the larger rocks and boulders that were waypoints in my mind had vanished under a white blanket. It took longer than it should have, our winding path leading us out of the way from time to time before I realized our mistake and righted us again. Sometimes it was Enja, recognizing something in the forest that I didn't and directing our way, or Siiva, who seemed determined to take a particular route that neither of us thought was correct. We had agreed to head south, to a small village I knew only vaguely. There were more villages north, and we would visit them all if need be, but from where we had started out this morning, this one would be the closest.

This was adventure, I realized as we walked. This was what I had daydreamed about for so long: escaping Sjørskall and striking out into the wilds of Skane to see what lay beyond the realm of familiarity in which I had grown up. This was what I had always wanted.

I kept a careful eye on Enja as we travelled, but her injuries seemed to have caused her no lasting damage. She was alert and filled with energy, the kind I wished she could share with me, as my mind tried to crawl into those dark recesses that are better off left alone. A cloud of doubt and worry threatened to drown out even the brightest light that the world had to offer, but I fought it back, finding hope and beauty in the brilliant snow, in the rich evergreen needles peeking out from beneath their wintry shroud. There was beauty in Skane that no darkness could consume, that would remain until the island crumbled away into nothingness, or sank once more beneath the waves.

A twinge of distant smoke reached my nose a short while later, as we crested a steep rise in the ground. Siiva sniffed the air, and Enja and I slowed our pace as we neared the village. After what had happened, the thought of once again being near people set me on edge, and I chewed on a nail while we inspected the area. There was no sign of a perimeter, no sign of campfires or guards ready to turn us away, no sign of a stake made ready to burn us. This wasn't Sjørskall, I told myself. It would not be the same here.

"What's that?" Enja asked, tearing me from my thoughts. I followed her gaze to a patch of darkness hidden in the shadows of a shrub.

The back of my neck tingled as I made my way over.

Blood was melting into the snow. It was smeared on leaves, the trunk of a tree, the surface of a rock. Siiva let out a low whine like I had never heard before, and shrank away behind Enja.

"An animal?" she asked half-heartedly, kneeling to pick up the fox.

"Perhaps," I replied, moving to follow the trail. A hunter had lost their wounded quarry, maybe, and we could save it from its misery and return it to the village. That would make our welcome at least a little bit warmer. Or perhaps our approach had frightened off an animal from its prey, and lay waiting nearby for us to pass.

The woods were thick here, undergrowth and tree roots intertwining into a tangle. I ducked under low-hanging branches, climbed over fallen tree trunks and boulders shooting from the ground, egged on by a sense of morbid curiosity. Something was dead or dying, and I needed to see, needed to know what or who it was, for reasons I couldn't quite understand.

My heart was thunder. My breaths were short.

There was a splutter, a wheeze, like someone trying and failing to breathe, and I knew, even before I rounded the tree before me, what I would find.

A body lay in the dirt and leaves, eyes red and swollen, blood running from his mouth and ears. His furs were thick with it, dark and viscous and gruesome. He didn't speak – couldn't speak – and I was not entirely sure whether he was aware of our presence or not. Death was here with us, surely, waiting in this clearing for the opportune moment. This man had only minutes left.

A hand clawed at the ground, writhing and desperate for air that would never come. He was far from water, yet drowning.

"Stay back," I said softly to Enja. I wanted to help the poor man, wanted to take him into my lap and hold him, offer him water, clean his face. How alone he must feel, trapped in his own dying body with no chance of help. But I couldn't. Even though I'd never seen it before, I knew that we were staring into the grisly face of the plague.

"We must do something," Enja said, and her voice cracked with sorrow. She reached out towards him, but dropped her hands again promptly.

We couldn't touch him. Couldn't go near enough to breathe the same air as him. Not unless we were ready to run the risk of infection ourselves. And even though I had been well all day; even though I knew my eyes were not red, and no blood ran from my ears, I felt suddenly unsure, intensely aware of every inch of my body. *Did I feel feverish? Too cold? Was that a rattling in my breath?*

Perhaps we were already standing too close. I could almost see the plague slithering across the ground between us, winding its way up my legs and creeping down my throat. I took a step back, grabbing at my neck as though to halt its progress.

No. If the plague was going to take me, too, I would not give it the pleasure of first consuming my mind. I had seen what this kind of fear did in my own village, and I would not succumb to it. I didn't give myself time to think, to find another option. I simply grabbed Enja's bow and an arrow from her quiver, and shot it into the poor soul's heart.

It was the only kind of mercy I could offer.

*

I would soon be fourteen. In my efforts to be as good as Eri, I was out in the woods teaching myself to hunt. I had tracked a fox all the way from the village – not to kill, but to catch – and while a small voice in the back of my mind told me I should turn back, that the nip in the air signalled snow, I pressed on, eager not to return empty-handed.

Ahead, I caught the flash of a reddish-grey tail and moved towards it, my feet slipping into the snow without a sound. A chill wind hit my face and I glanced up through the tangle of needles overhead to where the sky was fast becoming dark grey. A storm was brewing – and quickly. I had seen skies like that one many times before, yet I was so close now. The creature could be mine within minutes, if only I could focus. . .

Another streak of movement, this time further afield. I picked up my pace, refusing to think about the snowflakes now making their way down through the trees from the sky. I was at least an hour from home. An hour's walk through this storm . . . but I pushed away thoughts of what my mother and father would say, of the scolding I would receive when I returned. If I brought something back with me, perhaps it would soften the blow.

My mind was at odds with itself, arguing back and forth about whether to continue tracking my quarry or to turn around and head towards safety.

A gust of wind snapped a small branch nearby. I stopped, swallowing hard. Ahead through the trees there were no more signs of the fox. Frustration fought to boil to the surface, but apprehension at the gusting wind and fast-falling snow pushed it back down. Casting one last glance around for any sign of russet fur, I turned back the way I had come.

When I was younger, my father had taught me that in a snowstorm, it's nearly impossible to tell in which direction you are travelling. With the wind and the snow and the lack of visibility, it is far too easy to head the wrong way and not realize it until it's too late. I had imagined several times what that would be like, stripped of all sense of direction and pressing on to the Goddess knows where, home and warmth waiting somewhere out of sight.

I didn't have to imagine it any more. Within minutes, the wind was roaring in my ears, the air sharply cold in my lungs. I wrapped my arms around myself to hold in any warmth that I could, but it did very little. I shivered like I had never shivered before as I tried to focus, tried to stay on my feet and keep pressing on. Before long, I wasn't sure if my feet were still carrying me in the direction of home. Had I turned slightly to the left back there, or was it my imagination? Was I leaning a bit to the right? It was impossible to tell, and my father's words seemed to be shouted into my ears by the wind.

I imagined the storm passing and finding myself far to the north, in unfamiliar woods with unfamiliar beasts roaming around – if I survived long enough to ride out the storm. My hair whipped wildly around; my clothing pressed tightly against my body with the force of the wind. Some small, frozen part of my mind considered coming to a standstill and collapsing to the ground. I could curl up into a ball and stay as warm as possible while the snow slowly covered me. There had to be worse ways to die.

Where did the birds go during storms like this? Where were the foxes and the deer and the rabbits? Maybe I could survive in the same way they did, in some small den or cave – where were my caves? Perhaps I could find one, but ... so cold. So bitterly cold. Thoughts tried to make their way into my mind, but they cracked and splintered before they could fully form.

The part of my mind that still functioned became vaguely aware that I had stopped nearly walking into trees. There were other shapes now, but I couldn't quite make out what they were.

Until my boots kicked against a solid wood door. I stood blinking for several moments, confused to my core. Home? Mine? Someone else's? It didn't matter. I kicked again, my arms too cold to raise my hands, and I kept kicking until someone cracked it open, pulled me inside, and shut it behind me.

It wasn't my village, and I didn't know the occupants, but it was a kind woman with fair hair and grey-green eyes, and her husband, who barely said a word. She put me by the fire and brought me food and a warm drink, and once feeling had returned to my bones, I'd slipped off to sleep.

147

Chapter 12

We continued on, our footsteps slow as we neared the village, our shadows growing long and the sky dipped in orange. Over the hours we walked, we spoke barely three times. The most recent occasion was when Enja asked if I knew where we were going, and I shrugged and said I thought so. But in the back of my mind, I had a suspicion that I knew where my feet were leading us, so I let them guide the way with little thought. The whole of my mind was consumed by the face of the person I'd shot; the face of agony and terror that would follow me to my own death.

And just behind that face were many others: my father's face, my mother's face, Ragna's face. What had become of them since we'd gone? Had they already forgotten about me and my supposed crime, overcome by death as the plague crept from one waiting body to another? Or had their fear driven them further into madness? Perhaps fear guided all humans, regardless of anything and everything. It was a spark we all carried inside us, fanned into flame by predators, mountains, tales of the past ... and by the red lós. Everything else paled in comparison to the dread those lights bred in our hearts, and for some it came before all else.

My footsteps grew heavier as my thoughts ran free, until the sound of my stomping in the snow pulled me back to the present, and back to the reality that I was now charged with the life of a girl a few years my junior, cast out of our village for ever, in the unforgiving depths of winter. *We will be fine*, I told myself, because I needed to hear it. We would try this village, and if we had no luck there, perhaps there were more of which I was unaware, or camps of loners who lived in the wilds. Perhaps we could find a cave in the forest, or return to the one down by the water. We would find somewhere to go, and we would make it through this winter.

Although, as my hand drifted to my face to brush away a stray hair, I couldn't help but picture the man again, bruises the colour of midnight and blood trickling from ears, mouth, eyes.

I heard a shuffling sound behind me, then a sharp squeal, and silence. I whirled around and started to run towards the noise, I stopped when all I found was Enja standing there, her face calm and cool, a rabbit in her hands. Its neck was broken.

"What happened?" I asked, flailing my arms out in the air in a show of exasperation at the start she had given me.

"I killed a rabbit," she replied, holding it out to me.

"I can see that." I didn't take the creature. "How? Why?"

She spun it around in her hand, staring at it. "I fell behind a little ways, and it made to cross my path. There's almost always a moment when prey meets predator when they freeze out of fear, unable to move. My father taught me to take advantage of it. To use it to survive."

My mouth hung open, dumbfounded. Perhaps I didn't need to be in charge of her after all, which relieved me somewhat. I still enjoyed the feeling of being alone. And perhaps my own survival skills were slight compared with hers. I glanced once more at the rabbit, opened my mouth to say something, and then turned away. Enja was strange and surprising, and since she couldn't see my face, I allowed myself a smile. That sisterly affection was working its way back into my heart, although I didn't have the courage to say it out loud.

An hour later, buildings up ahead peeked through the trees. In the distance, I could hear the crash of waves and the cry of seabirds. I had only been to this village once before, as a child that night I had become lost in a storm and was taken in by two strangers. I didn't even know which house was theirs, or how to find them. Walking through the village was like revisiting an old dream, one that isn't quite like you'd grown to remember it. And that night, the snow had been swirling and the wind had been crying, and I could hardly tell right from left. I led us to the centre of the village and stopped. A few passers-by eyed us uncertainly, even stopping altogether to stare. Enja took a step closer to me, the rabbit hanging at her side, while Siiva sniffed the air all around us.

Worry prickled in my mind at the sight of people, at the memory of the last time I had seen so many faces at once. Torchlight flickered on the edges of my vision, and the trees dotted between houses became the stakes where I should have burned alive. But these people had no reason to hate me. No reason to burn me.

"What are you after?" asked an old man from his doorway.

"Who are you?" asked a woman.

"I am looking for someone," I replied, searching each face for a sign of familiarity. Had I expected to recognize her after all these years? Could I even picture her face in my mind any more? I thought I could, but when I went to look for the memory, I found only shadows. I eyed all the surrounding houses, but nothing struck me as something I had seen before. Nothing. Perhaps it was the wrong village...

A door to my right opened and a man emerged. He was much older, more lines criss-crossing his face, but I knew him instantly. In some way he didn't seem to be quite sure about, recognition toyed with his features. I stepped forward.

"Please," I said, gesturing to Enja behind me. "A word? You wouldn't remember me, but you took me in when I got caught out in a storm many years ago. You and your wife. And we ... we have nowhere to go."

"Is it the plague?" he asked gruffly, distrust burning hot in his eyes. "Has it reached your village?"

"Not ours, to my knowledge," I said quickly. "There were no signs of it. We are here for other reasons."

He stared at me for a long moment, and then at Enja. I could feel the "no" rising on his throat, but before he could reply, his wife appeared in the doorway behind him, a wave of warmth and comfort following behind her.

"It's you!" she said, pushing past him and moving to embrace me. Golden hair framed a gentle face, and sparkling green eyes shone with recognition. "I'd remember that hair anywhere." She ran a hand over my matted tangles, and her smile melted some of the ice I'd been building since we had narrowly escaped burning. As she embraced me, I felt the bump of her stomach that had been mostly hidden by her wraps and clothing.

"Careful," the man whispered to her, taking her hand

and gently pulling her back. "After the lights ... you never know who might be carrying it."

"Hush, you," she said to him, and opened their door wider. "Come in." There was a glow about her like nothing I had ever felt or seen, like those first rays of sunshine after a long winter storm. She was the sort of person who made you feel as if you didn't always have to be the strong one, as if there was someone who could instead care for you.

Their home was warm and set up just as I had remembered it, with a few small new additions here and there, including a small daughter, who played with wooden toys in the corner. The woman hurried around as we sat down on folded blankets by the fire, offering us bowls of soup and tumblers of water before cleaning the rabbit. I drank and ate gratefully, the icy rage I had been carrying all day beginning to quiet. It was impossible to be angry here, in her presence. Every time she spoke was another warm blanket wrapped around my cold shoulders.

Siiva, having been allowed in, rested quietly beside Enja.

"Now tell us what has happened," she said finally after we were fed and watered to our content, while her husband stood lurking nearby. He had softened a bit since we arrived, but not enough to get too close. He reminded me of the people from my own village, although I hoped less murderous.

The woman's hand rested gently on the bulge of her stomach.

Amid such warmth and kindness, I felt like a child again, and I wanted nothing more than to lie down before the fire and fall asleep while she told us a story of some distant danger that would never be real, and I could sleep without darkened dreams or worries drenched in red. I wanted to forget the lós, the burning, the villagers who had risked everything to get us out, the dying man in the woods who had been consumed by the plague.

The man I'd had to kill.

I missed my good memories, suddenly and violently, as the weight of recent events – not only the burning and the lós, but a year ago, when I lost Sølvi – became far too heavy.

I drew in a long breath and told her everything. I didn't know why, exactly, but she was so warm and kind and I was so cold and tired that pouring it all out before her took a great weight off my chest. I told her about the man who had died – Fiak – and how I didn't know him. About Ragna, and the people of our village, and how we had narrowly escaped burning. I could hear the poison in my words as I spoke of them. I told her of the cliff, Enja's fall, the cave – and I told her of the man in the forest, careful to emphasize the distance we had kept, although her husband still prickled. Enja offered small bits here and there to fill in the story while Siiva slept by the fire, and when we had finished, I could have sworn a tear lingered in her eye.

"It's a tragedy, these lights," she said, shaking her head. "And not only for the things they bring, but for the things they cause humanity to do. Families casting out families, villages closing off their borders to even those who might need it. After the red lights show and long before the plague even arrives, we've lost ourselves to fear and hate." She coughed, a small, simple cough that sparked something to life in the back of my mind.

"You are expecting," I said, trying to offer a small smile. "Again." I glanced to the little girl in the corner.

"Yes, she was born almost two years ago, and this one... Well, this one will be here any week now. Not long left." She patted her belly fondly, and something in me ached. What a time to be born. What a time to enter this world, during such worry and hostility, and a plague that might take their life before they even had a chance to truly live. "If I were allowed one wish in all of this chaos," she continued, her eyes tight with sadness, "it would be that this one"– she patted her belly – "never has to see the red lós. And that she never has to see them again." Her eyes fell lovingly on the girl in the corner. "I wish long lives for both of them, under a calm blue sky, where the plague is nothing but a memory."

There was a weight to her words that gripped my heart, that made me think she would not be around to see them grow up. A tear ran down my face at the injustice of it all, if that were to happen. Her startlingly genuine kindness in a time when others had been swallowed by fear meant she deserved the world and everything in it. She was a gem of a person, standing in stark contrast to Ragna, and if ever Skane needed a leader, it should be someone like her.

If there was a way to make it happen, I wanted nothing more than to make her wish come true. And homeless as I was, impending plague notwithstanding, I had nothing but time to see it through. This unborn baby, the young girl in the corner – they could never know the plague. Perhaps it was my utter exhaustion or the heat from the fire, but in that moment, I felt so certain I could have staked my life upon it.

Memories of Sølvi's last moments fluttered in my mind, thoughts of the promise I had made to myself, to pay off the debt I owed.

"Well, you may both sleep here for the night, and tomorrow we will discuss what's to be done with you. I have blankets enough for a village, and fish enough to feed the island. You will not go hungry or cold under this roof."

Her words wrapped me in warmth and comfort, welcome after the past few days.

"May Siiva stay, as well?" Enja asked.

Her eyes darted to the fox, who lay curled on the

floor, ears twitching. "If he promises to behave," she said.

Our host coughed again, and something in me started to crack. It was such a simple thing, such a quiet cough, that it should have been no cause for alarm, and yet I felt my pulse begin to race. Was it the cold that had got to her lungs? Had the smoke from the fire dried out her throat? I wanted it to be true, more than anything, but I had seen that man in the woods, seen him coughing and gagging on his own blood, and the sight would not leave me be.

Late into the night, long after the sounds of snoring had begun to fill the large room, I still lay awake, staring at the roof and unable to quiet my mind.

Chapter 13

Morning arrived, although I hadn't realized I'd fallen asleep. Only Enja and I were still in bed, but her eyes were open and she lay on her side stroking Siiva. I propped myself up on an elbow and glanced around, my eyes falling on the woman where she sat by the fire, most of the colour drained from her face.

"Good morning," I said after I had crawled out from beneath the pile of furs and blankets, holding my hands out to the fire.

"Good morning, love," she replied, offering me a small smile.

"You look unwell," I said, unable to contain it any longer.

"Oh, it's just what happens when you are this far along. Everything makes you ill and tired." She said it so certainly, so convincingly that I almost believed her. Relief started to trickle into my mind, a melting icicle that quickly froze again.

I had seen pregnant women before. I had seen how they looked, felt, acted. This didn't seem like what I remembered, but I couldn't tell if she knew that or not. Couldn't tell if she was lying to herself, or only to me. If it was meant to calm my worries, it didn't.

"What's been left behind, then?" she asked, forcing a smile that reached nowhere but her mouth. "Siblings? Lovers? Who do you carry with you here?" She gently touched her heart.

I met Enja's heavy gaze for a few long seconds, unsure if this was part of the story I was ready to tell. The more I told it, the more it reinforced that he was gone and, with everything that had happened over the past few days, I wasn't sure if I was ready to face that. Not being in the village, not seeing his house that was devoid of his voice and laughter, made it almost possible to believe that he was still there. That it was I who had left, not him.

And yet, being around this woman's gentle nature, hearing her loving voice, had weakened my defences. A growing part of me wanted nothing more than to let my pent-up thoughts and feelings pour out like a waterfall until there was no pain left. No pressure still held inside me.

"I—" I started, but choked and cleared my throat.

"I have no brothers or sisters. If anyone were to be my sister, it would have been Enja. I was . . . her brother and I . . . we were—"

"I'm sorry," she interrupted.

I nodded. "Thank you. It was last year, but it still feels like yesterday. I think it always will."

Enja stayed silent.

"People are afraid that admitting they are healing means leaving the loved one behind. Forgetting them, or erasing their place in the world. But healing is part of being human, and if you aren't healing, you're withering. They would not want you to wither. Always remember that."

A bubble of sobs and tears and feelings welled up in my chest, so I nodded and took in a long breath as my head swam with memories.

"And you," she said to Enja, softly. "He was your brother?"

Enja nodded.

"I am sorry. Losing a brother or sister is like losing a part of yourself. You're both different and one and the same."

Enja nodded again, and her usually cool eyes shone with tears. It had been a year, but a year in which the both of us had dodged one another, avoided speaking at all costs and shrunk away into ourselves until we could see nothing but our own pain. Regret flexed its claws and began to dig away at my gut.

"We should have spoken more," I said aloud. "I shouldn't have run away from you when you were hurting."

Enja shifted uncomfortably. I knew she didn't like conversations like these, but it was necessary, especially if we would have to survive together over the coming weeks.

"You knew him and loved him longer than I did, and I forgot that," I told her.

She distracted herself for a long moment by avoiding my gaze and petting Siiva's fur. "I've never loved like you have," she said eventually "Not in that way. I've never wanted to. I didn't understand what you were going through, and I guess I didn't try to."

I breathed through the tightness in my chest as the conversation died out. This was neither the time nor the place for it, but the unspoken words remained, lurking just beneath the surface every time we spoke.

Her husband came through the door just then, his brows knitted together. His mouth was set in a firm line, his eyes darting around nervously, as though he didn't know what to say or do. He had the face of a man who knew hard work, and who carried many worries on his shoulders.

Enja crawled out from the blankets and joined me by the fire, Siiva following close at her side.

"My wife is unwell," the man announced, silencing her with a firm look. "She may give birth any day, and you should not be here for that. You will have to find somewhere else to go."

"E—" she started, but he held up a hand.

"No. Enough. This is my decision. We are in no time or place to take in stragglers, and you are in no condition to look after them." He placed a gentle hand on her shoulder, and for a moment, I could see how much he loved her, beneath the gruff outer layers.

I spoke up quickly, piecing together messy thoughts and trying to organize them into a plan. "No, I understand," I said. "I think I have distant family in another village." A lie. "We will seek them out. We only wish you well." I didn't know a soul in any other villages, but our time here had come to an end. We needed to move on. But my eyes trailed to her belly, to the baby still clinging to life within. The mother was ill – very, in fact. It was evident in the beads of sweat along her forehead, and the pallid wash of her lean face. If she ... Goddess forbid, if she had come down with the plague, that baby would never make it, and that fact made my eyes burn with tears.

She sighed, resigned and perhaps too weak to argue, and then laid her head back in her chair.

I crossed my legs and sat on my hands, watching as a bead of sweat rolled down her cheek from her forehead. My chest felt like it might burst, both with sadness and desperation. I couldn't take the plague from her veins, but if there was anything else to be done, even if only to bring her comfort, I would find out what that was.

I twitched and sat up straighter, a fragment of

something, a few words I had nearly forgotten amidst the chaos of the past few days, echoing through my mind. I saw them in my mind like a punch to the gut.

Do not let her die.

We stood outside the village, our one faint hope for safety and a home now behind us, and the wild forests of Skane before us. Enja stood tall, her head held high and a sort of determination on her face that I had never seen before. She was in this as well. She wanted the same thing – to help one of the only people to show kindness since the red lights had shown – and she would help me do it, no matter what. Even Siiva darted about anxiously, ready to get a move on to wherever we were going. And even though I didn't know what we would find there, or if it would be of any help in saving the poor woman's life, I knew where we needed to go.

Chapter 14

Trekking back to the cave by the sea was long and arduous, as was trying to find that hidden entrance through which we had sneaked the first time. Not only that, but the sudden silence of the birds and the way the sun had slowly been blotted out spoke of an oncoming storm, for which I had very little patience. I'd been overcome with a sort of intense determination, even if I didn't fully know what I was going to do, and I didn't want to sit idly by and wait for a storm to pass.

My mind was far away as we walked, so far that I saw no trees or snow around us, only shadows and stone. That song the villagers were going to sing to me before I died crept back to me, all cold and damp with blood and fear.

May the river of death be shallow and calm

And may the god in the shadows forgive you your wrongs.

We didn't speak about such a god, if he did exist, only the Goddess and her brilliant, entrancing stars. But she was all light and beauty and kindness, what with the warnings she gave us in the sky. I needed someone who dealt with death, though a plan had not yet come together in my mind.

"Janna, I can see you thinking, but I deserve to know what we're doing," Enja said from where she trudged on a few steps behind me. "I am part of this now."

She was right, of course.

"I want to get back to that cave. It's the only safety I can think of."

"Obviously," she said, since we had nearly reached it by now. "I was looking more for a reason."

I was thinking about how to best answer her when, finally, the dark entrance loomed before us, though we remained hidden behind boulders, trees, and snowdrifts from past storms, approaching cautiously. The memory of the giant wolf was fresh on my mind, and I didn't fancy a run-in with it if it could be avoided. We waited, listened, stared into the woods around us, and then listened some more before quietly stepping out of hiding and into the entrance of the cave. I kept a close eye on Siiva, watched the way his ears twitched and waited for any sign that he might hear something approaching. But as far as I could tell, we were on our own.

To fight off the darkness of the cave, I lit a small candle tucked away in one of my pockets, and the flame flickered in the blackness around us. It did little by way of lighting our path for much of a distance, but there was a comfort in not being swallowed by shadows. The flame licked the air, dancing and waving in a stark contrast to our tight, nervous movements in the cave.

The sunlight had only just disappeared behind us when Siiva froze. His ears stopped twitching, his head stood tall, and not a muscle on his body moved. Enja and I stood perfectly still, watching him, as my pulse quickened. There were precious few places to hide. Siiva seemed to be more concerned with something behind us than in front of us, and even though if it were wolves they would be able to pick up our scent, I wanted us to be out of sight.

"Come on," I whispered hurriedly, moving further into the cave. If we could keep ahead of it and find shelter, we may stand a better chance. I tried not to think about the large form, claws nearly as long as my fingers or its teeth like the icicles that formed outside our doors after storms. I just hurried us through the stone labyrinth of the cave, thinking of almost nothing but the kind woman and her baby, of her pale face and the sweat on her brow. It wasn't the baby making her ill, it wasn't, and I wouldn't let . . . couldn't let. . .

We rounded a bend in the tunnel and before us

rose a few tall pillars of naturally formed stone. I didn't think, I just pointed for Enja to duck behind one, and extinguished my candle. I heard her gently sweep Siiva up into her arms, perhaps in a vain effort to try to mask his scent somewhat, but it would do very little. Beasts of that size would wield senses of equal power, and how we had escaped the last time was still a mystery.

And not an accident, I was fairly certain.

I could see nothing in the cave, but I heard their presence only moments after we had hidden ourselves. Heavy – but still somehow light – paws tapped against the icy stone of the tunnel, coming closer and closer. This time, there wasn't just one of them. Judging by the sounds of their footsteps, there were at least two. I held my breath, stood as still as I could, and feared to even move my eyes until the sounds of their movement began to fade away.

Then they stopped.

All sound of their movement ceased entirely, and a moment later, the subtle scraping of their claws on the floor told me that they had turned around. They'd sensed us. Smelled us. Something had given us away. If I thought I had been still before, I was almost certain that now even my heart stopped beating.

There was no sound in the cave. I was surrounded by the deafening silence as if I had fallen into a deep snowbank and been left there. I shivered as I imagined them silently creeping along the tunnel, their gaping mouths opening to bite into my neck, my shoulder, and any moment now they could clamp down. Any second, I could feel those long, treacherous teeth sinking into my skin, and once they were done with me, they would move on to Enja...

Not if I could help it. Perhaps if they found me, they would look no further. They knew something was in the cave, but maybe that was all. One would be enough.

So I did the most reckless, foolhardy thing I could think to do, and I lit the candle. The brightness of the flame blinded me for a moment, but I tried to blink it away and focus on what waited nearby. A few yards away, four glowing eyes stared back at me, set into large, shadowed forms that the light from the candle couldn't reach. Their gazes were nearly at my own eye level, a fact that hit me like a punch in the gut. I had known they were large; I had seen them before in that clearing with Eri, but...

One, then the other, took a few steps closer to me. I heard Enja draw in her breath, but they seemed to take no notice of her. Their eyes remained locked on me as they approached. They had been further away than I thought, the sounds no doubt magnified by the quiet and the closeness of the cave. If perhaps I waited a little bit longer, if perhaps I hadn't lit the candle, then maybe they would have continued on their way. Maybe I wouldn't be facing them right now, fear setting my hands to shaking.

We faced off for a long moment, none of us moving.

I held my breath, stared into their glowing eyes, and waited. Did wolves not fear fire? Perhaps the flame was too small and I was too near, prey far too easy to let go.

The glowing eyes moved suddenly, their great heads turning to glance at one another in a bizarre, unspoken conversation. Then one circled to stand behind me and pushed me forward with its snout. I stumbled on the slippery rock and turned to the one who'd pushed me, shaking like a dead leaf. I opened my mouth to ask a question, and then caught myself. They couldn't understand me, of course.

Again, the wolf pushed me forward, and the other came to stand beside me. So, surrounded by fur and teeth and claws, I walked with them along the tunnel to some unknown destination.

Glowing blue lights lit up the room, and again my skin tingled as I found myself in the presence of those strange markings on the wall, dancing and flickering like flames hidden behind the stone. I'd wanted to come back, to study these very symbols and see what answers they held, but I hadn't expected to be led in by wolves. A surge of questions rose up within me, but I stayed silent, waiting to see what they would do. To see why they had brought me here. I laced my fingers together as though I were praying and squeezed, desperate to dissipate some of the anxiety.

One of the wolves, the one who'd been nudging me

along, moved to the centre of the room and raised its head, so impossibly tall. Then, as the markings around us began to glow brighter and flicker faster, it let out a powerful drawn-out howl that shook the very stone beneath my feet. I stared at the walls, dumbstruck, as the shape morphed and changed, the letters and symbols rewriting themselves into ones that, the longer I gazed at them, I realized I could read.

Slowly, and in pieces, they'd transformed into runes. The ones we read and wrote on cave walls. The common language of those who had come before us: symbols and pictures that told stories and relayed important information. A language that could last for aeons, carved into stone that would never decay.

I stared at each of the symbols in turn, trying to understand their meaning, their context, what they were trying to tell me.

Questions, I guessed. *Answers. You seek answers.*

I nodded, once, twice, then over and over again. "Yes. Yes, I want answers."

Another howl split through the cave, and the markings changed again. I watched them, going back and forth as I fought to piece together the message. It was never designed as a language for detailed conversations. It was meant to be scratched on a wall and left, telling stories of great hunts and long winters. It was never read immediately, used to speak.

The sky. Blood. Red. I worked to connect one to the next quickly, and though I could be wrong, I suspected I knew their meaning. "The red lights," I said, and I waved my shaking hands up towards the invisible sky. It was then that I realized the runes weren't changing when I spoke, only when they howled. Could they understand my words?

Woman.

Baby.

And then the wretched, skull-like symbol for death.

I sank back a step, shaking.

How did they know?

"She's dying."

Her kind, warm face hung before me, smiling through her illness. It wasn't right. It wasn't fair. How could someone as cruel and wretched as Ragna walk free and well, while the kind woman tumbled towards her death?

There was a long pause, and the air grew heavy with sadness that was not only mine.

North.

Fire.

Again, the symbol for death.

It had been sneaking up on me over the past day or two, or perhaps since I was nearly burned alive, and I'd heard that song about the god.

May the river of death be shallow and calm
And may the god in the shadows forgive you your wrongs.

A few years ago, Sølvi had traded an ornately carved bow with a hunter in exchange for a story from the man's grandmother. One of those murky stories no one was supposed to tell. *If it isn't making us stronger, it is making us weaker*, the village had said. And so some stories were forbidden: the ones that bore no lesson, no warning about the island, or the ones that enticed us away.

It was about a god, and fire, and a man who had tried to sell his soul in exchange for food during an especially hard winter. The man never returned, but spring came early that year, and until his story was forbidden, people used to whisper of travelling to the cave of fire, seeking this or that, or just to see if it held any truth.

I had thought of it more and more, as memories of what had happened to Sølvi tried to smother me.

"The god," I said. "The god of death. He can help?" I didn't explain everything to them; how my life had been saved once, in a way I could never repay. My throat tightened and tears threatened to well up. I couldn't let another innocent person die if I could do anything to stop it. "Who are you?"

But the blue lights began to fade and the wolves moved away from the centre of the room.

"Wait," I said. "Why have you come? How do you know me?"

I'd never been terribly far from my village, despite my habit of leaving it. I'd never gone far enough to know that there was anything out there other than forest, except, of course, for the sea. I could have left the village, if that was truly what I had wanted. But running away from home would not take me away from myself, and that was what tormented me. The memories. The thoughts. The questions that sneaked in with every breath, and hung above my head at night while sleep lurked just beyond reach.

But neither of the beasts seemed to hear me. They simply kept walking, on and on until they had disappeared down the tunnel, and all sounds had vanished.

Moments later, Enja and Siiva shuffled towards me, their eyes wide.

North.

I filled Enja in with a rush of words that, spoken aloud, made no sense. She stared in disbelief at the now dull blue markings that covered the walls. They had faded almost to the point of nonsense, carrying no meaning. I comitted the words to memory, determined to forget none of it. Somehow, it all made sense. They had shown me something, something that I could do, if I was willing. It was as if they knew what weighed down my heart, the guilt that had pressed against me for the past year. Like they knew what had happened to Sølvi.

I told Enja, in a whisper, the story of the god that I had heard from her brother. And this time, as I said it out loud, the words carried a spark that told me it was more than just a story. There was more to it, perhaps, more detail than we knew, but whatever those details were, I would find out.

When we reached the opening of the cave once more, there was no sign of the wolves, but the sky had finally begun to unleash its snow. It swirled this way and that, dancing and taunting me and begging me to come out and play. But I'd seen too many people dance with winter before, only to wind up blue and stiff, their eyes glassy with death. That wouldn't be me. Couldn't be me. I was driven by a bonfire deep within my chest, compelling every movement. I wouldn't let this land, this season, trip me up and end it all too soon. Not now that I knew what I had to do.

So we decamped back to the room with all of the Löskan artefacts, and I sat down with a sharp bit of stone and scratched out a map containing everything I knew about Skane. Which, it turned out as I stared at my small markings, wasn't all that much. It was trees, mostly, and my village and the one by the sea. The one with the kind woman who was ill.

North.

None of us knew very much about the north. There were mountains, we knew, from stories told by those who had long ago tried to reach them. Many died, and some turned back before the mountains could claim them, to come and tell us what they had seen, which was very little. Many were taken by storms, or beasts, and some of the stories were so peculiar or unusual that we assumed the cold had confused them. Some of those odd stories had been transformed and used in bedtime stories or warnings for children. Like the one about Grulla.

We were told if we misbehaved, a snow troll named Grulla would come down from the mountains and steal us away in the night. It frightened me at first, but as I grew older I found the thought of being stolen away to the distant, unknown mountains more intriguing than frightening. But that wasn't the intended effect, so I had kept it to myself.

"My uncle once ventured north," Enja said from where she sat in the corner staring at a piece of parchment. Siiva rested his head on her lap. "He never came back."

I stared at her for a moment, and then looked back at my map. "Well, that's ... grim," I replied, deflated. "It isn't safe," I continued. "We know that much, and you do not have to come with me. I don't know what we'll find, or what will happen. I don't know where the rest of the journey will lead. As the closest thing I have to a sister, I cannot ask you to come on a search with me for a death god."

"I'm coming with you," Enja said, her voice heavy with a sense of finality that seemed out of character.

"Why?"

She paused for a long moment. "I've never known

much about much. I think, like you, I was always better known for leaving the village than helping it. I never liked staying inside." Seeing that flash of myself in her brought a small smile to my lips. "So I never contributed much. Never helped with much. And this time I can."

"We aren't helping our village, though," I reminded her. "We're doing this for the woman" – I had never remembered to ask her name – "and her baby."

"I know." The glint in her eyes told me just what she thought of our own village.

"We might not make it through the forest. I can't even be sure we'll make it out of this cave. You know what Skane is like. More die trying than succeeding."

"But those who don't try never succeed. Just think how lucky you'll be to have two pairs of eyes to watch out for danger, instead of just one. Three, in fact." She motioned to Siiva.

I pinched the bridge of my nose and rolled back to crouch on my heels. It was like arguing with Sølvi sometimes, and as frustrating as it was, I could not fault her for it.

It was one of those nights when Skane fought to stay hidden, shrouding the moon until it was little more than a dull glow behind a mantle of sombre clouds. Somewhere behind them hung the stars, brisk and vigilant, but they were shy tonight. Sometimes I wondered, on nights like these, if we couldn't see the stars, were they still there?

Our footsteps were light in the forest, a gentle padding beneath the trees. Now and then our hands brushed together as we walked, gently, uncertainly, as though they were trying to come together of their own free will. Now and then, Sølvi's lantern illuminated a pair of small glowing eyes through the trees that disappeared in a flash. But it was a reminder that, while the village slept, the forest was very much alive.

We reached a clearing in the trees, and I fell to the ground and lay on my back, staring up through the darkness to the shadowed treetops. For a moment, Sølvi stood over me, filling part of my vision with his face lit up by the lantern, until he lay down beside me and silence fell. The hoot of an owl erupted nearby, eerie and beautiful all at once. Something small, probably a rabbit, rustled through some bushes. A breeze made the fir needles whisper to one another.

"I don't want to live in a village," I said presently, shattering the silence. I could hear him roll his head so he could see me. "I want to live in the forest, build a small house in a clearing just like this one. Live alone."

"Ah," he said, looking away again. "I take it that's not an invitation, then."

I smiled. "I'll allow you in. But no one else. Just us."

He thought for a moment. "I like the sound of that, but the village will hate it."

"I know."

"It doesn't have to be much, just something small and comfortable." He launched into a description of how he could do it, how he could build it, and it seemed suddenly almost attainable, as if that sort of happiness were just barely within reach. I could see it hovering just an inch or so beyond my grasp, beyond the mundane existence that had awaited me all my life. Within reach was the village, the rows of houses all alike; the superstitions and the unease and the leaders breathing down my neck.

I pictured our little earth-and-wood house standing in this very clearing, nights sitting under the trees right outside our door, a warm fire within, and my heart blossomed with joy.

"Children, I'd imagine," I heard Sølvi say, and then, much quieter, "well, one day, I suppose. No rush." He cleared his throat.

"How many?"

"How many what?"

"Children."

"Hmm." A thoughtful pause. "Two. Maybe three."

"I hope it's just one, like me." I had never given much thought to not having brothers and sisters, because I had never felt a loneliness without them.

"One, then, though I suppose the Goddess will have something to say about that."

"Perhaps," I said, though I was never quite certain exactly how many things the Goddess could control. Children

178

seemed as though they would be uninteresting to a goddess, who had far greater things to think about. It didn't matter, though, because right in that moment, I thought I would never feel so whole, so content, again.

Hours later, as I sneaked back into the warmth and quiet of home, I could feel the wide-awake presence of my father before I had fully closed the door. He sat on a stool by the fire, staring into the flames, though he looked up at me when I turned to him. Half of his face was cast in shadow, and the other half was lit up a fiery orange.

"Out late," he said, and it was neither a statement nor a question. There wasn't anger in his voice, I noted – my father rarely got angry – but a sort of resigned heaviness as though he were terribly displeased.

"I wasn't alone," I hurried to assure him. "I was with Sølvi."

"I guessed as much." He poked at the fire for a moment while I removed my cloak and boots. Mother lay on their bed nearby, though I couldn't hear the steady breathing of someone who was asleep. Listening, perhaps.

"I'm back now," I said. "Safe and sound." I made to move towards my bed, the weight of sleep finally pulling at my eyes, but my father spoke up.

"We must speak, Janna," he said calmly. "Perhaps not tonight, but tomorrow. It's ... important."

I stopped walking and looked at him through the glow of

the fire. I hated the tenderness I found in his eyes, because I knew that whatever he had to say, he would say it from a place of love and honesty, and I couldn't fight that. Or, I could, but I would almost certainly lose. "Speak now," I said, filling my voice with a challenging sort of strength. "We are both awake, after all."

"It would be better after some sleep," he cautioned me.

"I understand, but please, go on." I sat cross-legged on the floor across from him. I heard my mother roll over, perhaps to hear better.

A long moment stretched away in the quiet room, the flames flickering and dancing on my father's face, and the occasional crack and pop of the fire bringing my wandering thoughts back to the present.

"I know ... I understand how you feel about Sølvi. You are young, and your feelings can sometimes—"

"Don't do that," I warned him.

"Don't do what?"

"Don't try to undermine my feelings by passing them off as childish."

He was quiet for a moment, drawing in a long, deep breath, and folding his hands in front of him, elbows resting on his knees. "You are young, Janna. Pretending that you are anything but is dishonest. Skane does not allow us the luxury of living however we choose, doing what we will, when we will it. If we do not bend to its rules, we will die, and that is a truth that, as a father, weighs heavy *on my mind. Your whole life we have had to watch your every move, never let you out of our sight, watch the signs of approaching storms when you were too young to read them yourself. We have held your hand and guided you to adulthood, and this is a final thing with which you should trust us."*

I could not fight the logic of his words, but I was so angry – so hurt – that I couldn't find another route, so I stayed silent.

"Sølvi is . . . kind, and a friend. I know. But kindness isn't everything, especially not in Skane. You need a fighter, a hunter, someone who can adapt along with a changing landscape, who can anticipate dangers—"

I stopped hearing him after "hunter", because, as though he had shouted the name in my ear, I knew who he was talking about. I knew where this was going. "I will never be with Eri," I said, more firmly than I'd ever said anything in my life.

My father bit his top lip and stared at me. "How can you, at such an age, be so completely certain that you are meant to be with one person? If you've never considered the possibility of anyone else, you are strictly limiting yourself. Eri is a good man, and a strong one, and the sort that you will want to have by your side in the life you will lead here."

"But I have no feelings towards him. None that are good, anyway. Sølvi understands my writing, my hopes, my fears. Eri speaks little, and often of himself. He's a good

enough sort of person, I'm sure, but I care little for him.
Not like I care for Sølvi."

"And have you tried to care for him?"

"I – no. I have no interest in speaking with Eri."

My father returned his gaze to the fire for a long while,
carefully considering his next words. "If you will not work
with us in this matter, Janna, then we'll have to work for
you. We are going to limit the time you spend with Sølvi,
one way or another."

"Go on," I dared him, rising and walking to my bed.
"And I'll still see him, one way or another."

I knew that, deep down, they only wanted what was
best for me. But it took them a long while to realize that
would be Sølvi.

Chapter 15

I awoke the next morning bursting with a sense of urgency to be underway. Voices in my dreams pressed at me to hurry, and even though they abated some when I opened my eyes, the urge to get away remained. The storm had dropped another foot or so of snow, just enough to slow our progress but not enough to stop it. With very little idea as to precisely where we were going, we struck out to the north and moved at a steady, determined pace, Siiva walking at the front so we could keep an eye on him should anything else be moving about in the woods.

It was a strange sort of day. Walking through the trees felt as though we could be anywhere – back near the village, collecting firewood, or taking a walk after the storm. Everything could be so normal in these moments, like it hadn't all been irrevocably changed. I let my fingertips brush against the trunk of a tree as we moved further away from the places I knew, a sort of silent goodbye that was both saddening and exhilarating. I tried to focus on other things for a time, more immediate things, like the sight of morning frost dying in the light of a waking sun, but my mind kept wandering back. Adventure is different in thought than in practice, when those imagined dangers grow teeth and become real.

This was what I'd always wanted, though: to be free. Free of village life. Free of the rules and superstitions that anchored us to our homes, forbidding us from seeing or learning too much. I had wanted this chance to travel, to discover, just perhaps not under these circumstances.

After the first couple of hours, we had reached a point in the forest that I no longer recognized, the trees strange and new. They also seemed to grow closer together, away from the villages and the people who had cut so many down to build houses and use for firewood. Here, the forest had endless reign to grow and thrive and watch over the island of which they'd been a part for centuries. What sort of things had they seen? I wondered as we trudged along, eyeing one giant of a tree, and then another. What did Skane look like when they were little more than saplings, struggling to survive in the winter?

That was how I thought of us sometimes, like saplings trying to survive in a world that wanted us dead. Between the Ør, the red lós, and the winters in Skane, it was a wonder that so many of my people had survived at all. We should be nothing more than an old story that nobody would tell; a memory for nothing but the trees and the snow.

"I heard the trees never end," Enja said, after what felt like hours of silence. I wasn't complaining; I enjoyed the silence, the chance for reflection. I was used to spending time alone, used to the safety of my own thoughts, and allowing myself to wander in them for hours on end. But here, now, I wasn't alone any longer. More than anything right now, Enja needed a friend.

"And maybe they don't," I said flippantly, although the longer we walked, with nothing but more forest visible ahead, I began to wonder if perhaps she was right. Perhaps we would wander a never-ending forest for hours or days to come, until we ran out of flint and the cold slowly claimed us, or we were smothered in a snowstorm and died in a silent, frozen tomb. "The forest will end," I amended quickly, and I held my head a bit higher, as though defying the trees. *I dare it not to*, I thought.

Hours dragged on. Snow blended with forest and sky, shrubs worked to tangle our feet and trip us up, and now and then, a wind so biting and vicious cut through the trees to lash at our skin. We would shrug our cloaks on tighter, recede into our hoods, and trudge on. Other times, the forest was silent, save for our footsteps, still and

185

aloof. My presence felt intrusive, trespassing on ground that wished me miles away.

Sundown slowly approached, the curtain of dark clouds overhead edging towards a charcoal grey. Still, there was nothing but forest ahead, tree after tree after tree. Even after the sun had slid below the horizon and stars began to peek through the clouds, the forest had not ended.

"We can go no further tonight," I announced, trying to hide my bitter disappointment. Every day and night that slipped by could be one night closer to the woman and her baby departing Skane for ever if they hadn't already, and the thought nearly made me kick a nearby tree trunk until I broke all my toes. What would happen if this was all for nothing? Would we return to that cave and live out our remaining days there? Beg for entry into another village? Our own was closed off, for returning meant only fire and death, even if some survived the plague. They would blame us for it; say we had conjured it from thin air, cast it upon them.

Home was behind us now, for ever.

I had never spent a night in the open forest before, but we were left with little hope for anything else. As far as I could tell, this part of the forest boasted no caves or rocky outcroppings in which we could huddle, so instead, I found the largest, roundest tree in the area and we set up camp against it.

"Can you climb trees?" I asked Enja, digging out an area to build a fire.

"Yes."

"Good. All the sticks and wood will be buried beneath the snow. We need to climb the trees and pull off as many small limbs as we can. They'll be the closest thing to dry that we're going to find."

I hauled myself up on to the first branch of a nearby tree, and then up a couple more until I found an area where small twigs and brittle limbs grew in abundance. It was slow work, pulling them off and tucking them into a satchel, but it would mean the difference between life and death tonight. There were few other options open to us. The work gave me something into which I could pour my attention, pushing aside thoughts of the never-ending forest and my frustrations with our progress. *We should have walked faster. We should have found horses. We should have done many things differently.*

Half an hour later, we both hopped down from our respective trees and compiled our lot of scraggly firewood. It wasn't much, but I'd rather have one solid small fire than a bonfire that would burn through it all within minutes. And the longer we kept it burning, the more likely it would be that forest predators would stay away – another concern that had been growing in the back of my mind. We were far from the safety of the village, far

187

from the light and noise that kept night-time creatures at bay. Out here, we were in their domain.

At first, my flint alone wouldn't light the sticks, but a bit of parchment paper offered by Enja had them blazing within moments. We piled more and more kindling on to it, and before long, it was a fire hot enough to finally give us some warmth. My body screamed with aches and pains as I slumped down into the snow after a full day of trudging through the woods. There was a long night ahead of us, during which someone would always have to be awake, but at least we had a fire and a place to rest, and Siiva to alert us if anything lurked nearby. He had already climbed into Enja's lap and fallen asleep.

As we nibbled on dried meat and bread – given to us before leaving the kind woman's house – I sat against the large trunk of the tree and stared into the flames, while Enja lay on her back staring up at what bits of the stars were visible through the trees.

"Do you know any stories?" she asked presently, without looking away from above. "Ones you would tell children. Pretend I am not fifteen."

Fifteen. I had forgotten how young she was, as the things she had been through, the pain she had suffered in losing her brother, had caused her to grow up before her time. She carried herself as someone far older, lacked that spark of childhood that should still be burning bright, and part of me mourned for that.

I kept staring into the fire and thought for a moment. I was never much of a storyteller, at least not out loud. I would write them on walls until my fingers bled, but I had never spent enough time around children to learn to tell them. "I know some," I said presently. "There's an old Löskan story I heard from ... I heard a few years ago." I couldn't bring myself to say his name. Not here. Not now.

She nestled down into the snow and stroked Siiva's head while he slept.

"They say we all have a sē, a spirit that follows us around and protects us if we're good or trips us up if we're bad. You can never see it, because our world was divided from the spirit world long ago, but they are always with us, always near. Sometimes when you wake up in the middle of the night because you thought you heard a noise, or when you think you are alone in the woods and you hear a stick break, it's your sē lurking somewhere nearby. They can give voice to your conscience and help you to know good from bad, but it is our choice to listen, or to ignore it." I paused for a moment in the way I had sometimes heard storytellers do, to let the listener take it all in – and to glance at the shadows flickering around us. "They say there was once a man who was so evil that his sē had abandoned him long ago, unable to be a silent witness to his actions any longer. He stole and murdered and lied as often as he drew breath, pushing everyone away from him until he was wholly alone. And then, one day, as he was standing atop a cliff wearing stolen clothing and stolen jewels, a fisherman far below saw something invisible push the man over the edge of the cliff, where he fell to his death in the sea."

Enja's eyes were wide as she stared up at the sky, and I took the opportunity to again glance around us and ensure that we were still alone. Perhaps I should have picked a story with less darkness, but many of our tales were steeped in death and warning. It kept us tame, in our small villages. Ensured that everyone knew what to expect from one another.

Was that movement through those trees, or my imagination playing tricks on me after the unnerving story I had just told? One of the village elders who had passed away a few years ago held that stories were dangerous. *They put things in your head that are not meant to be there, ideas, people you were never meant to know.* I'd always hated his words in my heart, but I could not help wondering if they held some small traces of truth.

I stared for another full minute before looking away.

"Do you believe we all have a sē?" Enja asked, returning to her stroking of Siiva.

I scraped a stick along the ground, back and forth, forming a rut in the snow and dirt. "I don't know," I answered. "I've never seen any proof of one, but then again, it's hard to prove the existence of something invisible." I thought back to the time when I had first heard that

190

story, when Sølvi was telling it to village children around a fire during a winter storm. During *that* winter. A boy had asked the very same question, and Sølvi had given the same answer.

"I'd like to think that we do," Enja said to the stars. "It would mean that we aren't truly alone out here. Not just the two of us, anyway. And you, Siiva." She gently stroked his fluffy head.

I snapped the stick in half and didn't say anything. Nothing about the forest around us made me feel like we were alone.

It was a restless night. I caught snatches of sleep in between staring into the trees and wondering if I was imagining the shapes I saw there, or if it was the shadowy form of my sē coming to haunt me. Or worse, kill me. Now and then, the harsh caw of a crow would split the night, and I would jump up in fright that it was signalling something's – or someone's – approach. But the darkness around us always just settled back into eerie silence. I tried to remember words my father had told me many years ago, about how in the darkness and quiet of night, our fears grow into monsters that turn dreams into nightmares. *Do not entertain dark thoughts once the sun has gone to bed,* he had said. I could feel it, too. Feel the small anxieties and worries of the day shifting and morphing into devils with claws and teeth. So I fought against it during the hours when I was awake, only to fall into restless slumber once I'd awoken Enja for her turn on the watch.

And when morning came, it was hard to believe that such fearful thoughts had ever tormented me as the first golden rays of sunlight danced through the trees overhead, and birds sang to one another in a never-ending chorus of joy. In the rosy light of morning, you find that the flashing teeth of wicked creatures are nothing more than starlight glancing off the snow, and the deep shadows that once seemed frightening are nothing more than the shivering bodies of fir trees set against the sky.

A well-rested Siiva darted through the trees before us, sticking his face into the snow now and then and shaking it off playfully. We followed behind him, using the sun to continue heading north while I wondered over and over again what we would find there. What awaited us. And, more than once, if I'd imagined my interaction with the wolves in the cave. Enja hadn't seen it the way I had, and as the trees carried on and on and the snow field never showed itself, doubt crept further and further into my mind.

Where are you going? The words hung before me, beside me, behind me. They were everywhere I looked: engraved into the bark of the trees, shaped into the clouds. *You are a fool.* We had been chased from our village; we should be finding somewhere to live, to survive. Staking out a cave as our own and gathering food for the next storm. Yet here we were, in the furthest reaches of the forest, following the instructions of wolves I'd convinced myself had spoken to me.

Because they did.

It was afternoon when the trees at last gave way to the largest stretch of snow and space I'd ever beheld. It stretched away from left to right, and far into the distance ahead until it ended at a line of uneven grey forms.

The mountains.

We seemed to shrink in size as we emerged from the trees and stopped before the expanse, our forms so small and insignificant in a space as large as this. In the face of something so grand, it was difficult to feel like more than a speck of dust.

"There's so much of . . . everything," Enja said quietly. "Snow. And space."

"It's a big island," I answered, though I knew little of its actual size. Between the storms in the winter and the predators that came out to hunt once it was over, we didn't travel much. But it was nice to imagine an expansive, rich island filled with detail and mystery that made our troubles seem small in comparison.

Siiva wasn't interested in the size of the snow field, or the mountains in the distance. His nose was to the ground, sniffing a set of what looked like tracks in the snow – tracks that led directly into the plain. I followed them with my eyes until they became muddled by the horizon, disappearing somewhere far to the northwest. They cut across at an angle, not directly across as my instincts suggested we go.

"The wolves, maybe," Enja said, kneeling to stroke Siiva's head approvingly. "Do we follow?"

I continued to stare out at the tracks and the horizon, thinking. If we stepped foot into that expansive field of snow, we would be turning our backs on whatever ephemeral safety the forest had offered us. There was no shelter out there, no tall objects to duck behind at the approach of danger. We would be visible to any searching eyes, and the thought of that alone made me shudder, even if I couldn't imagine what things might be watching. And, more importantly, how long would it take us to cross the plain on foot?

"Yes," I said, because I couldn't wait another minute for a storm to clear, or for the sun to rise, while the plague settled into the bones of a woman who had saved my life. "Yes," I repeated. "We follow them now."

Enja nodded her agreement. I thought I'd find fear in her face, trepidation as we set off across this vast plain for the distant mountains, but instead, a glimmer of hope and determination shone in her eyes, like the sparkling of freshly fallen snow under a winter sun. I knew, as I stared at her face flushed red from the cold and our long walk, that she was doing this for her brother. There was no doubt that her first thought upon seeing those mountains had been of Sølvi, as mine was, and how desperately he had longed to see them. That was why she showed no fear, why only unyielding resolve lit up her deep blue eyes.

And I wanted nothing more than to be like her.

A footstep sounded behind us.

We both whirled.

Eri stepped out from behind a tree. "Don't go," he said, and I shut my eyes, frustration dampening my will, and fear flickering to life. Was he here to finish what the village had started?

"Why are you here, Eri?"

"I've..."

"I can guess," I said quickly. "You've been following us." I remembered how I thought I'd seen something in the woods the night before, but had written it off as my mind playing tricks on me after the story I'd told Enja.

He didn't answer, so I took that as confirmation. "I thought no one could come or go from the village." My rising anger was almost subdued at the memory of what great lengths he had gone through to get us out.

He shrugged and looked away from me. "I left with your family. I've set them up in a cave south of the village. You could always go back there and find them. They want to see you."

I turned and looked at the plain, snow piled on snow and ending only at those chilling mountains.

"Please, Janna," he said, and something about the way he said it, the way he spoke my name, reminded me of the old Eri. The one I'd known when Sølvi was still alive. I swallowed a lump in my throat and turned slowly around to face him again. "Why? Why would you be crossing the plain? Only the mountains await you."

"Is that what those are?" Enja quipped, looking at the mountains as though she had just seen them for the first time, and shielding her eyes from the sun. "We are so lucky you were here to tell us."

"Honestly," Eri said. "All you have to do is wait it out. I can help you find a cave. I'll bring you food and firewood, and I won't tell anyone. I'll come and get you the moment it's safe to return to the village. They'll forget about Fiak once the plague hits."

I tilted my head to the side and took in his face. His hair needed cutting weeks ago, and it blew gently in the wind. His eyebrows were knitted together in that way they do when people appear to be telling the truth. "Why would you do that?" I asked, genuine curiosity raising the question to my lips. "It's been a year, hasn't it? Why now?"

"Because you need me now."

A flash of anger seared through me, so hot it almost felt cold. I wanted to snatch those words from his mouth and break them into pieces. I didn't *need* Eri. I'd never *needed* Eri, though it seemed like everyone in the village hoped I did. What I needed – answers, and a way to stop

196

that woman from dying – were things he couldn't give me. Things I had to find on my own. His connection with me, no matter how he viewed it, had to end.

Even if he had helped me to escape.

"Come with me," I said, and I motioned for him to walk a little way with me along the tree line. He did it slowly, reluctantly, and I waited to speak until we were out of earshot of Enja. I wasn't desperate for privacy, but he might have been. She watched us go, slowly and deliberately running a hand along Siiva's coat in a way one could easily interpret as menacing.

I did not wish to be harsh with Eri. He was not being unkind to me, and so, as desperate as the anger within me was to be unleashed, I would not be unkind to him. But he could never understand the certainty I felt that I was doing the right thing, in the same way I was certain of who I was, that my skin tingled from the cold, or that the trees around us bent because of the wind. Although I was not without fear, there was a calm in my heart that I could not put into words.

"I know how much you cared for me, Eri. And perhaps how much you still do. I don't know whether you feel guilt over Sølvi's death or you genuinely wish to help me, but the help I need cannot come from you. I am leaving this forest, our village, all of it behind, and Enja and I are going to the mountains. I'm not quite certain where our path will lead, but our minds are made up, and nothing you can do or say will stop us. This storm has already begun. Go back home and ride it out. Tell them, if you must. If it will keep you from following us. Tell my mother and father I still love them, and I always will..." I cleared my throat. "But I am choosing this journey, Eri, and it is not up to you to stop me. Our paths diverged a long time ago. You cannot keep trying to force them back together."

Sadness clung to his eyes, like with every word I spoke I was crushing some deep hope he had been harbouring for longer than I had suspected. Pity toyed with my heart, but not enough to change my mind.

"Janna, we must go," Enja called, eyeing the sky and the stretching day.

"I'm coming," I called, and I looked Eri in the eyes. "I'm sorry for your loss, Eri," I whispered to him. "For your father, your closest friend. I know you've suffered, as many of us have, and I hope you find peace soon."

He reached out a hand as if to stroke my face but ended up resting it on my shoulder instead. "I'm sorry, Janna," he said. "So sorry. I've seen how much you've been hurting since he died, and I wish I could have done something."

"It was my pain to endure," I told him, and then I smiled a little. "We could fill oceans with the tears we've cried, but we haven't let them drown us."

He took in a long breath, still looking at me. "At the

very least, please accept this." He withdrew a beautiful knife from somewhere in his cloak – the handle carved of beautiful wood by a hand I recognized well. "He made it for me years ago, as a gift. I think ... I think you should have it."

I took it slowly, eyeing the intricate pattern and lovingly crafted design. "Are you certain?" I asked.

"I've never been more certain of anything."

For a moment I thought he would hug me, but he just stared long and hard, threw a wave to Enja, and disappeared back into the trees.

I didn't know if he would meet an end with the plague or be slaughtered by the village for his role in helping us to escape, but I had a feeling in the pit of my stomach that this might be the last time I saw him alive.

Chapter 16

Time had passed in a blend of monotony and happiness, in the way it does as someone passes through their teenage years. My mother and father's worries over my time with Sølvi had eventually vanished after several failed attempts to arrange more time with Eri. By sixteen, Sølvi was far and away my closest friend, and wherever I went, he went with me.

Including to my beloved caves.

The darkness of the cave deepened around us as we pressed forward slowly, but our torches kept us shrouded in light. In this particular area, we had to duck our heads down to keep from hitting the roof, which made it difficult to examine the walls around us for writings. Sølvi walked behind me, his shuffling footsteps a comfort in the unfamiliar territory of the cave. It wasn't terribly far from the village –

about an hour's walk in the crisp autumn air that would only grow colder as the year was plunged into winter. Any new cave begged to be explored, to have whatever secrets lay within its shadows discovered.

There was always that small voice in the back of my mind that said we shouldn't be here, that these caves were sacred refuges from long gone days, and that whatever words were written no longer carried any meaning for us. Voices that whispered to let the darkness sleep, and let the shadows lie.

But these caves were ours as much as they were the past's.

"I doubt very many people came in here to write," Sølvi said as the cave briefly grew narrower. "Unless they were children."

"You would be surprised," I said, slipping through a neck barely big enough for a body to pass through and emerging into a much larger room. "Secrets are often hidden in hard-to-reach areas." Vague satisfaction settled over me as our eyes fell on a few markings here and there on the walls. Nothing too extravagant, but enough to make the journey worth our while.

"You seem to have some sort of . . . sense about these things," he said softly. "As if you know where to find them."

I tilted my head, thinking for a moment. "I think perhaps it's just a passion," I told him. "Perhaps passion offers you a sense other people might not possess."

He walked in a slow circle around the room, studying a marking here and there, a scratching almost too faint to read, and then turned back to me. His long furs swished about his legs. "Why, Janna? Why do you love these so much?"

I met his gaze for a few long seconds, feeling that pressure in my chest whenever he spoke my name and stared at me the way he was now. His dark brown hair was raven black in the torch light, dishevelled and perfect. One of these days, one day soon, I would tell him how I felt. I would. Returning my gaze to the stone, I said, "I like to think about when they came over here, the others. I like to imagine them living in these caves for safety and warmth until they could build homes, scratching their stories into the walls so that they wouldn't be lost. Imagine... Imagine having done something so incredible, having fled the only country your people had ever known to somewhere far away and uncharted, somewhere you didn't even know existed when you left home. Imagine staking your life, your everything, on a hope. On a chance. You would want that to be known. You would want to remember the names of the brave ones, the ones who gave their lives, the ones lost to the sea or the snow or the red sky. History is only memories, and memories die if they aren't written down. I want them to have a voice. I want them to have a reader."

My words bounced off the cave around us before settling, silence seeping in for a long moment. Sølvi took a step towards me. The air between us grew heavy, and I tried to draw in a deep breath, my heart was racing.

"You care about things," he said, his voice just barely above a whisper. "More than most."

"I care about the dead," I told him, running a palm down my side. "I care that someone listens to them."

"You care about being remembered?"

"No," I said. "Not myself. I care that they are remembered." I gestured to the wall. "None of us would be here without them."

"But you don't want to be remembered?"

"I have done nothing worth remembering."

"You will," he told me, without a shadow of a doubt. "You have. These people, they've been dead for generations. No one alive today knew them, yet here we are, talking about them. Reading their stories. Because of you."

"The dead were alive once, like you and I. Our voices shouldn't stop with our last breath."

He smiled, and I was almost certain there were tears shining in his eyes. "So, don't," he said.

"Don't what?"

"Don't let your voice stop with your last breath."

Something in the way he spoke, in the earnest way he stared into my eyes, like he could see beyond them, in the way he understood me, and why I was here, and what I cared for, propelled me forward until my lips touched his for the first time.

The snow that lay on the plain came up to my knees as we trudged onwards, following the tracks before us. It was difficult work, struggling against it without rest, and our breathlessness kept us quiet as we walked. I hadn't quite understood how vast it was, and how much time it would take to cross, but as the sun slipped lower in the sky and the air grew colder, I tried to set an example to Enja and Siiva to hurry up their pace. This kind of open exposure could not bode well at nightfall, and I didn't want to place them into serious danger before the journey was even fully underway.

This is madness, said the voice somewhere in the back of my mind. *Why have you brought them here? Why do you carry on?* I reached up to cover my ears, as though it would block out the sound and clear my head, but it only carried on. My thighs burned, my feet ached, and my lungs felt full of tiny shards of ice, but I forced myself on. Just one more step. Just one more yard. Just one more mile.

"I know it's tough going," I said breathlessly, "but we need to hurry."

Enja didn't reply, but she seemed to fight the snow a little bit harder, pressing onwards with everything she had, and that was enough.

By the hand of the Goddess, only hours after sunset, the once-distance mountains embraced us.

Chapter 17

The charred pall of clouds overhead cast even the white snow into a sallow grey, snowflakes falling and swirling in the slight wind, although it didn't feel like a storm. Vast valleys of white, broken now and then by protruding bits of rock or the occasional lone fir tree, separated the peaks, which seemed to carry on and on and on into oblivion. Barren. It was the only word that seemed fit to describe the widespread bleakness that stretched before us.

"I'm glad," Enja said, hugging herself as we stopped to take in the view, "that I'm not here alone. I don't think I could stand it."

I nodded, although I wasn't sure I felt the same. I imagined standing in the middle of the widest valley in the middle of the swirling snow, screaming my thoughts to the wind.

Siiva had continued without us, shuffling through the snow with his nose to the ground, so I moved onwards to follow him.

Distances had always been simple growing up: I knew how long it took to get through the village, or to get to my favourite caves through the forest. I knew exactly how many steps it took to get from my house to Sølvi's – sixteen – and how many to get to our favourite tree outside the village – fifty-two. But out here in the mountains, where spaces were so immense that it left me feeling utterly minuscule, my mind began to wander with all manner of possibilities. Like here, where snow married with stone and sky, what sort of things would make such a deserted wasteland their home? Childhood stories came to life: beasts with glimmering eyes that roamed only in the coldest parts of the world, and ones with great wings that could take to the sky at will. Stories like that, of things we had never seen but that could exist somewhere out of sight, had kept me awake at night as a child, dreaming up all the possibilities of what things our small corner of the world might harbour.

Now and then, a sudden gust of wind would beat against us from one side, trying to tear us off our feet. We struggled onwards. I missed the sun, the blue sky, the feeling of openness when the sky was clear. Here, it was impossible to imagine that it ever saw the sun, the dismal surroundings steeped in a grey so solid that I wondered if even fresh sunlight could alter it.

"What do you suppose those are?" Enja asked. She stood still and pointed to the ground, where deep impressions broke up the snow.

They were a set of tracks, to all appearances, but not ones like we had seen before. They were certainly not wolf tracks, nor human, nor fox, nor anything else that we would expect to see. The wind had blown snow into them, making their shape difficult to read. Siiva sniffed them for a long moment, as if unsure himself what might have passed by here and left them behind. When he stood up straight again and put his nose to the wind, he seemed unconcerned, as though there was nothing near enough to cause him any alarm.

"It's probably nothing," I told her, moving past the footprints to continue on our way. *It's definitely something,* my mind whispered. "But let's keep an eye out anyway, yes?" My words brushed it off, but my vision flickered with images, possibilities of what might have left those prints behind, and it made me shudder.

We pressed on, the coldness growing so intense that, at times, the surface of the snow was frozen over and our feet had to break through a layer of ice. I didn't like the crunching, splitting sound it gave off that could be carried away by the wind and to the ears of whatever creature had left those tracks, but there was no other way through. As always, I kept a close eye on Siiva, gauging his movements and actions and searching for any sign of alarm, but all seemed normal with him.

This place, these hills and valleys, they did not feel like a part of Skane. Not the Skane I knew, anyway. I thought of trees with rich green needles, rivers that rushed to get somewhere far away, smoke curling up to a clear blue sky. But when I looked around me, surrounded by a bone-white wilderness where life seemed entirely impossible, it felt like another world.

By evening, the clouds overhead miraculously began to dissipate, revealing bits of a dark blue sky. Our legs ached more than they had ever done so before, and when we found a small nook carved out of rock, we decided that it would have to do for a place of rest. We couldn't walk through the night, as much as our lack of time made it desirable for us to do so, so we dropped our things in the rocky crevice and I hiked a short distance away to another lone fir tree to tear off any twigs, loose bark, or dried needles that could serve for a small fire. We'd been in the cold for so long that I wasn't sure I would ever feel my hands again. The thought of a warm fire, even a brief one, gave me enough energy to carry on.

Exhaustion had swamped my mind. Tomorrow, I could think about how I'd seen no sign of the wolves, about how we had wandered out here with little to no plan, in search of a god that almost certainly only existed in songs and stories, and I could wonder whether the kind woman was still alive.

Tomorrow.

I managed to return to the hollow with an armful of various dried bits of tree, and after scooping out snow and clearing away a rocky surface, I soon had a small fire going. It danced and bent with the wind, but the heat it gave off, slowly soaking into my hands and returning them to life, was magical. We ate dried rabbit as we sat there, just enough to take the edge off our hunger, as the clouds continued to sweep away and reveal the brilliant stars. Both of our heads were tilted back to take in the view, so vivid and stark so far from a village. Here, atop the mountains and far from home, I could easily believe it was another night sky altogether, nothing like the one I'd grown up gazing at, and about which I'd heard so many stories. But that thought, that here, even the stars were unfamiliar, made me shiver.

The wind blew. The clouds ebbed away. The stars glittered ferociously. Their perfect beauty nearly brought tears to my eyes – or perhaps it was the thoughts of Sølvi I'd spent a good part of the day trying to stave off. I remembered his dream of coming to mountains, of seeing and exploring everything he could find and returning home with story after story. Stories he would tell our children, our friends; stories that would pass down through generation after generation until no one was quite certain where they had come from in the first place. Sølvi had wanted that. He had dreamed of it so often, and now I was here without him, for reasons neither of us could have ever foreseen.

I reached into the pocket of my cloak and wrapped my fingers around the bit of paper I'd rescued from my parents' house. He was with me, in a way.

"I made it," I whispered to the stars, recalling how we had wondered if they were the souls of those we loved watching over us. "If you are up there, Sølvi, I made it." I had things to accomplish down here on earth, but if it was true, and Sølvi was up there watching over me now, then I suddenly wanted more than anything to join him. *I miss you*, I thought, because my chest heaved with emotion and I couldn't speak it aloud. *I want to swim in darkness with you and drown in the stars. I do not want to be alone down here. I do not want to be alone.* Tears slipped from my eyes, but I could feel them starting to freeze, so I wiped them away.

Enja carried on staring at the sky, oblivious to my struggle only a few feet away.

I volunteered for the first watch. I wasn't done admiring the stars overhead – more in number than I'd ever seen before – and I wanted to eke that last bit of fire I could out of the rapidly reducing pile of tree bits. All around us, dark rises and valleys ended abruptly at the stark night sky, lit only faintly by the array of stars set into the moonless heavens. It was all so grand, boundless flecks of hope and possibility that defied the night with an unapologetic spirit. That was what I wanted, I realized, burdened with thoughts of love and loss and things that would never be. I could defy the night, if I tried, square my shoulders and push away the dark thoughts that wriggled their way unbidden into my mind. It didn't mean pushing away Sølvi, just the endless spiral of heartache that came with him.

Love is like a river, my mother once said. *Steady. Sure.*

But it wasn't. To me, love was like the winter. Unpredictable. Frightening. Wild.

Exhilarating.

Love is waking up to sunshine and falling asleep in a blizzard. Love is the bone-deep crush of the cold when you think you might lose it. Love is never knowing what will come next, and the incessant, determined wind forever shrieking their name somewhere in the back of your mind. And lost love is the memories encased in ice, there for you to look at, but to never touch again.

I picked out one single star in the sky and didn't look away. I imagined that was Sølvi, that the star had only blinked to life when he had released his final breath, his soul climbing high into the sky to its eternal resting place among the stars. "I love you," I whispered to the star, "more than the snow loves the cold. More than the stars love the sky. More than anything."

And somehow, as I stared at the distant light that flickered in the shivering cold, I felt better.

I touched the paper in my pocket again, remembering when he had given it to me the day before he died. I'd seen him jotting something down on paper from time to time, and he would always tuck it away out of sight when I got close. Then he gave it to me and told me to read it when I felt alone, and I wanted to before everything broke. Before Skane stole him away from me on one especially cold winter's night. And after that, I could not bring myself to look at it. To read it. They would be the last words he ever spoke to me that weren't already a memory. The last new words he could utter. I hadn't been ready to rob myself of that gift over the past year, and I wasn't ready tonight. I didn't know if I'd ever be ready.

I turned where I sat to check on Enja, wrapped tightly in her cloak with Siiva snuggled against her, sleeping soundly. All seemed peaceful and quiet, just us, alone, in the middle of nowhere, only the stars aware of our presence.

When I turned back to face the wilds around us, two glowing eyes peered out from beside a tall rock, fixed unflinchingly on me.

Chapter 18

My thoughts immediately fell to Enja, sound asleep on the ground. She wouldn't have enough time to wake up, to understand the danger and to react before the creature was upon us. Perhaps it would even go for her first, the one on the ground with her guard down. Easier prey. Why hadn't Siiva alerted us to its approach? I realized the answer almost immediately: as if it knew how to avoid detection, the creature stood perfectly downwind of our little hollow.

I stood very slowly, terrified to make any sudden movements that might encourage it to attack. If I said Enja's name to wake her, she might see the eyes and jump. I had to get it away from the camp. Siiva stirred where he lay, even raised his head and briefly sniffed the air, then spun around and returned to sleep. When I was finally on my feet, I froze. Could I reach for my knife before it came for me? Could I turn and try to outrun it? The fire had died down and there wasn't enough light from the stars to see its size or shape. All I could see were those eyes, round and terrifying in the near darkness.

Slowly, I took one gentle step sideways out of the hollow – and the creature mirrored my step almost exactly. I took another one. As did the beast. Though my heart pounded, this was what I'd wanted. I'd wanted to lure it away, to keep it so focused on me that it paid no attention to the girl asleep on the ground. Slowly, slowly, one step at a time, sideways, now backwards, ascending a snowy hill away from the hollow. It slinked after me, and the longer I focused on it, the more about its shape I could tell. It was feline. White, though I was almost certain its fur was covered in small dark spots. But perhaps its most notable feature were the two white fangs that protruded from its mouth, gleaming now and then in the starlight.

My knife no longer seemed to hold any use, not when this animal had two teeth as long as my face, and claws that likely rested somewhere inside those powerful paws. No, whatever this thing was, it was bred to hunt at night, to take down prey before it had the time to think. If it wanted me dead, it would find a way to kill me. As it followed me up the hill, its head held low to the ground in a way that was both graceful and unnerving, I slowly bent until my hand had

214

wrapped around the blade tucked safely into my boot. I slid it up my arm a ways so the creature wouldn't see the glimmer in the faint light. It may well have no idea what it was, but just in case, I didn't want to do anything to sound the alarm.

My right foot slid on a patch of ice I couldn't see, and my body nearly hit the ground. Driven by my sudden movement, the creature darted forward a few steps, closing the distance between us with frightening speed. At such a close proximity, it stood nearly to my shoulders – a fact that made my hands begin to tremble so fiercely it was a struggle to keep hold of my knife. I could hear its claws now, sinking into the snow and ice a little as it took a step. This creature belonged out here, in the frozen wastes of the mountains. It had grown to adapt, to survive, even to thrive. And I ... I was far away from my element, with little to protect or defend me. Out here, I was at the mercy of the mountains, and of this dreadful, elegant creature.

A sudden sense of imbalance made me stop short. I glanced away from the creature just for a moment to find myself almost on the edge of what could only be a ravine. The ground on which I was standing stopped suddenly and gave way to bottomless darkness. It stretched out of sight in either direction, though I could see across the gorge to where the rock and snow started up again. The creature had allowed me to come this way, had backed me up to an edge so that I would have nowhere else to go. It knew this was here.

From the hollow, a high-pitched yipping sound rose into the night. Siiva must have finally seen the beast and was warning Enja. The hunter's head spun around to stare back towards where I could just make out the fox standing on top of a rock.

The creature seemed torn now, aware of much smaller and easier prey in the vicinity, but so close to me that it might as well continue as planned. After a moment of deliberation, it turned its speckled face back towards me and slowly lowered its head. My heart skipped a beat at the sight; something seeming to change in the beast's posture making me realize its hunt was about to start in earnest. I didn't bother moving slowly any more – I couldn't afford the time. I raised my knife up and held it between us, daring it to come any closer. The weapon was barely any longer than one of the creature's fangs, but it would have to do. It was all I had.

An arrow shot out of the darkness and just barely whizzed past the animal's head, disappearing over the side of the ravine. For a split second, my mind went to Eri, of that arrow he'd shot in the woods when he had nearly killed one of those wolves, but it was Enja, I realized. She had brought her bow with her and hadn't had much of a need for it until now. The creature hissed at the sudden disturbance but didn't back down. I swung my knife from left to right, vaguely hoping to show some intimidation, but it only moved closer.

Why had it not yet killed me? A voice in the dark corners of my mind answered for me: it savoured the game. It enjoyed toying with its prey, knowing it had the power to destroy.

In a quick, mighty movement, it swiped one paw through the air towards me, only barely missing my midsection. I took a step backwards, my left heel hanging over the edge of the ravine. If I didn't get some ground to either side of me, I'd either be taken out by its next strike or go tumbling over the edge into oblivion. The thought enraged me. We had come too far and there was too much at stake for it all to end here.

Drawing in on myself and standing as tall as I could, I charged towards the beast, swinging my knife around as viciously as my strength allowed. Some small part of me had hoped that a sudden attack might throw it off its guard, surprise it just enough to give me the upper hand, but it did no such thing. As I approached, it swung one great foreleg through the air and knocked me from my feet, tumbling sideways into the snow with no breath left in my lungs. I struggled to suck in air, gulped for it as the world spun and I rolled a few times, but air remained just out of reach. My vision blurred, my body in shock from the force of the blow, but I could just barely make out the shape of the beast looming over me, surrounded

217

by hazy stars. I still couldn't breathe, though I tried with everything I had left. Fangs glimmered, coming closer.

A paw rested on my chest, keeping me in place.

Traces of air filled my lungs, but not enough to give me any strength.

In the distance, the howl of a wolf.

The sky was clear and the late autumn night chilling to the bone, but those were always the best nights to see the lights. Enja, Sølvi and I made our way through the snowy woods, loaded down with blankets and knitwear and flasks of warm drinks. Our mothers and fathers did not mind so much, as long as we were gone together. These were our nights, when the air was still just too warm to claim our lives, but cold and clear enough that night sky shone like sunlight on a diamond sea. These were not nights to be missed.

"It's cold as Ragna's heart out here," Enja said as we walked, shuddering.

"Enja," Sølvi said scoldingly. "That's rude... Not even winter is that cold."

Enja laughed, and I separated from them briefly to make my way around a large boulder stuck into the ground. We were climbing up, up, up, to the top of a cliff where we could see the sky uninhibited by trees or rises in the land. Sølvi and I came here sometimes, but it was nice to have the company of his sister, and she was thrilled to have been invited along. I didn't have a sister – or a brother – but over time, she had grown to be as close to me as I'd imagined a sister would be. I cherished her company in a tender way not unlike my parents – with the love of a family.

Around us, the trees were living shadows, watching every footstep we took and every breath we breathed: guardians on the island that knew everything at once.

"How do we know it's an island?" I asked, and Sølvi looked at me from a short distance away. I could not see details in the darkness, but the subtle glow of his face looked curious.

"What do you mean?"

"The Löskans landed here and wandered a few miles until they set up camp and built the villages. Some tried to go to the mountains and either never returned or ran back."

"Oh, is that what happened? It's almost as if we grew up in the same village." Sølvi's voice carried with it the sounds of a smile.

"You know what I mean. No one has travelled very far. So how do we know it's an island and not something as big as Löska and its surrounding countries?"

There was a pause, then Enja said, "I have to say, you have my attention."

"And mine," Sølvi said, "but what does it matter? Our villages are here, the mountains are north. That's what we know, and all we need to know."

I grunted my disapproval, but we had reached the top of the cliff and dropped our things on the ground. We wrapped ourselves in blankets and knits, keeping close together as we lay on the ground and looked up. The night sky sprawled out above us, legions of stars shimmering and far too numerous to count. A shiver caressed my skin as I was reminded of the great things at work beyond our world, reminded that there were things – the stars, for example – that were so grand and far and would always remain a mystery. And that was all right.

"Pick a star," Sølvi said, and he raised an arm to point upward. "I pick that one."

"I can't tell which one you're pointing to," Enja said, leaning closer to try and line up their eyesight.

"That one, right there. To the left of the Warrior's blade. The bright one."

"Sure, I see it," Enja replied. "I'll take the one just above it, so I can keep an eye on you. Mother and Father would be proud."

Sølvi grunted. "Mine is brighter than yours."

"You were always the favourite child." She looked over at me. "What about you, Janna?"

I scanned the sky. "I'll take that one, beside the Goddess but before you reach that little cluster. The one that looks like it's twinkling."

"Maybe it is," Sølvi said. "Just for you."

"Ugh," Enja groaned, but her brother's hand quietly found mine and squeezed it, and I couldn't help but smile.

Subtly at first, a faint bit of colour seemed to play with our eyesight in our most northern view of the sky, but within a few minutes it couldn't be missed. A gentle, spring green lit up the raven sky, a kind of beauty for which we didn't have words. Lines of the coloured light seemed to descend towards us from the darkness behind it, like it was falling from the void behind the stars but dying before it could reach us. We knew – or at least, my people had always suspected – that the Goddess was behind it, that it was her way of blessing us or warning us, but what were the lights themselves? Little bits of divine light slipping through cracks between the world of gods and goddesses and our own? Thousands of spirits gathering to dance away the night? Sunlight that refused to give itself up for the darkness? My questions were as many as the stars that still shone dimly behind the enigmatic lights.

The howl of a wolf ruptured our quiet. We all sat up in unison and looked around; Sølvi nimbly drew a knife from his cloak and held it at the ready.

"It wasn't close," I said. "Loud, but not close. We're safe for the moment."

"I don't like it," Sølvi said quietly. "We should return home."

"After all that work to get here?" Enja said.

"Yes," her brother replied simply. So we gathered our things.

It would be a long time before I heard that howl again.

Chapter 19

Daylight pierced my sleep, sharp and unrelenting. I was still partly unconscious, dreaming of warmth and fire and family, so real and close. I tried to roll over and lull myself back into the comfort of dreams, but an ache wrenched me back into the cold light of day. Rock and ice surrounded me – the hollow where we had set up camp.

I sat up quickly, my body giving complaint.

Enja sat nearby, her legs pulled up to her chest and her brows knitted in worry. There was no sign of the creature anywhere nearby, though Siiva stood atop a rock with his nose in the air, smelling and watching. Everything was so quiet, but the last thing I remembered ... I was about to die.

"What happened?" I asked. I moved to stand up, but everything ached. "Where did it go?"

"It was all ... so fast," Enja replied, shaking her head like she was still trying to understand it herself. "You were on the ground. I kept trying to shoot arrows but I was so scared and cold that I kept missing. Then I started running over to you, but..."

"Wolves." I remembered the howling suddenly, the last sound I'd heard before I went under.

She nodded. "They must have been nearby. They arrived so quickly, running out of the valleys and shadows. It didn't take them long. That ... that creature didn't stand a chance." She stopped, as if remembering what she had seen. "Then they just left."

I finally managed to haul myself to my feet and looked around at the stark, bright day. The hills and valleys rose and fell in a blanket of white all around us. Here and there, wind whipped the snow into spirals that rose and disappeared within seconds. Not far off, I could see where the ground gave way to the ravine, which I hadn't seen the night before while we were setting up our camp. I'd come so close to falling over the edge. I remembered that part.

"Which way did the wolves go?" I asked. She pointed to the northwest, where I could now see an abundance of tracks in the snow. "How many were there?"

"I don't know. Six, maybe. Eight. It was hard to tell."

Dark thoughts crept into my mind as I stared out at the snow, remembering the night before. Perhaps these mountains were evil after all. Perhaps we should just turn back now. When the sun only rises to illuminate the way of evil, and the moon ducks behind clouds to give dark things the run of the night, why go on?

Because I cannot let her die.

I took in a long, renewing breath as I stared at the tracks, and then turned back to Enja. "Let's get out of here," I said, and we left the hollow behind.

A sort of blackened forest clung to the sides of a hill. There was no evidence of fire, but the trees themselves stood raven dark against the pale landscape, out of place. They did not offer me the same comfort that my trees back in the forest gave me; these were angled and crooked, skeletons of what they could be.

Enja's grandfather once told us a story of a dark wood just like this one, guarded by a man with no face, in a cloak of shadows, on a horse made of midnight and smoke. At the time we were safe and warm inside, and all thoughts of such a man were far away and indistinct, but here, in a crow-black forest stuck to the side of a hill and far from home, I fancied I could see him walking between two trees, smoke curling from the nostrils of his steed.

I wondered if Enja remembered the story, though I dared not bring it up.

Large, imposing rocks and rises protruded from the icy

earth, partly obscured by the mist and fog that pressed against the ground. It reminded me of smoke. Everything about the land around us seemed strangely detached, as though we were seeing it through the disjointed eyes of a dream. We stayed close together, moving slowly around rocks and corners where the ground rose sharply upward. I couldn't tell exactly what I expected to see each time we turned a corner, but there were faint visions in my mind, visions of the stone come to life, and of monsters that my mind couldn't quite make real. Siiva moved slowly, deliberately, ears alert and twitching, and nose sensing things about which I was unaware. They said that about animals – that they had a sense which we humans lacked, so I kept an eye on him at all times and let him take the lead.

Somewhere behind the fog and mist, the mountains towered overhead, snowy peaks sensing our presence and bidding the land around us to be quiet. Once upon a time I'd loved the quiet, the peacefulness of the outdoors far away from the village, but not today. Today, I longed for a familiar sound to break through the lonely silence that haunted everything around us. If there was an afterlife, this was a taste of its isolation.

My hair rustled a bit, and something whispered in my ear.

I stopped moving.

Sssss, something hissed again. Wordless, indistinct,

but real. Each time the sound came, my hair stirred some, like a gentle breeze that moved of its own accord.

"Did ... did you say something?" Enja whispered beside me, her words barely audible despite her close proximity to me.

"Sshh," I whispered back. "No."

Siiva had stopped walking.

Another breeze ruffled my hair, and a voice breathed in my ear. "Welcome. Weellcome." As if fear itself was a thing made real, an icy hand trailed up and down my spine until every inch of my body trembled.

"Don't stop," I whispered to Enja. "Keep moving."

The fog seemed to intensify, growing thicker and heavier until I could no longer tell in which direction we headed. This rock could be familiar, and we could have rounded that corner many times now, but I refused to let us stop. Each time we slowed down, that voice, that breeze, again reached for my ears, and with every step I wondered if I left a little more of my sanity behind me.

On and on. Round and round. Terror urged us on, but to where, I didn't know. Yet we made no progress, and nothing new presented itself through the fog. Finally, I allowed my feet to stop moving.

"I don't know where we are," I told Enja under my breath. "And I don't know where we're going."

"Perhaps we can mark our way," she said, tearing off a small bit of paper from something in her cloak and dropping it to the ground. No sooner had it settled onto the rock and ice than a breeze I couldn't feel whisked it up and away, depositing it somewhere far out of sight.

I drew in a long, steadying breath and flexed my fingers. Whatever this living breeze was, it would not see the end of our journey.

I hear your thoughtssss. I know your feelings. If you run, I will follow, and if you fall, I will devour.

I held on to my hair to keep it from blowing about as the voice tormented me. "Enja, when I say go, run forward with Siiva, and I'll follow. Do not stop until we're away from this place. Do you understand me? Do not stop."

She nodded a few times, standing up taller in preparation to run. I waited until my hair settled after a moment, until I couldn't feel the caress of movement against my face, and then I said, "Run."

We took off together, Siiva following closely behind us as we darted around rocks and boulders dripping with ice. The voice of the breeze sounded just out of reach, trailing behind us so closely that if we stopped, it would instantly be upon us. Onwards, only ever onwards, slipping on treacherous ground, tearing around bends, half-tumbling over boulders in the ground. Until, with a sudden thud and a sickening moment of falling through the air, my boot caught on invisible ice and I plunged to the ground like a ton of rocks.

"Don't stop!" I shouted to Enja, but she had already turned and reached a hand out to draw me up.

You belong to us now. Welcome to the mountainssss.

"Go, Enja, go," I ordered her, but she took my hand and hauled me to my feet as the voices around us grew in number. Then, suddenly, she stood straighter, head turned in the direction we had been running, listening.

I opened my mouth to ask her what it was, trying desperately to ignore the words hissed into my ear, until I heard it, too.

Howling.

Faint, disembodied howls wafted to us on the cold air, far away but distinct. I was suddenly back in the woods near my village, hearing the howling of wolves far to the north and desperate to answer their call. I couldn't answer it then, not really. But now, now I *needed* to.

"Follow it," I told Enja, scrambling to get to my feet. "Follow the sound."

I blocked all hisses and whispers from my mind, listening only to the howling of the wolves, however far away it may be, and followed it at a run over rock and ice. Enja ran beside me, her breath short as we refused to slow down. I could sense the voices close at hand, catch a faint hiss now and then, which only encouraged me to run faster.

Ahead, a dark outline began to take shape, and from it, the still distant call of the wolves seemed to emanate. A cave? A tunnel? It didn't matter. "In there," I shouted, pointing as we ran. Enja didn't respond, only shifted her direction until she made directly for the opening. It appeared to be some sort of hollowed-out rock, though whether it was naturally so or made by something I lacked the energy to fathom, I didn't know. The closer we drew, however, the larger it loomed, until, as we finally passed through it, the roof yawned so far overhead I couldn't quite make it out.

But my wonderment was overshadowed by my relief, as we stopped running and came to a halt, all sounds of hissing and whispering having disappeared. Near silence engulfed us, broken only by the sound of our heavy breathing and the gentle panting of Siiva at our feet.

Enja fell to a heap on the ground, trying to catch her breath. I remained standing and turned in a slow circle to take in the large cave as my eyes began to adjust to the darkness. It was mostly empty, save for the nearby trickling of a spring, and a large pile of boulders resting in one corner. A naturally formed cave, then. It had to be. I relaxed a little and sat down beside Enja, resting my elbows on my knees.

"What...?" she started, and then stopped, shaking her head. There was no use asking what it was. Neither of us knew, and part of me... Part of me didn't want to know. If such evil things existed, as long as we were safe, let them remain a mystery.

But if this was the road to the god of death, I couldn't help but wonder how much worse it would be.

"I don't know," I said, turning to look back towards the entrance to the cave. I remembered the stories about the mountains.

They are where all the evil things in Skane were gathered long ago, and they are better off left alone.

After the events of today, I could nearly believe that last one.

As we sat in a long silence, breath slowly returning to normal and fear calming some, a thought crept its way into my mind and rooted itself there, solid and unmoving. That breeze, those voices, they had followed us even when we ran. They had pursued us, close at our heels and inescapable. They had said they would pursue us. Why, then, had they not followed us into this cave?

There was something about clear winter nights that pulled me from the village and into the welcoming darkness of the woods. Sølvi walked at my side, our feet crunching lightly in yesterday's snow. Through every break in the trees overhead, crisp stars watched our every move, eyes in the sky that missed nothing.

"I convinced a boy today that he was a dragon," Sølvi told me, laughing softly as he said it. "I told him that white burst of air when he breathed was from a fire in his belly."

I smiled. "Did it make him cry?"

"No, he thought it was wonderful. Went off to tell all

his friends. He'll realize his mistake when he sees that they can all do the same thing."

"So, you lied to a child."

"Well, it's what my own father told me. I was simply passing it on."

We fell into silence as our path led steadily uphill, drawing strained breaths from our lungs and slowing our pace somewhat. He had never been here before, but I knew the way by heart. Nearby, the lonely hoot of an owl sounded in the trees, repeating a few times before falling silent once again. Animals were scarce around us, likely hearing our footsteps and scampering off before we approached.

A short while later, we reached the rocky summit of the hill. I hoisted myself on to a boulder as Sølvi climbed up beside me, and overhead, an infinite number of stars glistened against a raven sky. There was no moon to shield their light, no village torches to hide them from view. Cold air licked my skin, burning like a flame, but I pulled my cloak tighter around my shoulders and shuffled closer to Sølvi.

"Cold?" he asked gently, wrapping an arm around my shoulders. I nodded into his chest. In a whisper, he began to sing a childhood song by my ear.

"Cold, so cold, the winter arrives
Chill as a witch's heart
Cutting as knives."

Also in a whisper, I joined in with him.

"Cold, so cold, the winter sets in

231

Warm fires beat the frost
Biting your skin.
Cold, so cold is the crystalline snow
Coating the land
Outside houses aglow.
Cold, so cold are the winter nights
While stars hang as sparks
Of celestial light."

Our whispers died out, and quiet settled in. I stared at the sky, thinking about everything and nothing.

"What do you suppose they are?" I asked eventually. "The stars."

He paused before answering. "Perhaps they are the eyes of the Goddess, so she can see everything we do."

"But they are only out at night. What about during the day?"

"During the day she uses the sun."

"What if it's cloudy?"

He thought for a moment. "Then perhaps they are the souls of everyone in the world who has ever died."

I didn't answer. That seemed much more likely, but the weight of that notion overruled a response.

"Perhaps one day," he said, "I will be up there too, watching over you."

"I would rather have you here," I said, pushing against him a little more. He didn't reply, and a sharp sadness moved us to silence.

Chapter 20

We knew it would be a hard winter, because in the spring, one of Alff's sheep had given birth to a blind lamb, and the third quarter of the year brought three days of fog. Some superstitions came over from Löska and stayed, like the belief that one must leave a candle burning through a snowstorm or it might never pass, or that nightmares meant an evil spirit was whispering into your ear as you slept. Others developed here in Skane, though whether they were formed in the mind of a yarn-spinner or born from mystical encounters, no one was ever certain.

But the ones involving nature, the ones that spoke of winter and the things it might hold, those were as sacred as the stars in the sky. So as the cold months slowly drew nearer, we hoarded food, dried meat, baked bread, and knitted warm clothing to keep the frost from our skin.

Firewood stacks grew tall along the walls of our homes, and chimneys never ceased to smoke.

Then, with all the vengeance of shrieking winds and swirling snow, drifts piling high against our houses and burying trees as if they were no more than stumps, winter arrived. Many swore they'd never seen anything like it, never felt a cold so brutal, seen snow so deep, or had storms more often than that winter. It was all anyone could talk about when the snow ceased enough for us to travel between homes.

"I reckon we might lose half our sheep."

"And even that's optimistic."

"If our firewood doesn't last, the whole village will riot. May have to start hiding some, just in case."

Storm after storm meant staying indoors with very little to do, so I filled up every inch of parchment paper I could find with writings that I would later etch into a cave wall. I spoke of winter, of the storms, of the things I heard people saying. If we never had another winter like this one, it would be worth remembering long after all of those who survived it had died out.

On one of the rare clear days, I walked beside Sølvi into the woods where we would gather buckets of clean, untrodden snow to boil over the fire. We moved slowly, letting the freedom of the outdoors sink in and drinking in the occasional birdsong overhead. It had been four days since we had last come outside, four days of wind and snow and a cold unlike anything I'd ever felt. But now, among the trees and laden shrubs of the forest, under the brilliant sun, it was hard to imagine that this was the same land as the one from yesterday.

"After a winter like this," Sølvi said, "I feel doubtful that the warmer months will ever arrive."

I nodded. "I fear that we'll be buried beneath this snow for the rest of our lives."

"We won't be," he assured me, and then paused for a long while. Our feet crunched into the deep snow, covered with a layer of ice. "In the spring," he said finally, considering his next words, "I think that things should change. We're young, I know, but. . ." He trailed off, and I held my breath, suspecting I knew his next words as I watched his face. I always liked his eyes best just before sunset, when the green-gold flecks shone in the golden light of a fading day. "I think we should finally—" Just then, voices rang out, crying for help.

We dropped our buckets and hurried as fast as we could through the deep snow in the direction of the voices, which came from the bank of a small river that cut through the forest. It wasn't deep, perhaps waist high on someone taller than me, but it was covered with a thin layer of ice, and beneath that, the current ran strong.

"Finni!" a woman screamed. I recognized her as his older sister, Inna. Finni was a boy from the village, maybe fourteen or fifteen, although I didn't know him well. Inna was crouched on her knees, reaching out towards a hole in the middle of the river where a few fingers poked from under the ice, clutching the edge of the hole.

"What happened?" Sølvi shouted over Inna's screeching, gently pushing her aside to reach out himself.

"He fell! He fell!" she cried, touching two shaking hands to her mouth. "He wanted to cross. Thought the ice could hold him. Oh, Goddess bless him, he can't breathe!"

The fingers slipped, losing some of their grip on the ice. Sølvi reached out as far as he could, but I could already see the problem. There would be no way to stand on the ice and pull Finni back out, because the ice wasn't strong enough to hold someone. We could break the ice with ice picks, but that could injure Finni, and he wouldn't survive that long. As it was, stuck beneath the surface in frigid, rushing water, he didn't have long left. Sølvi reached out further and further, and I knelt and held on to his waist to give him more flexibility, but the seconds ticked by, and we were out of ideas.

Then, as quietly and unceremoniously as a leaf falling from a tree, the fingers disappeared, and Finni was gone.

Inna shrieked and collapsed into the snow. My heart thundered in my chest as I fought away tears, and Sølvi stared silently at the place where, only seconds ago, the boy had still been holding on for his life.

But this was winter in Skane, where death lurked in every shadow and frostbite hung ready in the air, eager to

*eat away at your skin. If you weren't careful, the land would
claim you, and as Finni would one day become, you'd be
turned into a cautionary tale to children.*

*"Never try to cross the ice of a rushing river, or you'll
be sucked beneath its surface and drown, like Finni."*

The dim light from the cave's entrance eventually began
to grow even fainter, until at last, night had fallen. I lit
a candle I'd kept in my cloak and propped it up with a
few stones. It was only a small flame, but it penetrated
the darkness around us like a torch and blanketed the
cave in comfort.

"How do you suppose the others are faring?" Enja
asked presently. We both stared at the flickering light,
watching it dance about as Siiva slept in her lap. "Back
home."

I shifted uncomfortably. "I don't know." She liked
to ask questions of me, I'd noticed, perhaps due to my
being the older one, yet more and more often I had no
answers. Only days ago, things were far simpler. We
gathered firewood to keep warm and ate dried meat for
dinner and huddled under blankets at night. Each day
was a predictable as the one before it, and while I had
long lamented that fact, a small part of me now wished
for it back. There's a certain dullness in repetition, but
also comfort. "Well, I hope." So much had happened
since we had left the village, so many strange encounters

and moments of terror that my mind was too full to give them much thought. It returned often to the woman and her baby, and then focused in again on the moment, on where we were, and how we would keep going. On an impulse, I said, "I'm sorry that you had to do this. That you had to come with me."

She eyed me for a long moment, before replying, "This was always about both of us. I would have never let you come here alone."

I smiled a little, my eyes growing heavy. "Would you like to sleep first?" I asked, moving to lie sideways and prop my head up on my elbow.

"No, you go first. I'll keep watch and cuddle Siiva for a while."

I should have tried harder and insisted on her going first, but the day had worn me out, and sleep came before I could formulate another sentence.

It was all but wholly dark. My eyes blinked open slowly, heavy with sleep. The candle had nearly burned out, little more than a stub with reddish embers keeping it from extinguishing altogether. Enja lay asleep with her head resting on one arm, Siiva curled in a ball against her belly. She should have alerted me before nodding off, but I couldn't blame her too harshly after such an exhausting day. All was silent, peaceful, and yet ... what had awoken me?

A sudden sense of urgency filled my veins as I became distinctly aware that something was out of place. Something had changed in the cave, and I was still too dumb with sleep to identify what it was. I sat up slowly, staring around me and trying to force my mind to remember what it had looked like when we had first entered it, to understand what had changed, but—

The large pile of rocks in the corner was gone. Missing. Boulders, they'd been. Far too large to simply be picked up and carried away. So how, then, had they moved?

My back was to the entrance, but something stirred the air behind me. Ever so slowly, breath caught in my lungs, I turned to find something impossibly large and gruesomely bulky looming over me. A creature, of sorts, made of a skin so grey and leathery it looked like stone, but tall enough to almost reach the roof. In the split second before I let out an involuntary yelp, my mind flashed with the stories we had been told about the things that lived in hiding in Skane – giants, trolls, devils of all sorts. The grey skin, if you could call it skin, and the dark, beady eyes fit nearly every story I had heard of the mountain trolls, but I wished to stare at it no longer.

My yelp had Enja and Siiva on their feet in seconds, and the moment she laid eyes on the creature, she shrieked. I was on my feet in a moment, but the troll – if that's truly what it was – stood between us and the entrance, leaving very little room to get around it.

Its eyes moved from me, to Enja, to Siiva, and it drew itself up taller, slowly rubbing its hands together with a sound that made my skin prickle. It was delighted, no doubt, that we had delivered ourselves to its doorstep. I should have given more thought to the total silence, to the signs that perhaps something lived here, but I had been too shaken and frightened to notice anything.

The troll grunted, which sounded more like a roar, and took a step towards us.

With the exit blocked, that left us with the only option of fleeing further into the tunnel, which would almost certainly lead to a dead end. At the very least, however, we might be able to find a space small enough in which to hide, buy ourselves some time until perhaps it went away – or until I could come up with a better plan.

Enja was ahead of me, already running towards the rear of the cave while sparking a flint to light a small torch. I took off after them, hearing a grating, sliding noise behind me as the troll gave pursuit. As the cave gave way to a tunnel that quickly became far more narrow, the footsteps behind us slowed, but did not stop.

"Keep going," I panted to Enja, glancing behind me. Wherever the troll was, it was just out of reach of the dim light. Enja turned to glance behind us as well, and lost her footing, stumbling forward a few steps. Ice.

I realized the trickling sound of the underground spring had grown louder despite our footsteps, and ahead, just barely visible in the light, I could see it cutting across our path. But it wasn't so much a creek as a fast-flowing river maybe eight feet wide. Centuries of flowing had worn it down into the rock, leaving the sides somewhat banked and rounded. If we did not jump far enough, our feet would slide off the bank and we'd disappear into the rush of the river for ever.

Memories of Finni, of the river swallowing him whole, rushed to the forefront of my thoughts until it was all I could see.

But the approaching footsteps behind us returned me to the moment.

There's no other way. There's no other way.

"We have to jump," I said, removing my cloak and pack and hurtling it across the river. They landed safely on the other side, leaving us enough room to land. "You go first so I can hold it off if it reaches us."

I expected her to fight back out of fear, to refuse to go first until I had attempted the jump, but she merely breathed, threw her things across, and nodded as if to convince herself. There was an air of courage about her that, although I was terrified and distracted, wasn't lost on me.

"Hurry," I urged, as the ground around us rattled.

With a running start of only a few steps, she leapt into the air over the river, landing with just enough space to catch her feet and propel herself forward. Without a word, I grabbed Siiva and hurled him across the river;

he landed in her arms with a few yelps. That left just me. With the footsteps now so loud that they could only be right behind me, I pushed off from the ground and hurled myself into the air.

The river rushed beneath me, sickeningly loud, and the ground on the other side came closer and closer until – there, my feet touched the rock, and I should have enough forward momentum to continue moving away from the edge. There was a moment of free fall that stretched away like a chasm; nowhere I could go, nothing I could do but wait for the second or two to drag by. Air at my ears. Footsteps at my back.

But the edge was icy, and one of my feet didn't quite find the purchase it needed. It began to slip away in what felt like an eternity. The seconds stretched into minutes and I saw so many things: Finni's face just before he disappeared. Sølvi, smiling at me in the crystalline light of a winter's day. One by one, I saw the faces of those we had lost, those who had crossed over to the other side at one point or another, just as I would now, while trying to cross this river. The rush of the water became the voice of death as it began to welcome me home.

And then I saw Enja, eyes slightly bloodshot, horror marking her face, as she reached for me while shouting words I couldn't hear. Her hand touched mine just as my foot left the edge, and she yanked me towards her, pulling me fiercely towards safety and life.

Solid ground met me. The sounds of the river returned to normal, and the faces of those who'd passed, those who hadn't been pulled to safety, one by one began to disappear. The footsteps following us had stopped, the river seeming to draw some sort of a line that the troll refused to – or could not – cross. I let my body fall against the stone beneath me, lying on my back and staring up at the dimly lit ceiling. In the space of hours, we had been chased by whispering winds and a giant mountain troll, and we were now somewhere that felt deep underground, so removed from everything familiar.

But every time I closed my eyes, I saw the kind woman's face, and the voice in my head echoed, *do not let her die.*

So I hauled myself to my feet, took a long look at the troll pacing back and forth on the other side of the river, and turned us away towards the darkness.

We moved gingerly through the tunnel, afraid of what every bend and every corner might hold. At times the ceiling was so low we were forced to walk with our heads down, and at other times the passageway was so narrow that we had to turn sideways to fit through. It was at times like that when my skin began to crawl, when the closeness of everything began to draw in even further and my breath got caught in my chest.

And then, much later, the tunnel gave way to a vast,

sweeping chamber of stone that stood so high and wide, our light left it in darkness. There was a certain kind of uncanniness in that, in being in a room – if indeed it could be called a room – so great that anything could be lurking just beyond the reaches of the light, and we would be none the wiser. It was far less cold here, and, well away from the noise of the river, utterly silent. I didn't like our footsteps. I didn't like hearing my own breath in my nostrils. There was something about this large, seemingly empty room that begged for us to leave it undisturbed. And yet, this was the way forward. We'd heard the distant cry of the wolves echoing from somewhere within the cave, so there was nothing to do but press on.

Ahead, on the edges of the light, some tall stone structure became visible. It didn't have the look of something natural, I realized with a tingling at the back of my neck, nor was it like anything I'd ever seen before. Whatever it was, or whatever it had been, was so large that our light only seemed to illuminate the bottom half as we approached. On a whim, far too curious to remain unenlightened, I struck the flint and lit a second small torch, holding it aloft.

It was a giant man, carved from smooth stone, with his head bowed, one knee and his hands resting on the floor. Even knelt as he was, the top of his head still towered far above us, a kind of size I had difficulty comprehending. Had he once been real, or was he always made of stone?

My heart and mind raced, and I fought back the urge to flee this room and this cave and the questions that flooded my mind.

"Look," Enja whispered, pointing to our left. I turned, and the edges of our light fell on another set of feet and hands, and another bowed head, only this time of a woman. They knelt side by side in this vast, forgotten room, the only signs of humans I had ever seen outside of our villages.

There were stories as ancient as the land itself, of a people who used to roam it, back when gods and goddess still walked the earth, and creatures long dead drank from its pools and flew through its skies. It was a different time, then, and perhaps one when the sky did not glow red, and a plague did not slip into our veins and take our lives by the dozens.

Or, perhaps that's how they had all disappeared. Perhaps the plague chased them away from this island, or claimed their lives one by one until there was no one left.

And quietly, I sent a prayer to the heavens that we wouldn't end up the same way; that we wouldn't be a whisper of a culture that would ultimately dissolve into the snow and ice shrouding our land and lay erased from the world for time immemorial.

"What are they?" Enja asked, but I could tell by the way she asked it that she knew I didn't have an answer.

"I wish I knew." I ran a hand along part of a stone foot,

half ensuring it was real. "It doesn't matter," I lied, hoping to offer her some comfort. "The only way is forward." I tore my eyes away from the statues and instead focused on the space in between them. The path disappeared into darkness, but somehow, I knew that was the way to go. These two people, kneeling as they were, gave me the distinct impression of some sort of gate, and while I did not know if I would like where it led, we still had to go through it. Perhaps whatever they welcomed us into – or whatever they guarded – was as forgotten as the people who had built it.

I squared my shoulders, and drew in a long breath.

Enja nodded to herself, standing up taller. "The only way is forward," she echoed, and this time, a sort of determination had settled into her voice.

"Forward," I repeated, and I took the first step.

Chapter 21

A shiver ran through my body as we passed the imposing statues, as though we had crossed some sort of perimeter within the mountains where the air changed. I didn't like how it felt, but curiosity and duty propelled me forward, onwards, until the statues were long behind us. Enja and I walked so closely together our shoulders brushed from time to time, neither of us finding any comfort in the yawning cavity of the mountain's belly, or the darkness that lurked just beyond our faint light. What things skulked beyond the reaches of the candle, watching, waiting? Or was it worse to imagine that we were the only living things in this mountain, other than the troll we had left behind? The possibility of that kind of isolation swirled as a shadowy fog in my mind, whispering *alone, alone, alone.*

"Who do you think made those statues?" Enja whispered. "I mean, who do you imagine?"

She knew I didn't have the real answer. She was after my thoughts, my speculations. I kept my whisper even quieter than hers. "I don't know." But those age-old stories of an ancient people who lived long before our memory, long before we fled Löska to find safety, permeated my thoughts. I could have told her that, told her what I knew, and we could have continued to muse and imagine what they had looked like, how they had acted, and what had become of them, but a voice in the back of my mind told me that it didn't matter. Who had built those statues was far less important than why, because what they bowed to – if it wasn't the Goddess – would be far more relevant in the coming moments or hours than whatever long-dead people had constructed them. "People like us, I imagine," I said finally. "Long ago."

We carried on.

"Always check behind you," I told her after a pause, as I glanced over my shoulder to ensure that we were alone. I wasn't quite sure why. Certainly these archaic rooms and stone passageways had not been walked in centuries or longer, and Siiva would surely hear if anything approached, but the events of the past few days had left me overcautious and on edge.

The room we were in seemed to narrow a bit, evidenced only by the change in the echo of our footsteps on whatever walls stood just out of sight. My mind tried to fill in the blanks, to map out the cavern where we walked and paint in the details that eluded my senses, but there were too many unknowns. Too many things that were impossible to know. The air grew closer, my sense of space less expansive, and then suddenly, we were descending. The floor banked at just enough of an angle to tell us we were headed down a sort of hill. Further into the mountains. I felt less like myself with every step, less like the girl who loved the lofty forests and magnificent icy hills of the land above. So, so far above, and so far away. Down below it was ... different. It was nothing like the land I knew, or the land I loved. The sense of space I'd grown to cherish, the sense of beauty and peace and wonder, was replaced by the creeping sense of unease and disquiet.

Do not let her die.

So onwards we walked.

The sounds of our footsteps changed once again, what felt like hours later but could have been minutes. Time was difficult to tell, and though I sometimes tried to count our footsteps in order to keep some track of its passing, my mind always began to wander. I could not place exactly what had changed in the soft sound of our footfalls, but I drew us slowly to a stop and held the small torch aloft for a better view. Nothing presented itself. Just a few paces of golden light flanked by darkness.

"Something's changing," I whispered to Enja, and then vaguely wondered at myself. We'd been whispering since we had entered the mountain, though perhaps we could have shouted and not a soul would have heard us. But I didn't know if that was more, or less comforting.

"I heard it, too," she said, watching Siiva for any hints or signs. He was sniffing the air ahead of him, curious, but seemingly calm.

"I have a third torch," I told her, tapping it gently within my cloak, "but we need to save it. Eventually we'll run out entirely, and we need to stretch out our light for as long as possible." I did not tell her something else that had been weighing on my mind: that if we didn't find something within the mountain to use for light, we would have nothing for the return journey.

She nodded, subtle fear glinting in the whites of her eyes.

"Just move slowly. Listen. I don't know what's ahead."

She nodded again, adjusting her grip on her torch to hold it more tightly. We were even more cautious when we again began to move, our boots barely making any sound at all as they made contact with the stone beneath us. Siiva crept along with his head down to the ground, sniffing and pausing every now and then to look up. Each time he did so I hesitated, imagining in visceral detail what shadowy things might be lurking beyond our pool of light. On any other day, I would give little thought to each individual step I took. But here, every inch my feet moved was deliberate, careful, slow to the point that my muscles gave frequent complaint.

The air, I realized suddenly, was curiously warm, lacking that icy tinge to it that my body had grown accustomed to over its eighteen years on this island. A bead of sweat, perhaps from my apprehension, trickled down my back between my shoulder blades.

Something on the ground pulled me to a stop, and I knelt to examine it. A sort of greenish film I recognized from four years back, when a warm summer left this odd growth on some of the rocks by the sea. It was a plant, perhaps, or at least it bore the colour of one, but if it was a plant that grew by the sea…

I stood and slowly took a few steps forward, holding the torch high.

And a velvety black body of water yawned before us, its surface as still and smooth as undisturbed snow. A lake, in the belly of a mountain.

I moved to stand close enough to it that the toes of my boots rested just shy of the water's edge. Siiva sniffed the inky water intently, his body rigid with a kind of focus I had not seen before. He lapped up a sip or two, and promptly spat it back out, making little coughing sounds and backing away.

Enja came to stand beside me, bending down to inspect the water. "It's difficult to tell if the water is black

251

or if it's just the lack of the light," she mused, refusing to get close enough to let her feet touch it. "But there must be a way to cross."

I looked at her quickly. "Why?" I had been entertaining the wretched sinking feeling that we would have to turn back, maybe find another way.

"Because clearly we aren't the first people to come here. Those statues opened the way to something, so others must have passed. This lake can't be the end of the road."

She stood tall and held her torch aloft. The flame flickered, bending to a faint breeze I couldn't feel. "That's why," she said. "There's something on the other side."

"Then find a crossing," I told her, turning to the left and treading along the water's edge with my torch. "I doubt they swam."

She travelled in the opposite direction, and our little circles of light followed us as we split ways. I examined the surface of the water carefully, looking for a ridge, a shallow area, anything that could allow us to cross. Doubts began to set in as we searched. *This lake could have formed since the last people walked here. Perhaps it did not exist so long ago.*

"Janna." Enja's voice shattered the silence, and I turned quickly and trotted over to where she stood. The distance was considerable, this lake spanning far wider than I had imagined.

When I stopped beside her, my eyes fell on a few irregularities in the water, small, flat surfaces that resembled to be … stepping stones. Enja reached out one foot and pressed gently against the first one. It held strong. "This just might be it."

I looked up from the stones and to the pitch blackness that lurked beyond the comfort of our pale lights. If we took this pathway and crossed these stones, what awaited us on the other side? And was there, indeed, another side? What if we carried on and on, our legs growing tired and our bodies growing weak, but there was no way to rest, no way to sleep? I thought of the lake back home, the Hornsträsk, with its expansive waters and sweeping depths. How much larger could this lake be? And, more importantly, what cost could we face in crossing it?

"Forward," Enja said, echoing my words from earlier. "We go forward until there is nowhere else to go. If there is a path, then we must take it."

This murky lake reeked of death and warning.

Do not let her die.

These stepping stones were narrow, and the faintest breeze could throw us off balance.

Do not let her die.

The distance was unknowable; the energy required substantial.

Do not let her die.

"Forward," I said, and I placed my foot on the first stone.

If you followed the Horn River south for a good ways, it reached a point where it went tumbling over a series of high cliffs, forming waterfalls as loud as thunder. The water was always white and churning, daring you to get too close so it could swallow you whole. No one who fell into that water would ever come out again, so we always gave it a wide birth.

But today, I had crept behind the crashing water at the point where it fell through the air away from the rock, and into the small cave set just behind it. Stone stood damp and strong at my back, and the roaring waterfall tumbled before me. It was loud, louder than anything else I had ever heard – but not loud enough to drown out my thoughts, as I'd hoped. As I stared at the falling water, listened to the roar as it plunged, I saw Finni's face before he had disappeared for ever. Why had I thought coming here would help? The rushing of the waterfall became the rushing of the river that had killed him, and my head spun.

He'd been so close. So close to living, to being saved, to surviving. He could be here right now, be in Skane with the rest of us; be going about his day, doing his chores, and never know that he'd very nearly died. I hadn't known him well, and yet I'd witnessed his last moments; witnessed his death and had to describe it to his mother and father while their tears fell like rain. Describing it was like reliving it all over again, and thinking about it now, set against the background of rushing water, made my stomach churn.

A second had always seemed so simple, so inconsequential, but what a difference it could make. It could draw a line between life and death, between here and there, between breathing and drowning. One second was all it took for his fingers to slip, to the current to pull him in, and for the river to consume him.

"Janna."

A voice cut through my thoughts, stabilizing me. It was a voice I wanted to hear, like a pillow to my heavy heart. Sølvi ducked behind the waterfall and sat down beside me, wrapping one arm around my shoulders. He said nothing at first, just sat there with me while I quietly let a few tears fall and soak into his cloak. I wanted to go back and save him, save Finni, take those fingers that were holding on so dearly and use them to pull him towards warmth and safety. Towards us. Towards life.

"I want to save him," I sobbed, and the tears came faster. Sølvi embraced me tighter, saying nothing. "I want to go back to the river and help him, risk falling in myself if I have to. I shouldn't have been afraid. His life was in danger, and he lost it, because I was afraid."

"Because I was afraid," Sølvi corrected, and I remembered suddenly that it had been him reaching out for the boy. "The ice would have never held either of us if it couldn't

hold Finni. I had to make a decision between losing two lives and losing one, and it was the hardest decision I've ever had to make."

I sat up and looked at him, suddenly aware of how much this must have been weighing on him. I'd been selfishly caught up in my own thoughts and my own pain that I hadn't even registered what he must have been going through.

"I'm so sorry, Sølvi," I said, my voice catching from crying. "It wasn't your fault. It wasn't anyone's fault, I suppose."

"I feel awful," he said, tracing a gloved finger along the stone. "Terrible. Every time I see his sister around the village, something inside me breaks apart. But I cannot change it. Skane is harsh, all ice and snow and cold. It demands respect, or it will take your life. Think of all the others, the first ones who came across the sea. More of them died once they arrived than lived to tell the tales. They were smothered by snow, froze to death at night, drowned in the frigid sea. The landscape is as much a villain as you allow it to be. Finni was unlucky. He let his guard down for a moment and in the blink of an eye, he was gone."

I stared at the water before us, mighty and powerful and, as Sølvi had said, demanding respect. Skane was vicious, as much as I desperately loved it, and if we weren't careful, it would weed out the weak ones among us, catch us when our guard was down even for a few seconds. It would always *be a fight to survive here, but it was a better existence than the one they had left behind in Löska.*

"I'm sorry," I said, my voice stronger. "I've just ... I've never seen someone die before. Not someone so young, anyway, and not like that."

He held me again, and I could feel my strength returning with every second. He sat there with me for a long while as we shed our sorrows and worries, until sunset began to threaten the sky and we were forced to leave, and while I did feel better, the guilt of watching Finni's fingers slip away towards death would haunt me for the rest of my life.

Chapter 22

The first few steps were easy enough. Each stone was slightly wider than both of my feet positioned side by side, and spaced just far enough apart so as to be a healthy, wide step without throwing me off balance. Enja had opted out of carrying Siiva after I had convinced her that she would be safer without him. He was agile enough and could hop from stone to stone even more easily than we could, but she required both arms and all of her strength to make it to the other side. She had agreed, but paused every few steps to turn and check on the fox, and though I couldn't see him, I suspected he was holding his own. On the crossing, we each had to fend for ourselves. There wasn't the space and comfort to be able to stop and turn easily, to allow enough of a distraction from balancing to start a conversation and check in. Focus. That was all we could do.

The crossing grew more unsettling when the bank upon which we had been standing disappeared, and nothing but inky water could be seen in all directions. I couldn't help but wonder, as I tried to keep my focus on the path ahead, how ancient this lake might be. If something, someone, long before our time had created a path across it, then surely it had lain here for hundreds upon hundreds of years. That was a long, long time, and anything could have since made the lake its home.

Could anything survive in a pitch-black lake, hidden far below the surface of the world?

After the things I had seen since arriving at the mountains, I could almost believe anything.

My right foot skidded slightly as it made contact with the next stepping stone – more of that greenish growth. Which was odd, because the surface of the stones lay just above the waterline, meaning that the only way water could have come to be on top of it was if ... it had been splashed there.

I stopped walking to consider that for a moment, but forced myself on a second or two later. If I stopped to explain it to Enja, it would take precious time that we could be using to get off the lake. That had to be our focus. Press onwards, and put this murky lake behind us.

"Be careful," I whispered. "It's slippery."

One stepping stone later, I stopped again. The water

below us ... it was moving. Gentle ripples were lapping against the stones, subtle, but distinct. I held the torch up to see if it was a breeze that caused the waters to move, but the movement of the flame was almost negligible. And the ripples were moving towards us – from the centre of the lake.

"Enja," I whispered, my hand drifting to my knife as though it would do us any good. "Stop moving."

I heard all sounds of movement cease behind me, and we stood deathly still, waiting. The silence pressed loud against my ears, overwhelming and heavy. Seconds seemed to stretch into hours as my heart hammered in my chest, my pulse thundering in my ears. We were vulnerable enough on solid ground in these cursed, foreign lands; the stones beneath our feet would be a sore disadvantage against whatever lurked in the abyssal depths.

A few breaths. Another lapse of unbearable silence.

Two dull, whitish-yellow eyes emerged from the lake many metres away, hovering just above the waterline and focused on us. I could make out little of the head, but from my distance it appeared to be little more than dark, filmy stone. If I thought it had been silent only a moment ago, then this was a taste of death itself; seconds of nothingness stretching away into infinity. A small yelp ruptured the quiet behind me, and I heard Enja's hand clamp over her mouth. Remaining undetected was no

260

longer an option.

"Enja, move. Move, and don't stop," I instructed her, stepping firmly on to the next stone. "We have to get off the lake." I couldn't remember being so scared in my life, not even with the whispering winds, or when I had come so close to being burned in the village. This was different, a primordial fear that did not belong in my world.

We could beat it, perhaps, if we were fast enough – fast enough without compromising our balance or our safety. *Forward. Forward. Forward. Don't look back.* We took stone after stone, finding a rhythm, a pace, using our fear as momentum. One stone. Two. Three. Four. Five. Still, only darkness and more steps ahead. Six. Seven. Eight. Nine. Ten. Only shadows and water visible in the light of the torch.

And the eyes drew nearer. I tried not to notice it, tried to force anything from my mind except for my concentration on the stepping stones, but the unmissable glow of those eyes grew larger and larger in my peripheral vision.

Eleven. Twelve. Thirteen. Fourteen. Fifteen.

Whatever beast to whom those eyes belonged began to undulate, sending ripples towards us that grew stronger and stronger. Water splashed over the stones and on to our boots, leaving dark patches behind that I tried to ignore. "Don't stop!" I shouted again, forcing myself forward and on to the next stone. The eyes were so close . . . so close. . .

A garbled cry echoed from behind me, and I whirled to see Siiva's head bobbing just above the surface of the water.

"Siiva!" Enja cried, turning and crouching to reach for him.

"Leave him!" I shouted, moving back a stone to pull on her cloak. "He can swim." Though I knew well he would not survive that beast – and neither would we if we delayed. "Come, Enja! You have to leave him!" Water continued to splash my feet, and the eyes moved closer and closer to the fox. I did not wish to leave him behind any more than she did, but there wasn't time to waste.

"Never," Enja said in a deadly harsh whisper. She leaned precariously far over the water and grabbed some fur at the back of his neck, pulling him with a sort of graceful speed towards her. He climbed up on to the stone beside Enja just as a large wave came hurtling towards us, black and silent.

"Watch out!" I shouted, and turned, setting my shoulder to the onslaught and closing my eyes. Enja crouched and lowered her head, drawing Siiva close to her chest. When the wave hit, my breath disappeared from my lungs like I'd taken a fall, and it was all I could do to remain on the stone. The world spun, up meeting down and left meeting right, my ears fuzzy and muffled. Through it, I wondered briefly at this creature: I had been expecting at any moment to see some sort of arm or leg, some claw-ridden limb protruding from the water to destroy us or a mouth with rows of razor-sharp teeth ready to swallow us whole. But I saw no such thing. It was just eyes and ... waves.

A spluttering cough jolted my head towards Enja – whose body had fallen into the water, though she held on to the stone with both arms. Siiva spun around on the stone, desperate to help but unsure how. The rolling waves grew taller, stronger, and I fought against them as I made my way to Enja's rock. So low to the waterline, she would struggle to breathe through the waves.

"Take my hand," I shouted. She coughed and coughed, and if I did not get her out of the water soon, she would certainly drown.

I couldn't watch another person drown before my eyes. Not when I had the power to save them.

Weakly, she reached up and clasped my hand, and I pulled with all the strength I had left. A wave crashed against my body, threatening to topple me over and send me into the water with her, but I fought with shaking limbs to remain on my feet, to stand strong and pull, pull, pull. Seconds later, Enja was standing on the stone beside me, our feet just barely able to fit side by side. I held her shoulders firmly while she breathed and coughed. Siiva whined at our feet.

"You have to walk," I said, posing it at as an order

rather than a question. "You have to walk quickly." She could rest later, but the waves would not wait.

She nodded, water still running down her face from her hair. I tried to ignore the glowing eyes moving behind her.

"Pay no mind to Siiva. He can take care of himself. Just *get off the lake*. Do you understand me?"

She nodded again, her resolve growing stronger by the second. I fumbled briefly with my flint and relit my torch, holding it aloft again and turning away. I moved carefully but quickly to the next stone. Water continued to pour over my feet, and sometimes I couldn't make out the next stone from the water of the lake, but slowly, steadily, we made our way forward.

Eight stones later, I saw the opposite shore. There was only a small distance between us, only a few more stones separating us from what I could only hope was safety. "We're almost there!" I said over my shoulder, and the quickening of footsteps told me that Enja had picked up her pace. We no longer whispered, and my words clanged about the stone chamber and came back to me, empty and detached.

With only three stones between us and the shore, the water below us seemed to shrink away suddenly as it was pulled into a wave much larger than any we'd seen before. It was like the seaside in winter when one of those blizzards rolled in from the east and bent the

264

ocean to its will. I knew the power of waves like that, and I knew we'd never stand a chance against it. "Run!" I screamed, as though we were not already doing so. I forced my feet to double their speed, the stones steadily disappearing behind me, my body rocking precariously as I stepped on to stones even before I was sure of their existence, and as soon as I could possibly do so without risking a fall into the water, I jumped the rest of the way.

Air rushed past my ears as the bank came closer and closer. My arms spun, and the torch threatened to go out. But my feet, at long last, connected with the stone of the shore, and I tumbled forward to a halt. Behind me, Enja pushed off from one of the last stones and propelled herself forward, the wave only inches behind her. Siiva had already landed, shaking himself off and panting after the exertion. I opened my mouth to say something, to shout for her to move faster, but nothing I could say would make a difference as the seconds of her jump seemed to stretch into hours.

Finally – finally – she tumbled on to the stone shore, and I held fast to her hand as the wave crashed over us. It beat against our bodies with an impossible force, but we remained on the shore, and as the waters slid away and the eyes receded back into the murky depths, I said a silent prayer that we would not have to cross the lake again.

Chapter 23

Every inch of Skane spoke of the approaching storm. The birds gathered in flocks to eat seeds and berries, more of them than I had ever seen together. A snowy owl sat perched on our neighbour's house for nearly a full day, and on one night the moon wore a vivid halo of light, a sure sign of snow unlike anything we'd seen that winter. I did not like the utter emptiness of the woods in the days leading up to it. I did not like the way even the rabbits remained in hiding, the way the song of the birds had all but ceased, and the distant howling of the wolves as they gathered to hunt down whatever creatures found themselves stranded out in the storm.

Here and there, children carried baskets through the trees, gathering whatever fallen sticks and bits of kindling they could find. Anything that could keep the cold out of our homes. There's the cold when you run outside to grab logs from the wood hut nearby during the night, wearing only thin wraps because it will only take a moment, and there's the cold where every second you spend outdoors burns your skin like you're being slowly lowered into a fire. Sometimes, when you're that cold, it's difficult to tell the difference between hot and cold. Sometimes you think you're warm when, in fact, your body can no longer sense the cold because it's giving in, giving up, and slipping away.

We ensured we were well away from the cursed lake before we let our bodies fall to the ground to rest. My legs screamed from their sudden disuse, and I rolled on to my back and lay flat on the cold stone. We could not risk running out of light, so we left the torches extinguished and lay in the dark, silent for the first few minutes. Even now, the glowing eyes of that beast pierced the blackness, watching, waiting. I couldn't shake the sight.

"I didn't think I'd miss home after what happened," Enja said. There was a catch to her voice that sparked something in the back of my mind. Concern, perhaps, or just an awareness of something I couldn't place. "I thought I'd never look back."

"Nor did I," I said softly, but somehow the memory of my bed, layered with furs and knits, and food cooking over the fire nearly reduced me to tears. Then the faces of the villagers – of Ragna, Alff, Oben, and those who had condemned me to burn for someone else's wrongdoing – filled my vision, and thoughts of home again soured my mouth.

"I wish it was a bonfire night," she continued. "I wish we were all in the village centre by a big, warm fire, eating food and telling stories and watching the children play. I wish..." She trailed off.

I waited a few moments, and then prompted, "You wish?"

"Hmm? Oh, yes. I wish we were safe again."

Something in the way she said it confirmed a fear I wasn't entirely sure I'd been harbouring: Enja wasn't well. She hadn't been well for a few days, yet we'd been too busy for me to fully take notice. The realization broke something within me, and a tear slid from my right eye down my face. She had taken that fall from the cliff, and I had been too distracted over recent days to give her the proper attention she needed. She should be resting, not trekking through the mountains in search of a god. I should not have let her come.

"I'm sorry," I whispered. I couldn't make a fire here, or cook her food or play games. But I could tell her a story. It was stories that kept us warm in the winter, wolves and witches and tales of the people who used to walk the world long before our time. Stories meant comfort, and home. I paused, cleared my throat, and started. "There were stories that came over from Löska, of fisherman who'd been out at sea. No one quite knew whether to

268

believe them, but they kept the stories just the same. They said that sometimes they'd find boats devoid of a single body, yet sailing as though it hosted an entire crew. Sometimes it would be a boat declared missing weeks ago, believed to have been destroyed in a storm or sunk by some other unhappy event. But they'd see the ships, sometimes rowed by invisible hands, sometimes with a sail being hoisted by no one. Those back in port said the sun had gone to their head, or they had spent too much time on the desolate sea and should spend more time at home. But they went to their death swearing on what they'd seen, swearing that those boats had never gone missing at all, and that they were still out there, still at sea, sailed by a phantom crew."

Enja drew in a long, deep breath.

"They began to call them the drüg, believing they were the spirits of those who had drowned at sea, and could never leave their ship. It turned some away from desiring to be fishermen, and inspired others. It's funny how stories of death work like that."

"Would you do it?" she asked sleepily.

"Would I do what?"

"Go out to sea, knowing that you might become a ghost."

I reached a hand up to place it behind my head. "No. But then again, I've never had much of an interest in going out to sea."

"Why not?"

I shrugged, even though she couldn't see me. "I love Skane. I've never given much thought to leaving."

"I have," she said. "I've always wanted to know what was out there, besides Löska. What if we built a boat and set sail off the western shore? What would we find if we survived for days or weeks? Nothing, perhaps. We might sail and sail and sail and eventually wind up back on this island, or on Löska, or worse ... the Ør Isles." I heard her shudder as she ended the conversation with herself.

Why had I never thought much about leaving? I supposed it was only because I'd never had much reason to do so. My mother and father were here, and Sølvi for those precious years he was with us, and I loved the forests and the snow and the hills. No part of me ever felt like that – not until Sølvi died, and the only thing I ever felt was longing. Longing for just a bit more time, a few more seconds, one last conversation. The trouble with hindsight is that you can never change what's been done. You can never undo the feelings of regret, of taking life for granted, of not truly realizing what you have until it's gone.

"What are you thinking about?" Enja asked, startling me from my reverie.

Swallowing, I said, "I was just thinking about taking life for granted."

"Mmm, yes. We all do that."

"I wish I hadn't," I said, vaguely aware that it wasn't my usual sort of thing to discuss such personal feelings with anyone. "I wish I hadn't while Sølvi was still alive. If I'd known he would die so soon, I would have done everything differently."

"We always say that when it's too late, yet we still know that time only moves in one direction. It is in our nature to simply ... keep waiting for the next thing. Waiting for tomorrow." Her voice took on a whispery sing-song sound, as though she were hovering on the edges of sleep. "Just another day becomes just another week, which gives way to just another month, just another season, just another year. Just another decade. And on and on, sunrise and sunset, moonrise and moonset, winter and summer and spring and harvest, bonfires and stargazing, weddings and funerals, births and deaths, something new and something old, a beginning and an end, all while we're waiting. Until just another day becomes just another lifetime, just another generation, just another age. Until the memories of us are crumbled to ash and whispered into nothingness by the wind."

Slowly, I rolled on to my side and propped my head up on one hand, staring through the darkness at where she lay. Her words bounced around in my head, breaking and reforming and breaking again. What *had* I been waiting for while I was with Sølvi? If I would have done things

271

differently, did that mean I hadn't truly been happy? I rubbed at an eye with my palm, desperate for sleep but now alive with thoughts. I wanted to answer my own questions, to understand why I would have changed things, but the only thing on which my mind could focus was the way I referred to him in the past. *While Sølvi was still alive.* Those words were so final, sitting heavy on my mind. In a way, it was as if I'd been lying to myself for the past year, and it was finally time to realize that I'd never see him again. *Never.* But that is such a long time. If I did see him, it would only be in dreams pulled from memories that had already been made. We'd never get the chance to make new ones. And somewhere deep down, I feared that I would stop dreaming about him. That a part of my mind would forget he ever existed as he became more and more removed from my everyday thoughts, until one day he'd be little more than a passing mention brought up irregularly in conversation; it would spark a memory here, a bit of nostalgia there, but it wouldn't hurt so bad.

And that was my biggest fear of all: that one day, I would stop hurting, because that would mean that he was really and truly gone.

"You're right," I whispered, rolling back on to the stone. "I shouldn't have spent so much time waiting."

But Enja was already asleep.

*

I recalled that earlier in the day I had seen Sølvi trudging out of the village, a bow in hand, but that was hours ago. I had assumed he had long since returned. And yet, though I waited and waited, I saw no sign of him. Perhaps he was still in the woods, or off in one of the caves I'd shown him for some time to himself. There was nothing like the total silence of the caverns to open the mind up to pathways of thought often left uncharted. But had he not seen the warning signs of the storm? Nonsense. We all had. Sølvi should have known enough to not put his life at risk – yet, where was he? Had he seen the signs and foolishly ignored them, trusting too greatly in his own capabilities? He wouldn't, because we all knew how that story ended: with a funeral pyre and a poem, and a name scratched from the village.

Unease toyed with my mind as I waited a bit longer, hoping that perhaps he had simply become caught up in some drawn-out chore and would, any moment now, come hurrying through the trees, bursting with apologies. More than once I thought perhaps I saw movement, that perhaps I saw his tall form hurrying towards me, but it was nothing more than my wishful mind, bending the tree branches just right or playing with shadows until I saw what I wanted to. The wind picked up, the sky grew ever darker, and there was still no sign of Sølvi.

He'd killed a deer, maybe, and it was taking time for him to bring it back to the village. He must have known we would need extra food during the storm, which would mean he was aware of it bearing down on us. That must be it.

I waited some more.

I hopped down from the tree, half thinking that perhaps I should stay just a little bit longer, and half convinced that he was never going to show up. Sølvi knew perhaps better than anyone the dangers of not respecting Skane, as he had once told me. When all the signs in nature were pointing towards a blizzard that could leave us stranded for days, he was not the sort to disappear into the wilds outside the village, and that fact crept into my mind like water slowly turning to ice.

For a long moment, I stood in the trees staring back towards the village and safety; back towards home, where my mother and father would be expecting me at any moment. They would worry soon, there was no doubt of that. With the wind already whipping around and the veil of ashen clouds overhead, snow would soon follow. Snow like we hadn't seen in a while, and that should only fall once we were all indoors, huddled by fires with food and family.

But I turned, pulling my cloak tighter around myself, and struck off into the woods.

Chapter 24

In the morning – no, when I awoke, for the Goddess only knew what time it was – my first thought was of Enja, of the way her voice had sounded the previous night, and the worry that had flooded my mind. While I was still concerned for her, something about having slept on it made the danger seem less immediate. She was still slumbering away when I sat up and lit a torch ... and my stomach churned. We were dangerously low on fuel, so low in fact that, if we did not find something to use in these mountains, we would never be able to find our way back through them. Unless we travelled via the outside, but then the cold and snow...

Stop, I ordered myself. There would be a time to worry about that. For now, our mission was not over yet.

"Enja, it's time to go," I said, gently shaking her by

the shoulder. Siiva stood and stretched, his mouth pulling open in a yawn. When she rolled over to face me, blinking blearily, some of the fear from the previous night returned. Goddess bless her, she was pale. Pale like snow, like something dead ... or dying.

She must have seen the concern in my face, because she touched a few fingers to her cheek and said, "What's wrong, Janna?"

"N–nothing," I told her. "How do you feel? Were you warm enough last night?"

She moved to sit up, swaying slightly. "I feel ... tired. Heavy. I think perhaps I didn't sleep very well." Her voice was steady but weak, in a way that sounded like there was no strength behind it. No life.

"You look unwell," I said quickly. How could I keep it from her? I needed her and she needed me. We trusted each other, and I would not – could not – break that trust by lying to her.

She eyed me for a moment, rubbing the back of her neck. "It has been a long few days," she said eventually. "Lots of walking and running and poor sleep. Poor food. And there was that fall from the cliff. I'm sure that's all."

I tried to find comfort in her words, tore them apart in search of something to quell my fear, but I found nothing. "Do you need a longer rest?" I asked, knowing full well that we had no time to do it. Our light source would soon run out, and more than that, it was impossible to know how much time had passed. The plague could long since reared its bloody head, and the woman and her baby...

I swallowed and shook away the thought.

She shook her head and rolled over to stand up. "I should move about," she said. "I'll find my feet once again."

I hoped she was right, but everything inside me was screaming that something was wrong.

It was impossible not to wonder, as we made our way through the labyrinthine tunnels, how they had come to be. I'd wondered such things many times, especially when we'd passed those two statues, but the further we walked, the longer the tunnels stretched out, the more powerful the question became. It wasn't simply a few carved-out rooms with a handful of tunnels leading to them; it was designed and lovingly crafted, often wide, cavernous pathways that wound through the mountains, seeming to never end. These were not natural, and that seemed more obvious than the red hair that sat on my dishevelled head. But the feeling of something ancient having been here, of a people I would never know – could never even comprehend – having worked so hard to build this, made me feel like an intruder somewhere sacred.

That same feeling often haunted me in the caves back near my village, but that was different. We were meant to find those writings, meant to read them and know their stories, despite the hallowed feeling of a place

277

that had not been entered in years. But here... This was different, on a scale much larger than I could fathom. It made me feel as if Skane was not my own, not in the way I had always thought. There was more to it, more lurking beneath its icy surface than my small mind could have ever dreamt up.

Something small caught my attention, but I couldn't quite place what it was for a few long moments. Then I saw it: beautiful, scrolling writing ran along the higher part of the walls close to the roof, a kind of writing I'd never seen during all my time spent in caves. It was not our language, and it was not the old Löskan language, but it *was* a language, I was certain. I stared and studied it, my suspicions only confirmed. A people had been here, even lived here, a people with a language all their own, who cared about this place and this land, who cared enough to leave something behind, even if I couldn't read it.

And then, though it caught me off guard, I realized I recognized it. It was the same writing from that cave with the wolves, the same writing that had glowed blue. So they had not just contained themselves to the mountains. They had explored this island and left something behind away to the south. They had walked the same forests as me, seen the same things as me, yet we were separated by the uncrossable chasm of time.

I glanced over my shoulder to ensure that Enja and Siiva were still following me, and they were. Enja's arms were crossed over her chest, and she gave me a small smile when I looked at her, but it did nothing to make me feel better. And I realized, in the brief seconds that I was turned around, that I had to strain my eyes a bit to see her, in the way I had to work to see inside the house in the wee hours of the morning when the fire was nothing but embers.

I looked quickly to my torch, to find the flame had shrunk in size considerably. We had only hours of it left, minutes, even. Something inside me went cold.

"Enja, what happened to that torch you had yesterday?" I asked, hope dancing some. I heard her steps slow as she felt around, searching for it, then a sickeningly long pause when she stopped walking. When I turned to face her, her eyes were large and round.

"What is it?" I said, somehow already knowing.

"The lake," she whispered. "When I fell in... It must have... Oh, Janna, I am so sorry. I didn't think about it." Her eyes began to glisten in the dim light, though whether it was from tears or terror, I didn't know.

My heart thundered in my chest, but I tried to smile calmly, tried to make it seem as though it wasn't the worst thing that could happen to us. "It was not your fault," I told her gently. "Don't worry. We will figure something else out." But what that "something else" would be, I hadn't a clue. Perhaps we could burn our clothing, or—

Later. I could push this until later, until after the

torch had gone out, take things one step at a time. "Let's hurry," I said flatly, matter-of-factly, standing taller and turning away. We had to use what light we had left to get as far as we could, to put as much distance behind us as possible before the darkness closed in. I could not tell by the smouldering flame exactly how long that would be, but it almost didn't matter. How much time we had left wouldn't change; the only thing we could control was how far we got while it lasted.

There was an urgency to our steps now that perhaps there always should have been. There had been times when we were rushing, hurrying to get away from something or to reach something, but in between, we'd been slow. We'd taken time to rest and recuperate, our feet moving at half the speed they should have been. *You fool.* I should have known that the light would run out. I did, in a way, but I didn't think about it enough. I didn't think it through. What would we do, two lost girls, stuck far beneath the mountains in darkness? We would wander in the shadows until we perished, unknown to anyone else. Perhaps decades from now – if anyone survived – someone would find their way down here for a reason entirely dissimilar to our own, on a mission or an adventure I would never know about, and stumble across the bones of two people who had failed in something that would for ever remain a mystery to their finder.

By that time, the kind woman would have died, along with her baby, and our failure – my failure – would for ever haunt these halls. If I didn't have the ability to save her life, what did I have? What could I do? Flashes from the night Sølvi died lit up the air around me, and I shook my head to clear them.

I didn't like it. Those thoughts, while I kept them to myself, infuriated me enough to move faster.

Behind me, Enja picked up the pace as well, keeping time with me. Siiva walked between us, after me but before her. Now and then I would glance at him, see how he was reacting to the space around us. If there was something nearby, if there was a sound that came from neither of us, he would be the first to hear it. Yet he just scurried on, nose to the ground as though he could smell things on the stone we would never understand.

I never knew, in all the times I'd heard about the mountains, when I'd first seen their seemingly small forms far across the plain, in the stories told of them by the elderly around bonfires, just how much lay beneath them. It was magnificent, in a way, but also eerie. Why? How? *Who?* They were questions I wished I could ask of the stone, as I trailed one finger along a jagged, pillar-like structure that reached from the floor to the ceiling far overhead. How did you come to be? Who used to walk these halls? For halls they felt like, sweeping and grand in a subtle, natural sort of way, yet unnatural all at once.

But the stone kept its secrets, sleeping and soundless, and somehow watchful. That was it – how I had felt over the past few days, even if I hadn't truly realized it or acknowledged it: like in some unexplainable way, the mountains knew we were here. Like the mountains, ancient, silent and sprawling as they were, had been waiting.

Chapter 25

The tunnel which we'd been traversing ended suddenly and unceremoniously at a high stone wall. In the remaining light from my torch, I stared at the stone before us, a barrier I had not been expecting, but that caused something inside me to wilt. An impasse, it seemed, and I stood back, holding my fading light aloft and examining every visible inch of the wall before us, but there was nothing to find.

"We aren't going back," Enja said, and I could see her shaking her head in my peripheral vision. "We cannot go back. We can only go forward."

Her echoing of my words, while heartfelt, would mean nothing if there was no more ground to travel. If there was no forward. It didn't make sense, though: why would all these tunnels, these ancient pathways carved from the Goddess-knows-what simply end at nothing? These tunnels had meant something, been a way to get somewhere, once upon a time. So why here? The questions stacked up, but answers remained distant, unattainable.

"I don't understand," I said, speaking aloud to work through my thoughts "We've followed these tunnels for days. They've all woven together and carried on, leading somewhere, and then it just ... ends here." I ran my hand along the stone before us. "No. I doubt it." Without a clear idea, I began to walk to the left, dragging my hand along the wall as I went. In the fading light, the stone just stretched on and on, never seeming to end – until it did, at a sort of corner with the tunnel, and that was it. Calmly, I turned to walk in the other direction, wondering if my eyes were playing tricks on me or if the light was fading faster now. I passed Enja and Siiva, carrying on past them to search the remainder of the wall, my hope nothing more than a dying ember that had little chance of being brought back to life. We'd never make it back through the tunnels, the cavernous rooms, the mountains, without light, and without more food. I had been hoping, somehow, that each new tunnel we entered would hold something of use, a candle, some dried food or something to hunt, yet now the idea seemed foolish. Ridiculous, even. Other than the lake, we'd seen no signs of life in days. There were no sounds, no animals, nothing but our own shadows, and endless, winding stone.

My hand slid on to wood, and I stopped moving. In the near darkness, a small wooden door stood before me, juxtaposed with the grandeur of the great stone halls around us. I expected to feel relief, to exclaim my excitement to Enja after having found a new way forward – but the only thoughts my mind could muster up were dark. *Why a door? Why the wall? What were they trying to keep out ... or in?* I stood for a long moment in bafflement, until the barely flickering torch in my hand urged me into action.

"Enja, over here," I said, my voice bouncing off the walls and back to my ears more than once. I didn't like how it sounded, didn't like the way it carried so far and could wind up in the ears of something unknown – not that we'd seen or heard anything. Siiva sniffed along the bottom of the door while Enja hurried over, out of breath in a way I tried not to think about. "I don't know where it goes, but it's a way forward," I told her. "It might be an answer, a way out, if nothing else." I hadn't thought much about the fact that soon, we might have to abandon this mission. I would carry on to risk my own life, but not Enja's. Not in the state she was in. She needed help, and I couldn't deny her that.

I was reaching for the stone handle of the door to pull it open when Siiva hissed and backed away, hairs on his neck standing up straight. My hand froze in the air, and we both stared at the fox, suddenly unsure of

285

what to do. A sort of garbled, almost human cry came from his throat, and he stood behind us as though hiding from whatever might come through the door. My skin tingled, my vision blurred momentarily as dread tore through my veins. Uncertainty. Confusion. Fear. What could be inside? We'd passed nothing in days. Nothing had come in or out. Could anything live so far from the surface without the need to leave?

The darkness around us seemed to grow darker, pressing against us until even the air felt thick and heavy. This was a fork in the road, and both directions held danger and death. We could turn around and go back, and slowly starve to death as we felt our way through the tunnels, or we could go through the door and face whatever lay on the other side, pressing on until the life was strangled from us.

"We have to," I whispered to Enja. "I'm so sorry. There's nowhere else to go, and if we turn back, we will die." The cold, hard truth of those words hung in the air between us for a long moment. Her eyes were glassy with worry, and maybe illness, but she nodded after a pause, knowing the crossroads that lay before us. Possible death or certain death. Turning back to die or going forward to danger. The decision was made for us. "I don't know what's in there," I told her again, swallowing. "I can't begin to imagine. But stay close. We're stronger if we're together."

She nodded again.

Tears welled up in my eyes as I saw the fear glistening in hers, as I felt it myself, deep in the pit of my stomach. We shouldn't be here. We were never meant to be here.

I put my hand on the door handle and began to pull. "Stay close," I repeated in a whisper. my body shuddering with a suppressed sob. She shuffled closer until our clothes were brushing, Siiva at our heels. I doubted very much that we could have coaxed him to enter the room if Enja hadn't been going in. He kept his head close to the ground, staring through our legs at whatever lay inside. In a swift, quiet movement, we entered through the door.

Darkness yawned in every direction beyond the dull light cast by my torch. The way our footsteps bounced away from us, echoing into oblivion, told me that this room was much larger than any we'd yet passed through. There didn't yet appear to be anything living in there save for the silence – but I felt, rather than saw, something move out of the corner of my eye. I spun to my right, holding the torch out further to inspect the area, but there was nothing. A low yelp came from Siiva, but I shushed him quickly.

"What is it?" Enja whispered beside me, barely audible.

"I don't know," I replied. "I thought I saw something."

I know I saw something.

We pressed onwards. Slow. Measured. I didn't know where we travelling to, but I tried to keep us moving in a straight line from where we had entered the room. It was impossible to know, in the near darkness, whether we had turned back to the right direction after I'd turned to investigate that movement. Perhaps at any moment, we would end up back at the door we first came through, and I almost expected to see it with each step we took. And suddenly I almost wanted to. I wanted to go back through it and into the tunnels we'd been travelling for days, back out into the familiarity that had settled in over time. I wanted to be away from this wretched place, and whatever that thing was I had seen a few moments ago.

Movement, again. This time to my left. I stopped short and stared into the curtain of blackness around us, waiting for my eyes to fall on whatever *thing* had just darted by. I stared and stared – and then realized that Enja was staring, as well.

"You saw it?" I whispered, so quietly I could barely hear it myself. She nodded ever so slightly.

There, directly in front of us, a shadow appeared for a fleeting second, and then vanished. The light around us danced as my hands shook wildly. I tried to control it, but fear had crept into my heart like frostbite and settled there, making every bit of my body shiver. It had been a shadow, but ... a shadow only, it seemed, cast by nothing. As with many other things we'd encountered on this journey, I couldn't force it to make sense, yet this

288

time it was darker, as if fear itself had taken a form that could be seen rather than just felt.

"Let's hurry," Enja whispered, taking another step. "Let's get out of here, Janna, please." She was on the brink of tears, and my heart ached. I felt tears trying to rise again to my own eyes, as well, as if crying would somehow make me feel better. Release the pressure within. But it wouldn't, damn it. Nothing would, except getting out of here.

"Go," I said, moving forward again. Our footsteps shuffled on the stone, louder now as desperation pushed us onwards. We couldn't be quick and silent. One had to be sacrificed.

Another flash of movement to our left, then our right, then a sort of whooshing sound behind us. A coldness I couldn't explain brushed against my skin, and pure dread flooded my mind, my heart, my fingertips and toes. "No," I heard myself saying. "No, go away." I didn't remember deciding to speak, or ordering my mouth to move, but words came out and my voice reached my ears. "Go. Go. Go."

"Janna," Enja said, but I couldn't respond to her, couldn't hear clearly. That coldness had returned, and my mind wasn't my own, filling with impressions of death and destruction, of a loneliness so complete it was like being the only human in the world, for eternity. These things, these shadows, I didn't know what they could be, *how* they could be, but something about them felt strangely familiar – humanlike, but certainly not human.

"Janna, the torch."

The torch. Was I even still holding it? I heard her shriek, and then again, "Janna, get rid of it."

Why? The light. I remembered needing it. I remembered worrying that we wouldn't have it. Why would I lose it? That warm glow, however faint, was the only thing that offered any warmth against this sudden bitter cold.

"Janna!" She was shouting now, and a moment later, a hand wrenched the torch from my own, and I saw it sailing through the air, far away. Movement followed it, shadows that tumbled over one another to chase it, until it clattered to the ground many yards away and nearly went out. "Hurry," she whispered beside me, and I shivered, that iciness disappearing. Her hand was on my shoulder, pulling me towards – what? Safety? Did safety even exist in here? I didn't know. Couldn't know. I just kept shivering at the thoughts of that chill, of that doom and desolation that had consumed me, until the floor gave way beneath my feet and we were descending steps. Down, down, down to only the Goddess knew where.

Sølvi's footsteps were easy enough to find at first, but they very quickly faded from sight as the heavy cloak of night settled in and the snow began to fall, blown about by the wind before at last finding a resting place. I stopped more than once and turned towards home, finding all manner of reasons to go back – he could find his own way home, or perhaps he'd already returned and would soon leave again to look for me – but he hadn't been there. He hadn't been at our meeting spot, and before the darkness had settled in, I had seen no return footprints. He might have been hurt alone in the woods, with no one to hear his cries for help, or he might have got lost and couldn't find his way back in the storm. Love and duty and determination urged me onwards. The world was wrought of stone, but my will was something stronger.

With the light went all traces of warmth. The bone-dry wind carried with it the voice of the devil, if the devil were made of ice that burned like fire. It scorched my skin with a kind of cutting cold I'd never felt – because I had never been out in a storm as bad as this one. This was a storm that we would one day tell stories about, that our children would hear with wide eyes and interested ears while we spoke of the wind, the cold, the many, many feet of snow. And this was a storm that would claim lives, if anyone dared to defy it.

Snowflakes raced each other to the ground, desperate to smother rock and earth. One minute, I was still contemplating whether I should turn around and go home, and the next, I knew with certainty that I could not turn back. Snow swirled in all directions, and the wind screamed so fiercely that it destroyed my sense of direction. There was no way to tell if the direction in which I was walking was still the same one I had been walking in a few minutes ago. Here and there I bumped into the trunk of a tree or tripped over a hedge, tumbling forward and hauling myself back to my feet against the wind that tried to keep me down.

There was no familiarity. I didn't know one tree from the next; every step was a step further into the unknown. Some small part of me that hadn't yet gone numb from the cold realized that this was it. This was every story of warning I had ever heard about Skane come to life. Soon, they would merely add my name to the list, mention me in passing as one of the many whom this island had claimed. Mention me alongside Finni, which would have brought tears to my eyes if I wasn't too cold to cry.

I couldn't – couldn't what? I was too cold to think, the wind whipping against me and carrying away my will to live. I couldn't ... I couldn't...

Die.

I fell forward onto the snowy forest floor, and this time, I didn't get up again.

Chapter 26

I had never seen a darkness so complete, so solid and enshrouding that I couldn't see so much as a finger before my face. Enja and I shuffled along, having many minutes ago reached the bottom of that staircase we had found in the room with those . . . creatures. Those moving shadows. That coldness. We'd passed through a door with a faded inscription we had done our best to piece together.

Spirits of the unburned. Enter in darkness.

Even the memory of it made me shiver, made me wonder if it was why we burned the bodies of the dead. Why we didn't bury them. Was that what would happen, shadows trapped on earth for eternity? The air around them had been unlike anything I could remember or describe, like I was enveloped in history so old it muddled my brain. Perhaps I was never meant to understand it.

The mountains *were* haunted, and I knew now why we had always left them alone.

Now and then, I could hear the soft padding of Siiva behind or beside us, hear the occasional click of his claws against the stone. It was comforting in a way, knowing that he was so close at hand. He could do precious little to protect us, being as small as he was, but he had senses and an agility that we could never have. And somehow, the way he cared so dearly for Enja made him seem almost like another human in our disparate group.

Our pace was achingly slow, as we had to take each step deliberately and feel around before us. Now and again, I'd strike the flint just for the sake of a few sparks, and we would catch a quick glimpse of the tunnel around us before it was plunged back into darkness. I noticed almost immediately, though, that something was different in this tunnel: it was unrefined, the walls rough and irregular, the distance from the floor to the ceiling frequently changed. This was not like the carefully designed, elegant halls through which we'd been traversing earlier. This felt more ... untouched. Forgotten.

Something about that, about the rough-hewn tunnel around us, set me on edge in an entirely new way. I didn't like how we'd unknowingly stumbled into it, as though it had been lying in wait to swallow us. The stairs had just appeared in that room, as though they fell away from the floor when they knew we'd entered. It wasn't right. Any of it. I wrapped my arms around myself momentarily, just to feel the comfort, but had to put them out again to feel the air close at hand. It was impossible to tell if there were vast spaces all surrounding us, distant and empty, or if at any moment, my head or hand or shoulder would knock against unforgiving stone. That sort of uncertainty made my stomach sick.

"This is awful," Enja whispered, though the whisper might as well have been a shout, the way it echoed around us. "It is like if the moon and stars disappeared from the night sky, and we were all left stumbling around in darkness."

A shiver fluttered up my spine. "But they haven't," I said firmly. I looked up, as if I could see the glorious night sky shining beyond the stone. "It's hard to believe in light in the midst of such darkness, but it's there." I was saying it more to myself than to anyone, trying to counter the chill that was settling into my heart, but it did little to warm me. The words felt hollow and unbelievable, yet, that light *was* still there. I tried to focus on it, to imagine the moon and the stars as we tiptoed through the shadows. I imagined its brilliant crescent lighting up a cold winter's night. I imagined the constellations all twinkling and vying for our attention on this world far below them. And I imagined the Goddess, dazzling and magnificent where she shone high overhead. Even if we couldn't see Her, She knew we were here, and that thought alone was enough to at least warm the icy fear that had entombed my mind.

"Strike the flint again," Enja whispered after a few moments. I hadn't done it recently and ever since that room upstairs, she had silently taken over as our leader, my nerves burned to bits. I had frozen up, put us in danger because something had … invaded my mind, filling it with misery and devastation. Enja had kept her head, powering on and leading us away. She'd had the quick thinking to throw the torch, and whatever those shadows were had followed it, leaving us alone for long enough to get away.

I fumbled around in my cloak for the flint, and just as I was preparing to strike it, a long, lonely howl split the silence.

We stood perfectly still for a long moment, staring off in the direction we'd been heading. No one spoke.

Siiva let out a low yowl, and I could picture his teeth on display in a snarl.

I thought those wolves had long ago abandoned us. There had been no sign of them in ages, no hints that they were still nearby. We'd just been walking and walking to *something*, to *somewhere*. In search of a god, or a river of death. Now, our primary goal was to survive.

And, somehow, to not let the woman die.

"I thought they were long gone," Enja breathed beside me. Her voice was rife with relief.

"So did I," I replied, finally striking the flint. The tunnel lit up around us momentarily, nearly identical to the last time we caught a glimpse of it, but this time, a carved statue of what looked like a giant bird of prey with the head of a man stood to our right. We both jumped, taking a step back as it was again shrouded in darkness. A lump in my throat threatened to choke me, so I tried to swallow it back as my shaking hands gripped the flint. "Shall I do it again?" I whispered, as quietly as I could.

"Wait a few moments," Enja replied, and, taking my elbow, she led me forward. "Let's get away from that thing."

I could have hugged her in that moment, if it hadn't been wildly out of place. The firm way she spoke, how she managed to find confidence even when I was crumbling to pieces. It gave me strength, in a way, at a time when I desperately needed it.

We carried onwards, using our brief glimpse of the tunnel to move at a quicker pace, knowing that nothing stood directly before us. My strength was short lived. My feet felt heavy now, weighed to the floor to the point that it was a struggle to lift them. My body was refusing to cooperate, feeding off the fear in my mind and freezing my muscles. If I did not get control of myself quickly, I would be the kiss of death to this entire journey.

It's only stone, I told myself reassuringly. *It cannot harm you. It cannot move. It has stood here for years, centuries, even, and it will continue to stand here long after you are gone. This darkness is temporary.*

It worked. The tension in my muscles eased up and walking became easier. I took in long, calming breaths as we travelled along, repeating over and over again to myself that stone couldn't move. I wanted desperately to believe it, and some small part of me did, or I would not have calmed down, but a larger part of me knew that in these mountains, anything could happen. The wind had whispered to us, a troll had chased us, shadows had tormented us. It was not so very difficult to believe that that stone statue could come to life.

The past year of trying to be strong had only made me tired. Weak. A growing part of me wanted to lie down on the stone, close my eyes, and give up.

"Strike it again," Enja said after we'd traversed a good way in silence. Even though we'd seen in the last strike that the tunnel simply carried on, slightly curved downwards, it was so easy to imagine the stone moving and reshaping itself. To imagine that a wall now stood before us, or another statue, blocking the way.

I struck the flint. The tunnel carried onwards, curving even more downhill, and another statue stood tall and imposing to our left. This time it depicted a man's body and the head of a bear, a tall rod with a pointed end in one hand. I fought back a gasp at the horror of it and shut my eyes, even though the tunnel had already gone dark. Even Enja let out a gasp, a low, breathy sound that spoke to the fear she must have felt. This time it was me who put a hand on her shoulder, calming her even if my own mind was in turmoil.

"It's nothing," I whispered, as if the statue would hear us. "It cannot move. It's just terrible to look at. Come."

I took a few steps away and heard her follow, trying to keep to the centre of the tunnel to avoid brushing against the walls or any outcroppings. The faster we could move, the faster we could get away from ... whatever those things were. I didn't like the thoughts they encouraged in my mind. Didn't like the way I couldn't shake the thought that if those kneeling statues from days ago had been some sort of entryway, some sort of gate, then these seemed a lot like guards. Watchers. The thought made me shudder.

There was a third guard when we next struck the match, a woman melded with a horse, but when the sparks died out a second later, a subtle glow seemed to remain. I blinked a few times, staring around us until my eyes settled on a slight glimmer of orange light much further down the tunnel. It was so faint, yet blinding the more I stared at it: the only source of light in total darkness.

"I see it," Enja said beside me. Her voice was breathy again, as if she had been running for several minutes straight. But she hadn't. I looked to study her face, but the distant light wasn't strong enough to do anything but outline her form. "Let's go," she said, moving forward without me. "I miss the light. I'm tired of the darkness."

She wasn't whispering any more, as if the sight of the light meant that whatever things we'd feared were listening had been left in the shadows behind us. I glanced around, ensuring that we were, in fact, still alone, and followed her down the tunnel.

Chapter 27

The light grew stronger with every step we took, nearly blinding against the blackness in which we'd been enclosed. The sight of it made me feel sick, either from its brightness or the sinking dread that crept into my body the closer we got to it. I didn't want to be here. The glow of the light should have given me comfort, but I didn't want to be anywhere near this place. Yet we'd heard the howl of the wolves. We'd been led here by them for a purpose, and it was too late to turn back now. Every step we'd taken since leaving the woman's home had been a step towards this place; a step towards these coming moments. We were almost there; I could feel it deep down in the centre of my bones.

There was a hissing, sliding sound that didn't let up – a whisper? a voice? – but no, it was only Enja's feet dragging on the ground between each step. Her legs seemed heavy, weighing her to the floor, although I didn't know if it was from her illness or her dread, like mine, at whatever lay before us. I should have been alarmed at her weakness, been aware of the fact that she seemed to be fading faster and faster, but the light was so bright, so intense, and I couldn't force my mind to form clear thoughts. Everything bore a haze, a bit of weighty confusion that muddled my mind.

Bitter, unforgiving cold gnawed at my body as I was pulled from the black chasm of unconsciousness. I wanted to crawl back into it, to disappear into the darkness and never be found. More than anything, I wanted to escape the cold. But the more awake I became, the more viciously it attacked.

I opened my eyes.

Utter darkness.

Cold stone pressed beneath my body, and somewhere not too far away, wind howled. I remembered the storm, the snow, the way I had been so sure I was about to give up. No, I had given up. I'd fallen, I'd succumbed. So why was I awake now?

I moved to sit up, aching and exhausted and so, so cold.

"Janna?"

I froze.

"Sølvi?"

"Yes."

His voice was deathly quiet, and very close at hand. I rolled over and felt him lying just behind me. "What happened?"

There was a long pause before he replied. "I was so foolish," he said, though it sounded more as if he was addressing himself than me. "I . . . I should have come back earlier. . ."

I sat up, shivering like I'd never shivered before. My cloak felt extra heavy, though I wasn't sure why. "Where are we? How did I get here?"

"A cave," he said, even quieter than before. "I . . . found you."

I looked around, still unable to see even the tiniest detail in the perfect darkness. "There's no fire," I said, trembling now. "It's so cold."

"I brought nothing to start one," he said. "I didn't mean to stay out this long. And there was nothing in your cloak." Something hung in his voice, something that seemed so obvious, but that I was too cold to fully recognize. Whatever it was, I didn't like it. It slithered up my spine like something cold and clammy.

"We need to get warm," I said, moving to stand up. "We'll readjust our layers. Something."

Sølvi didn't move, and I realized as I was trying to stand that my cloak hadn't got heavier; I was wearing two. "Sølvi," I said quietly, slowly. "Where is your cloak?"

He said something I couldn't quite make out, but I

303

didn't need to hear it. I knew I was wearing his cloak. Terror — for him, for us, for everything — split my mind like cracking ice. With shaking hands, I wordlessly pulled his heavy cloak from my shoulders.

"Don't you dare," he said, his voice the strongest it had sounded since I had woken up.

"Sølvi, you will die without it," I told him. I wasn't crying, but a sob welled up from deep within me and burst out in a weak whimper.

"If you take it off, we'll both die."

I tried to say something, to fight his words with some of my own, but the cold was unbearable, sinking deeper and deeper into my body until parts of it were numb.

"Put the cloak back on," he said.

I wanted to see his face, wanted to hold his hands and look into his eyes and tell him that everything was going to be all right. "I can't," I said, stifling another sob. "I can't do that to you. You need it."

"Please, Janna." And I realized what was in his voice that I couldn't place earlier: acceptance. He knew... He knew he was dying, and he knew the only way we wouldn't both die was if one of us could stay just warm enough to live.

"You can't make this decision for me," I said. I wanted to sound resolute, strong, but I was too cold to say it in anything but a whisper. A tear welled in my eye, but I could already feel it freezing. I wiped it away. "It isn't yours to make."

"I've made my decision, Janna, and you can make yours. We do not both have to die in here tonight. I don't know what comes after this life but I would never be able to live with myself if you followed me. I am going to die in here. Please do one thing..." His voice trailed off, weak and empty. "Please live. Not for my sake, or for anyone's. But for yours. Just live."

I fell back to the floor, shivering and sobbing, and tried to put the cloak over him in the dark. He pushed me away weakly. "No. I won't have it."

"Please, Sølvi," I begged him. "Please take it."

"I can't."

I slumped forward, my eyes burning with cold tears. This couldn't be happening. I must still be asleep. I fell down in the woods, I remembered that. Perhaps I had never got up, never been found, and I still lay there slowly freezing to death. But maybe Sølvi was well, somewhere warm at home or in a cave and this was all just a terrible dream born from ice and wind.

"Janna," he said, and I hated the way he spoke my name so gently, so calm and certain that he was doing the right thing. An arm reached out and grabbed one of my hands – they were mittened, but stiff and unfamiliar, so unlike the ones that had long held mine while we meandered through the woods or explored caves that delved deep into darkness. "Allow me this. Allow me to die knowing you will live. And just ... just talk to me. I'll miss talking to you."

305

I squeezed his hand with everything I had, holding it close to my body. It was a wicked thought that I was not ready to entertain, the idea of never talking to him again. He was my love, my every day, my morning and evening and everything in between. He was always there, always an ear or a shoulder when I needed it most. How could I lose that, and go on? "Talk about what?" I said between sobs.

"Anything."

I nodded, even though he couldn't see me, and searched desperately through my cold mind for a happier time. "I was just ... I was thinking about that time when we were younger, laying outside under the stars and wondering what they were. Telling stories about the constellations."

"I remember it," he said, and it sounded like he was smiling. "I wonder if the Horned Horse ever found her foal."

I laughed a little, and it felt grossly out of place. "I hope she did."

"I remember another night, up on a hill talking about the stars. We sang a song about winter."

"We did," I replied. "I remember you saying you thought the stars were the souls of ... of everyone who had passed."

"I still think that," he whispered. "I hope it's true."

A new wave of tears built up in my eyes. "Don't say that," I said. "I know what you're thinking."

"What am I thinking?"

"That you'll be up there soon."

A quick release of breath that might have been a laugh.

"I know I will. And I can't wait to see. . ." He trailed off, either from emotion or the energy it took him to speak.

"Here, Sølvi." I held out his cloak again. "Please take it. If you wait too long, you won't be able to undo it. We can even share it, hug each other under them."

"No. I'm already too cold, Janna. I can't warm you."

Silence fell, and I could feel my heart breaking, slowly, as I realized he was leaving me.

"If you could wish for anything right now, what would it be, Janna?" His voice was weak, cracking a little as he spoke. "What's the one thing that you would wish for?"

I blinked tears from my eyes. "I don't know. You. I'd wish for you to live. With me. For ever."

His voice grew quieter with each word he spoke. "No. You should wish for something better. They say that when someone dies, you get a wish. Just one, but it should be a good one."

"You're still here," I said firmly, shaking my head. "I can't make a wish."

"But make sure that you do. And make it good. There's that saying. I think it was Löskan. Burn my body, and blow a wish into the night on the embers of my soul. So when I am gone, Janna, make a wish. All right?"

I couldn't stop the tears now, so I nodded through a sob. "All right. I will."

A long pause followed, the howling wind outside the cave the only sound.

"Stars above, snow below," Sølvi whispered, and my chest tightened. It was an old poem recited at deathbeds to bless the departing.

"Hear the echoes of my soul," I joined in.

"Raging sea and summer rain, don't let the world forget my name." We finished it together.

"I love you, Janna," he whispered.

"I love you more, Sølvi."

He died quietly during the night, as easily as if he'd fallen asleep. I could follow him anywhere on this island, into the woods, through the winding passageways of a cave, even to the distant mountains if we wished. But I couldn't follow him any more, and I wasn't prepared for the bone-crushing loneliness that gripped my soul the moment it realized his was gone. I sat awake and stared into the darkness, wishing everything was different. Wishing him back. Wishing myself with him. If a new star blinked to light in the night sky, I missed it, sitting alone in a cave in the middle of a storm, buried beneath two cloaks that kept me alive.

Chapter 28

I thought of the moments of Sølvi's death as we approached the light, of the pain I had felt slowly consuming me, and of how he had told me to make a wish. And I had. After his funeral, as sparks rose into the night sky and smoke curled away from what had once been his body, I had wished to truly live, and that my life, though small and insignificant in such a grand and frightening world, would be used for something important. Sølvi had saved my life, and every dawn was one more than he would ever get to see. That meant something, and until I, too, was nothing but ash on a funeral pyre, I wished that my life would have meaning.

The room was lit by a fire so blinding I could hardly see details at first. Something tall and terrifying stood in the middle – stone, I thought, but I had to blink a few times to be sure. It was hot, hotter than anything I'd ever felt before. Searing, sweating, burning hot. More statues lined the far walls, dreadful creatures torn apart and pieced back together again, but the one in the centre, shaped like a man, stood much larger than the rest. He towered over us, so tall that we had to tilt back our heads to see his face. Tall like the statues we'd passed what felt like a lifetime ago.

And unlike the others, he moved.

When I looked up into his face, our eyes met in a way that told me with absolute certainty that he was in some way alive. I said nothing, rendered to silence by confusion, and the searing heat, but somewhere, words teased my aching mind.

May the god in the shadows forgive you your wrongs.

"Human."

His voice was everywhere and nowhere, inside my head and filling the room all at once. It grated, rough and deep, and every bit the voice of ancient stone.

"Two humans, and a beast."

My eyes began to adjust to the brightness – though a crushing headache had begun to sink in – and I noticed for the first time that eight wolves stood in the room, as well. I stared at them, confused, and yet grateful for something to look at that wasn't the man made of stone. Something about him made my insides twist, like my small human body was never meant to be in the presence of something so dark and evil. He was the devil, if the devil were moulded from rock and fire.

I grasped at whatever strength I had left and stood taller. Words felt weak and powerless, but if I must face him, let me at least be strong. My body longed for the snow and ice in which it had grown up, for a cool breeze to caress its skin and send shivers down my spine. I was never meant to be this hot, sweat beading on my skin and making my eyes blur.

His eyes bored into mine, fully grey, and dreadful.

"What is it that brings eight immortals and two mortals to my door?"

I fell to my knees, exhausted, hot, and dizzied by his hideous voice. I stared at the ground beneath my feet, grey stone with streaks of darkness where fire had touched it. Eight immortals. The statues?

No.

Of course.

Had I guessed that, or had I been too blind? Too focused on other things? It was difficult to tell, and nearly impossible to think in such brightness and heat.

The wolves.

A howl erupted from one of the wolves, but in this room, it transformed into words that reached my ears. "You deal in death and ruin, here in the pit of the island. But there is a life that must be spared."

The god rubbed his hands together, a horrid grating sound that raised hairs on my arms. "Why would you come to me, and not to her?"

I knew, somehow, to which Her he was referring, and I clung to the image of Her bright stars in the night sky. It made me think of freezing nights and ground covered in snow, and I longed to be cold again, even if only for a moment.

"She cannot touch things on the island," the immortal replied. "If there is a life to be saved, only you can help us."

"I do not make a business of saving lives, Særvar," the god said in a quieter tone, though he seemed pleased to be needed. "Far from it. If someone is to die, let them die. There will always be another."

"This one does not deserve to die."

Their words held meaning that I could not quite grasp. I had my own reasons to save the woman, to finally stop a death that is within my power to stop. She had saved me once, and Sølvi saved me, and damn it, I wanted one chance to help someone. To truly live, no matter what that looked like. But these wolves, they seemed to have other ideas.

Something bright and beautiful cut through the heat around me, but no one else seemed aware. A warm, white light approached, and I wondered briefly if this was what dying looked like. If this was my soul headed not to the underworld, but to somewhere far more beautiful, filled with light and song. I reached out towards nothing, as a voice sounded not in the room, but somewhere within me.

You cannot affect the future until you know what that future will be.

And then the light grew even brighter, blindingly bright, until it was all I could see and I had to squint after days in darkness. And then through the light, shadows began to take shape. There was a baby alone in a house, a girl sitting in the corner crying. Then the baby, older, flowing curls behind her as she watched a boat leave the harbour of her village. My vision of her wasn't clear, but I was certain that tears lit up her eyes. A second later, she was older still, and I saw her here, in the mountains, lying on her back and speaking to the stars. Then it was all a blur, obscure shapes and movement. *A beach,* I thought, *and a battle.* Stars streamed down from the sky, fires burned, people screamed. And then a victory that I couldn't see, but I could feel. The girl with the curly hair looked happy, and she was smiling despite the battle that just raged around her. She had done something that would change everything, and even if I didn't know exactly what it was, I knew that it needed to happen.

One day a storm would come to Skane, a storm of ice and stars where powers would clash like giants in battle, and the cosmos and earth would come together. If I could be the first breeze to rustle the fir needles, the first snowflake to fall from the sky, or the distant

313

rumble of an impending roar, then my death would not be in vain. If I could never again step foot on the island, but could run with the stars knowing its future was sure, then eternity could not come soon enough. And so, as simply as a candle flickers in the dark, and as ferociously as winter waves crashed against Skane's beloved shores, my decision was made.

Words rang out in my soul, soft and beautiful, and as I listened, hope began to spark and grow until it filled every corner of my aching body. I listened, rapt, until the last note died down, and then, with a knowing smile, I looked up at the god.

I felt something dying inside of me, subtle at first, like when one or two brown leaves cling to their vibrant green brethren, hoping not to be noticed. Hoping that perhaps your eye will travel right over them and you'll be none the wiser, until all of a sudden, every single rustling, whispering leaf has perished. But I did notice it, because no matter how tiny the dead leaves are, how few of them there may be, you cannot help but notice them. I think Janna didn't want to see it at first, but eventually she couldn't miss it, in the same way that I'd tried. I'd been unwell for most of our journey, so in a perverse way, our village was right to push us out. I hated that.

I looked to Janna, and I saw in her face that she knew. She knew how this needed to end. What mortal lives needed to be exchanged to save the woman and her baby. And as long as the god did not find out I was dying anyway, we could do it. We could trade our lives for those of others, just as Sølvi or anyone else would do.

"I know," I said to her, but my voice was small. "I know, and it's all right." I thought of Sølvi again, wondered if this was how he'd felt in that cave before the end, a sort of peaceful understanding of what was to come. "If you can take my life," I said, louder this time, "and save the woman's, then it is yours." Let him think my life was still one to give, that it wasn't already ending as we spoke.

Breathing was a struggle, as if my lungs had been slowly filling with water over the past few days, and every breath was shorter than the one before it. I knew, though, with a sort of grim certainty I couldn't shake, that it wasn't water. I knew how this story ended: with blood and bruises and gasps for air, and a slow, winding descent into death. Whatever thread of love and life existed between a brother and a sister, I could feel it begin to tug, as though, wherever he was, Sølvi knew I was coming home.

I stared at Enja while the god spoke, and she stared back at me. A conversation passed between us, though I didn't know how. We'd both decided something over the past few minutes, something I couldn't put into words, but something wonderful disguised as something terrible. I knew more than she did: I knew just how badly that baby needed to live. I knew she would grow up to be great, and that in some indistinct way, she would save this island, and those in the future who still called it home.

"And mine," I said, "for the baby's."

The god was silent for a long while, head tilted sideways in thought. "Cursing you immortals to animals did little to rid me of the thorn in my side you have become over these centuries. Removing you altogether, and at your own request, is something I never dared to hope could be." He fell silent again. Some conversation must have passed by while I'd been watching Enja, something involving the immortals. "So, in exchange for replacing their lives" – he waved a giant arm to us, carelessly – "I will get all of you?"

The wolves nodded in unison.

The god smiled.

"I think we have a deal."

"But not here," I said, loudly and firmly. The Goddess's voice had instilled in me some kind of strength which I desperately needed. "I will not die here, below ground, surrounded by fire. I will die in the open, under the stars, by the sea."

Chapter 29

It was a crisp night, the kind I had always loved. If we were back home, and things were as they had always been, I would have sneaked out of doors by now and would be traipsing through the woods, off to find some high point from where I could see the stars. I would spend hours searching for the one I had dubbed as Sølvi, tell him hello, ask how he'd been. Tell him I missed him. And in the early morning hours I would make my way back home, with a heart that felt both empty and full.

But this wasn't one of those nights. Tonight, I walked a wide ridge in mountains on our way to the sea, the stars raging like a hundred thousand fires to illuminate the darkness. I felt comfort in their presence, like they were old friends who were glad to see me after my descent into the mountains. And somewhere deep down in my heart, I could see the face of that girl, the one I needed to save, and I could feel how desperately she would love the stars as well. Right now they were mine, burning for me and those I loved, but one day they would belong to her, and she would command them in a way I could never imagine. I wished I could see it, but just knowing what would happen filled my heart with peace.

A firm determination burned through my veins, a mixture of fire and ice. I wanted a wedding and I got a funeral. I wanted a family and I got all-consuming loneliness. Life wasn't in the habit of making my dreams come true, so I made a new dream, a dream to save someone I would never know, and I would fight for it until the last beat of my heart echoed in that cursed god's ear.

The god was no longer stone, but shadow and flame that walked before us, both there and not. The orange glow of the flames looked sickly against the bluish light of the night. He kept his eyes on the ground ahead of him, never looking up, and I suspected it was because he didn't want to see the Goddess. Light always makes evil uneasy.

We had said goodbye to Siiva in the foothills. One of the wolves had spoken to him, and he had climbed into Enja's arms for a final embrace before he left us, tiny footsteps trailing to the south. Whether back to the village or somewhere they had instructed him, I didn't know, but there was a peace in my heart that told me he would be safe.

Enja trailed behind us, so I slowed to match her pace.

"I'm sorry," I said, placing an arm around her shoulder. How much she must have been suffering.

"For what?" she asked, and there was more strength in her voice than I would have supposed.

"For ... everything. Everything." I shook my head and felt suddenly as though I was about to cry. I stopped walking and turned to face her, starlight glistening in her eyes. "For your brother. I am sorry you lost him, and for my sake." Tears blurred my vision, and I pushed knotted hair from my face. "He might still be here if it wasn't for me."

She put two hands on my shoulders and looked me in the eyes. I blinked away the tears to better see her. "Janna," she said softly, "you have nothing to be sorry for. You loved fiercely and lost greatly, and for that, *I* will always be sorry. I have missed my brother every day since he died, but I have never once blamed you."

As she spoke, a weight lifted from my chest and disappeared into the cold night air. A sob shook my body, and I hugged her like I had never hugged anyone. In a world filled with terrible things, she was a small piece of goodness. "Thank you," I said, and then repeated it over and over and over again. "Thank you. Thank you. Thank you."

She was a friend – my closest, dearest friend, but knowing what was in her heart, knowing she did not hold me responsible for her brother's death, lightened my heart enough to make the coming events just a little less frightening. I smoothed her matted hair away from her tired face, wishing there was something I could do to make her a little more comfortable, a little less pained.

I turned away to keep walking, and Enja fell to the ground. She coughed and coughed, and droplets of blood fell on to the snow and rock around us. The image of that person in the woods back near that village, of the red blood marring the white snow, and the strangled noises coming from their throat, took shape before me, but I pushed it far away.

"Enja," I said, and I crashed to my knees beside her. "I'm here. It's all right." Even in the darkness I could see how pale she was, all life and colour drained away.

"Janna," she said, and held tight to my hand, the whites of her eyes sparkling with fear. "Please don't let another moment go by where you think it was your fault. It wasn't. It was never your fault."

I brushed her hair from her face, losing a battle to hold back my tears. "I won't," I said. "I promise."

"I don't know where I'll go after this, but I hope Sølvi's there." She knew. She knew what was happening, and I couldn't lie to her. I would soon be gone as well, but not like this. Not in such a wretched, violent way, and my heart ached to watch it.

"I'm sure he will be. Tell him I miss him." I laughed a little, and she smiled.

"Stars above, snow below," she whispered, and I joined her.

"Hear the echoes of my soul.

Raging sea and summer rain,

Don't let the world forget my name."

"I'm sorry," I started to say, but stopped when she shuddered. "Enja?"

She didn't speak again.

"That changes things," the god said as I stared at Enja's face, lit only by starlight.

She had come so far and done so much. I would never have made it without her, never have found the god who could save the baby, not be on this ridge, surrounded by eight immortals if she hadn't given it everything she had. We had hardly spoken in a year, and then over a matter of days, she had become my dearest friend. And now she was gone, so simply, like a candle blown out by a breeze.

"You now have only your life to give," the god continued, and I stood slowly, lying Enja gently on the ground. "So who will it be: the woman, or her baby?"

Overhead, the stars twinkled and danced, as though making plans for a future so distant I would never be a part of it. And that was all right. I was here to do something big in a small way, a way that might never be known by another living soul on this island. Every word, every action, every breath trickles down through time and changes the world in some small way. The tide doesn't

321

crash against the coast in one thundering motion; it drifts in, so subtle at first that it might escape your notice, until, little bit by little bit, it has drowned the shores.

"We save the baby," I said, and I had never been more certain of anything in my life. If the mother were here, she would make the same choice. That baby would do great things, and right here, right now, I could ensure that those things happened. My vision flashed suddenly, and as if these dealings with a god had ruptured something in time, I was filled with images of the girl with light hair, on a boat in a storm, in a cave late at night, plucking the stars from the sky to use in her battle. It was as though she were living right now, all around me, as though our two stories had managed to collide.

We climbed a cliff that sat high above the sea, so high it was nothing more than a shadowed expanse far below. Up here, I felt as though I could fly, or touch the stars, or see distant lands which we knew nothing about. It was freeing, and knowing that I would never again touch the island made me sad that I had spent so little time by the sea.

I looked up at the stars of the Goddess, all worry and fear dissipating. I knew what I needed to do, and I knew how to do it. I knew where I was going, and I knew that I would be happy. It wasn't death, but a new life far from here, and because of that, there was no reason to be afraid.

Remember, the beautiful voice said. *So long as you do*

not touch the island, I can take your hand.

This was the end of a story, and the start of another. A transition from one era to the next. The beginning of the end of the fear in which Skane had been forced to live. And even though no one knew it yet, it brought me comfort and joy.

I reached into my pocket and drew out the paper I had carried around for the past year. Sølvi's last new words to me. I had never truly wanted to read them until now, to accept his final gift and put an end to the new memories we could make. But it was time. I unfolded the paper, and I read.

The letters on the page ebbed and flowed, a quick but elegant hand that stung with familiarity. I read every word, and then read them again.

Tears burned my eyes, but they weren't tears of pain, as they had so often been. For the first time since Sølvi had died, I finally felt peace.

I turned to the immortals, lined up and waiting, waiting for the sacrifice they would never have to make, but had offered so willingly. That was goodness, in its purest form. That was the sort of love and kindness I wished my village could learn.

"Thank you," I said to them, looking into each of their eyes in turn. "Your Goddess thanks you for what you are willing to do, and I thank you, on behalf of Skane. Such selflessness is rare and beautiful." They all bowed their heads to me one by one, in a wave of grace and elegance.

Then I turned to the god. "Do you know what destroys paper?" I asked, and the flames drew back in confusion, and a moment of silence yawned between us.

"I do not understand the question."

"Fire," I said. "Fire consumes paper, wood, almost everything. I've seen it destroy. Seen what it leaves behind. It nearly ended my own life, not so long ago."

Silence.

"Do you know what consumes darkness?"

He said nothing.

"Light. It floods the shadows," I answered. "A candle in a dark room might as well be the sun on a summer's day. It devours the darkness." I sighed, and quietly took in the stars for a moment, admiring how brightly they shone against the black sky behind them. "And do you know what destroys evil?" I asked.

"This is foolishness," he replied. "The heat has gone to your head."

"Good. Good destroys evil." I remembered, faint though they were at the time, the feelings of admiration and warmth when Eri had crested that hill to stop Ragna, the way their two souls had clashed for all to see. One good, one evil. I was only standing here because he had won.

More silence. I moved closer to the god, closer to the precarious edge of the cliff, and I took in a breath.

"Do you know what destroys fire?" I asked in a

whisper. My heart beat like thunder, all noise vanishing for a handful of seconds as I focused on what it truly felt like to live, to be alive, and to be me. I let my life play out from beginning to end in a flash, all the memories I would ever have from my time in Skane, all living one final time in my mind. This was the end of the Janna as she was, and the start of the Janna she would be for the rest of time. "Water."

And I ran at him with all the strength my body had left, and in a rush of air and flames, we both went tumbling over the edge of the cliff.

I fell and fell and fell, the cliff shrinking further and further away, and while I soon heard the crash as the god disappeared into the depths of the sea, that crash never came for me. I just continued to fall, the cliff and the island growing smaller and smaller until it had disappeared altogether. She couldn't help me while I remained on the island, but I was not on the island any more. There was a void where my life should be, a void that would be filled by the baby, born tonight, who would grow up to rule the sky.

As I fell, the darkness around me was slowly replaced by stars, and I was falling through the night sky I had spent so long admiring from below. And a voice echoed off the stars and lit up the darkness around me, and I could see Her constellation shimmering before me.

Come with me, Janna. Come to the stars, that you may

watch over the island for ever. At last, you will find peace.

And beside her, another star flickered and shone, and in it, I could see him. I could see him, and I wanted nothing more than to go to him.

"Take me," I said, and I reached up to the stars that burned above me. "Take me with you."

The lights overhead grew bigger and brighter, and then Sølvi's voice welcomed me home.

Far away across the island, a baby was born. She let out a weak cry, one that barely registered in the ears of her father, who sat shuddering with sobs by the fire as a neighbour wrapped the baby in blankets to keep her warm – a neighbour who quietly gave her the name Ósa, and whispered it tenderly into her ear. She would never know her mother, never know how desperately she had been loved, loved by the woman who had birthed her. Loved by a girl who had given her life to a Goddess. Loved so that her cry could echo off the mountains, the trees, the walls of every cave on the island and let everything within it know she had arrived. A baby's cry that could bring evil crashing to its knees.

A baby's cry that made the stars tremble.

After – Eri

Janna and Enja never did return to the village, but I left their families somewhere safe and remote, and returned to watch one by one as the plague took life after life, creeping in from only the Goddess knew where. They had forgotten the girls within hours of the failed burning on Døv Hill, when the first signs of the plague arrived.

Ragna. She was the first to go. It started out simple, her face paling, her eyes growing redder by the hour, until she lay writhing around on the ground, blood spewing from her lungs and trickling from both of her ears. She tried to speak, and I sat nearby watching, because I couldn't look away. I was torn between thinking about how much she deserved this and wondering if anyone deserved it at all. It was simple, but violent and gruesome. None of the stories I had heard could have prepared me for it.

Ragna died after a few hours, a mess of blood and bruises and too-pale skin.

Half the village died in the following week. I kept waking up in the morning and looking down at myself, prepared to see all the signs of the plague having settled into my body during the night, but in some unknowable way, I was spared For weeks, bodies lay dead in the streets, all the nearby snow stained red. Houses reeked of death and decay, and those who were still well dared not touch them. It wasn't until the last infected person had died, coughing up blood on the threshold of their home, that we let ourselves hope it had passed us by. Slowly, we used horses to drag them away, burning the bodies on great pyres, and depositing what remained in distant caves that we marked with symbols of death.

And only after the last of the bodies had been burned, houses cleaned out, and some semblance of normalcy had returned to the village, did I place my mother on the back of a horse, set the village of Sjørskall behind us, and set off for the western horizon.

SØLVI'S POEM TO JANNA

If love is a storm, let me drown in the snow
And if love is a fire, let me burn in the glow
If love is the sky, let us dance with the stars
And if love is a wound, let me tend to your
*   scars*
If love is a wind, may you whisper to me
And if love is a cage, may you always be free
If love is a wave, may you soon reach my shores,
And if love is a battle, may we never see war.

Thank you to:

Of course, my agent, Silvia Molteni, and my editor, Lauren Fortune. Without you both, this wouldn't be a book. Thank you to everyone else at Scholastic who has worked to bring this book into the world.

My family, near and far, and particularly my mom and dad, who are always my greatest source of encouragement.

Alex, again, for being an early reader and always being supportive; Schuyler, for seventeen years of the best friendship I could ask for; Reina, for always being ready to talk about writing; Shari, for her support and for being our travel buddy to the launch of book one; Debbie, for being such a dear and supportive friend; Rachel and Mik, for reading and loving my work and cheering me on; Claire and Samantha, for being absolute darlings and always being ready to help chat through writing problems with me; and to all of my other friends who have in any way helped and supported me. I am thankful for every single one of you.

I had two surgeries while writing this book, so I want to thank the doctors and nurses who worked so hard to get me through a difficult time. I have so much respect for you.

Phil, Ruth and Erin, always.

And to Thomas. Thank you for everything, and I love you.

A *Storm of Ice and Stars* Pronunciation Guide

While the accent marks may be familiar, I have taken some liberties with how they are used in the world of *A Storm of Ice and Stars*.

Janna – YAHN-ah

Sølvi – SOUL-vee

Enja – EN-ya

Eri – AIR-ee

Sjørskall – SYORS-kall

Sívar – SEE-var

Ragna – RAG-na

Löska – LOW-ska

Siiva – SEE-va

Lós – LOHS

Jot – YOT

Ør – Or

Døv Hill - DOVE Hill *(rhymes with drove)*

Have you read Lisa Lueddecke's
other tale of the island of Skane?

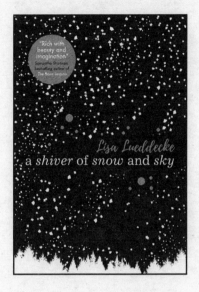

Turn over for an extract

Chapter 1

Skane was built on superstition. Always enter your home right foot first. When you sneeze, someone who bears you ill will has just spoken your name. Don't whistle while looking towards the sun or you might bring on rain.

But mostly, the superstitions were about the lights. Bright, colourful lights that danced for us in the clear night sky.

Green was common. It meant the Goddess was happy, and everything was as it should be.

Blue meant snow, and lots of it. Best round up your sheep and haul in some firewood before those first few flurries started to fly.

And then there was red. Red was different, rarer.

Red was a warning.

*

The lights danced. The lós, most called it, a word given to us by the old rune singers who translated it from symbols and pictures etched into cave walls. They waved and morphed and rippled like the sky was a lake into which someone had dropped a pebble.

"What are they?" I would ask my father every night as a child.

Every night he would answer differently. "They are the last remnants of the setting sun dancing for the moon." "They're the light of the stars reflecting off the sea." "They just ... are." Eventually, I realized he didn't know. No one knew. The Goddess could change their colour; that was the only certainty. What they were, why they were there – those were still mysteries to us. Perhaps they always would be.

Between those of us who were staring up at them now, the air grew still, charged, as if we were on a mountaintop and the breeze had stopped.

I'd joined a few other villagers who were seated on the large rocks that fell away into the sea. On nights like this one, when the lights shone so vibrantly that they lit up the snow in vivid greens and blues, groups of us would gather to gaze at them. When the sky demanded our attention, we obeyed.

"They're changing," Ivar said beside me, but his words were a fading echo, distant and hollow. My eyes were fixed on the sky, and I didn't miss the subtle shifts here and there as the bright blues became pinks and purples. They were deep too, reminiscent of a sunset.

My skin prickled, hairs standing on end, but not from the cold. This hue was dreadfully close to another, drawing ever nearer to a shade none of us in Skane wanted to see again.

It had happened seventeen years ago, the sky glowing crimson only days before a fever outbreak had ravaged our villages. Once it set in, nearly two hundred people died in a matter of days. I was born, and lived. My mother birthed me, and died. They said I was lucky. One quarter of those who perished were children.

Lucky. I'd never know her. Lucky. I'd had to be passed around other mothers who'd recently given birth – mothers whose children would know them, know what they looked like. How they sounded. Have memories of them to cherish. I was nursed to health by strangers.

Lucky.

Seventeen years was a long time, but no one had forgotten. Whenever the lights in the sky shifted away from green, even for just a few seconds, the villagers held their breath.

"Ivar," I whispered, but his name felt strange on my tongue. Meaningless, foreign, as my throat began to constrict. His presence usually grounded me, was my guiding point of comfort when life tried to smother me, but tonight, it did nothing. I may as well have been alone on a boat in the middle of the sea.

He drew in a long breath, one mitten-clad hand just barely touching mine.

The edges of the tendrils were changing. Shifting. Deepening. One particular whorl high overhead, waving like a scrap of cloth in the wind, was almost wholly crimson. It seemed to bleed out from there, infecting all the nearby branches with its blood-red disease. My body went cold, as if the colour had been stolen directly from my veins. Mist from the crashing waves stung my eyes, but I couldn't close them. I raced to find parts of the lights that hadn't changed, that were still uncorrupted, like I could singlehandedly prevent it from progressing.

It took mere minutes. Minutes for the entire sky to stain red. It bore down on us, a presage, a desperate but wordless warning we had no way to translate. *It's coming*, it screamed. *The plague is coming*. It was always the devastating plague, haunting us every few decades since we'd first arrived in Skane. But *why* it was coming was as knowable as how many snowflakes would make up the next storm, or how many raindrops it took to fill the sea.

I clutched at the icy rock beneath me, my fingers long since numb through my mittens. I suddenly felt keenly conscious of the scale of the lós, and of my own fragility in comparison. What does one tiny, useless form matter in a world where such dark things can happen? How many of these poor souls around me would be dead within days? Weeks? A wave of confusion and sickness came over me, and I couldn't tell the sky from the land. Doubling over, my head spinning as though I were falling through the dark places between the stars, I closed my eyes and forced cold, crisp air into my lungs.

Breathe in. Breathe out.

I recovered my orientation slowly, gripping the rock and setting my eyes on the stars that managed to shine through the cursed red lights. I expected fear to take hold of my heart and mind, paralysing me after all the stories I'd heard about the blood red sky, but it wasn't fear that gripped me. Instead, anger surged to life like a springtime river, refilling my frozen veins. Anger, because I didn't know why it was happening. Anger, because I knew the sky didn't portend that a handful of fishermen would drown at sea or a child would get lost in the woods and be found days later, buried under the snow. Anger, because when the lights glowed red, it meant the lives of everyone I knew and loved were at stake, and I had a greater chance of thawing Lake Hornsträsk in midwinter than stopping it.

Anger, because when the red lós shone, it meant that somewhere in Skane the plague was brewing once more and it was hungry for bodies.

Somewhere nearby, but just far enough away to be distorted by the breeze, someone began to chant the words. I'd heard them innumerable times before. Knew every word and nuance by heart, forward and backwards. Without looking away from the sky, I let my voice join in.

> *"Green, green, the lights glow green*
> *Happy is our gracious queen*
> *Blue, blue, the lights glow blue*
> *A vicious storm nearby does brew*
> *Red, red, the lights glow red*
> *Beware the dangers up ahead."*